The suspects included the most interesting people ...

When she entered, the young man was leaning back in his desk chair with his ankles propped on the unmade bed. He wore a blue crew-neck sweater, charcoal slacks, no socks, and loafers. The slacks and sweater hung loosely on his lanky frame.

Mary said, "Mr. Kennedy?"

The young man smiled toothily. "Jack," he said, setting down his chair and rising to offer his hand. Mary felt her own palm disappear in his warm greeting.

"I don't know if you remember me. Officer Shanley."

"We met the other day, didn't we? In George's office."

"Mr. St. John's?"

"He prefers 'Headmaster.' But unless my memory fails me, you're a New York City detective. And this is the state of Connecticut."

"So I haven't any jurisdiction here. That's true. But your father is about to be named to the Court of St. James. So let's talk privately, you and I. Unless you think he would enjoy denying public allegations in the papers."

"I don't see any joy in that."

"I thought not."

"Then—what should we talk about?"

"Your father has been trying to stop my investigation, through Tammany Hall. Have you any idea why he might do something like that?"

Jack sat on the edge of his mattress and offered her the chair. "No. But I suspect you do, Miss Shanley."

"I have an idea."

"Then why don't you share it?"

"I think he was trying to protect you, Jack. He knows—or believes he knows—that you were involved with a pretty young lady in New York City, whose body was found a few nights ago in the tunnel to New Jersey."

Pages 106-107

Books by Richard Fliegel

The Next to Die
The Art of Death
The Organ Grinder's Monkey
Time to Kill
A Semi-Private Doom
A Minyan for the Dead
The Man Who Murdered Himself
Clerical Errors: Tales of Murder and Ministry
Defending Her Honor

Death of a Charity Girl

Chelmsford Press   Briarcliff Manor, New York

Chelmsford Press
Briarcliff Manor, New York

ISBN-13: 978-0615847467
ISBN-10: 0615847463

Death of a Charity Girl

A New York Novel

by

Richard Fliegel

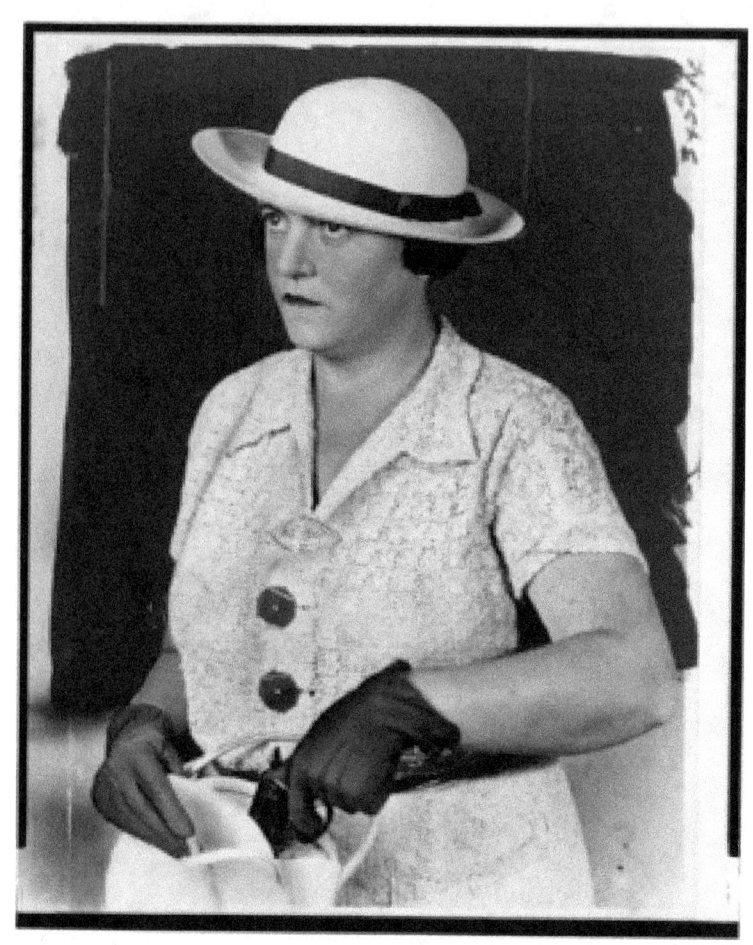

Mary Agnes Shanley

Member of the
NYPD Pickpocket Squad, 1937

"Today it is possible for the city of modern times, the happy city, the radiant city, to be born."

~ Le Corbusier, visiting New York City in 1936

Death of a Charity Girl

One. Tompkins Square

On the first warm day of spring 1937, Mary Agnes Shanley
sat on a bench in Tompkins Square Park and watched a
Brownshirt on a soapbox assail the Jews of New York. Mary
was a big-boned woman, broad through the hips and shoulders,
a hundred sixty pounds on a five-foot eight-inch frame. A fox-
fur collar made her look even bigger, and the ladies' derby she
wore tipped to the left lent her the air of a speakeasy bouncer.
Her woolen coat was open on account of the weather, revealing
a collared shirt-dress that fell to her shins, cotton stockings and
sensibly low-heeled shoes. The shade of an elm tree provided
some cover, but a careful lookout might have caught her
copper-green eyes blinking above the *New York World* folded
in her lap.

The *World* began running 'word-cross puzzles' in 1913.
Eleven years later, a fledgling publisher issued a collection of
World puzzles, launching Simon and Schuster and starting a
national craze. Nearly every paper in the country ran a
crossword puzzle in the 'thirties, except the *New York Times*,
whose editors refused to print one on principle.

The corner clue in the *World* this morning was *Con*. Mary
ran through all the slang for a *jailbird, stir bird, lagger,* even
trustee—none were four letters long. She might have solved
the whole puzzle sooner if most of her attention had not been
focused on the Nazi.

Not that the Brownshirt noticed, as he shuffled on his
wooden crate. It had once held Borden's milk rather than soap,
and the slats sagged under his shoes. *Not his boots.* It was the
first thing that made the hairs tingle in Mary's ears, a signal she
never ignored. The second was the strap of leather that crossed
his chest from his right shoulder to his left hip. It was buckled
too tightly, and his shirt still showed a crease from its
packaging. The third was his location. The German-American
Bund had grown more active in New York City since Hitler
was named Chancellor of Germany, and its American cousin,

the Christian Front, included cops who looked away when a gang of Christian Mobilizers had some fun with a Jew. Still, Mary thought Tompkins Square a curious place to see a swastika raised over a milk-box.

Tompkins Square Park comprised ten acres of grass, beech, and elm trees in East Greenwich Village, between Avenues A and B, Seventh and Tenth Streets. The square had been named for Daniel Tompkins, Governor of New York State, then Vice President to James Monroe. The park had a hundred-year history as the scene of political dissent, but that had always come from the left of the spectrum. In 1874, radicals staged a protest there for public-service jobs, broken up by a charge from New York mounted police. In 1877, five thousand people gathered in the park to support a railroad strike in Virginia— only to be met by the billy-clubs of seven hundred policemen. Justus Schwab's saloon, just off the square, had been the place to find Johann Most, the publisher of the *Freiheit*, a friend of Emma Goldman's and the face of revolutionary, European socialism for turn-of-the-century America.

Nazis were socialists too, weren't they? Mary wasn't sure. The word was written into the name of their party, but real socialists never seemed to like them. Mary's politics rarely reached beyond the gossip at Tammany Hall, but she had an eye for peculiar details, and knew her way around the town. And the badly dressed Nazi in this particular park was making her hairs tingle violently.

"Scam," she said aloud—and penciled it into her puzzle.

Only a year before, in 1936, Parks Commissioner Robert Moses had redesigned the park, dividing the space to prevent assemblies of thousands of people and riots by or against the police. Yet a restless crowd was gathering around the Brownshirt now. It was the lunch hour, in fine weather. The benches were full of working people eating sandwiches and fruit over cloth napkins spread across the green wooden slats. But the crowd who responded to the Brownshirt's provocations included a lot of bearded men wearing full-length coats despite the warmth of the day. And their eyes were growing black as their gabardine.

"Who do you think is to blame for this Depression?" he was saying. "Who controls the money? Not the people camped out in Central Park. Ask them—ask the folks in Hoovervilles, who do they think put them there? What will you get? A shrug. In Germany today, we have a party in power who know how to answer those questions." His gaze left no doubt what their answers might be.

Tompkins Square had a special meaning, too, for the German population of the city. Near the park had been the Weiss Garten encircled by white picket fences, once the heart of New York's "Little Germany." In 1904, thirteen hundred fifty people boarded the *General Slocum*, a three-decked steamer, and sailed up the Hudson River with a band playing Strauss. They were German women and children headed for a church picnic. As the ship passed the Upper East Side, a fire broke out. The captain did not pull into any of the docks nearby, fearful of spreading the flames, but headed for a beach at North Brother Island. The citizens of New York watched in horror as the steamer entered the wind and currents of Hell Gate. A thousand corpses finally reached the shore in the worst disaster in the city's history. The German community of Kleindeutchland dissolved in grief, settling over the next thirty years uptown in Yorkville. At the southern end of the park a monument now stood to "earth's purest children, young and fair," who perished that day on the *Slocum*.

It was a place for Jewish protest and German mourning. So what was a Brownshirt doing on a milk crate there?

Mary had her suspicions. What had Michael called her? *The most suspicious woman west of Kilkee*? He meant to exclude her grandmother, buried in County Clare. Mary hadn't always been so suspicious. Not when he brought her home, as a bride. But night after night of his workaday stories had changed her view of the street. And when Michael fell victim himself one night...

Mary cleared her throat to refocus her mind. The characters were taking their places and the curtain going up on the poor little drama in the park. Beneath the *World* she unclasped her handbag, a neat leather clutch large enough for her change purse, lipstick, and a few other items.

The Brownshirt was straining his voice now, raising a finger above the crowd that might have indicted them all. The men in black coats were not listening calmly but shouting back at the speaker in Yiddish and German, shaking fists and jostling each other as they closed around his milk-crate.

Mary watched the crowd, and picked out two more suspects.

In the front row was a young woman with her hair in a blue *babushka*, wearing a hand-made sweater over a skirt that fell to her ankles. As the men in the crowd surged forward, she turned and pushed them back, afraid it seemed of being trampled underfoot. She blinked—but her lashes were too long and dark to be natural. She had foresworn lipstick, it was true, but Mary saw a blush on her upper cheek that could only have come from rouge. The men in the front row felt her hand on their chests and backed off a step in respect. The shrill voice of the Brownshirt went up a pitch, and their faces swung back towards him.

As they did, the woman in the blue *babushka* passed a man near the fence, whose shoulders strained the fabric of his overcoat. This palooka wore his hat tipped low over eyes that squinted at the crowd but never lifted to the Brownshirt. When the woman in the headscarf passed, he reached into his coat and kept his hand inside. His pipe-joint of an elbow forced his coat open, and he tried to rebutton it. But his left hand was caught—cuffed to the fence behind him.

His head swiveled toward the chain links and then back around to the woman in the blue *babushka*, with the blank stare of a horned lizard trapped on a rock.

"What the…?"

He tugged the chain at his wrist. It jangled, and the fence bent, but its links held the handcuff wire. The second loop cut into his skin and pinched when he twisted it. He didn't even notice Mary moving out of reach, as he pulled it even deeper into his flesh.

"Hey, Flora—"

But Flora was in no state to help her partner. Her attention was fixed on the snub-nose of a 32-calibre revolver pressed against her spine. She stood frozen in place, with a wallet still in one hand and a whispered brogue in her ear.

"You can breathe again, dearie. But you're pinched."

Flora sniffed and scented a fox-fur collar. When she saw the Irish eyes glinting above it, she turned in panic to the Brownshirt wobbling on his soapbox. The crowd hadn't frightened him, but Flora's face did, and he paled when he spotted Mary standing close behind her.

"Thank you for your attention, gentlemen. We'll have to talk this out. But now, I'm afraid, I really must be going." He gave them a half-hearted *Seig Heil* and hopped off his milk-crate with surprising agility.

The crowd hesitated, and that gave him the chance to push his way through the listeners who had gathered in the space behind him.

"Excuse me," he said, and then, encountering a red-faced man who hugged him, added, "Yeah, yeah. *Deutchland uber alles.*" In three strides he shoved past the lonely fascist sympathizer and crossed the path halfway to the park's southern entrance.

The crowd started after him, but their shouts were cut short by a sudden *bang!* that echoed through the air. It was followed by the sharp smell of cordite and a second report. The first could have been the backfire from a car exhaust, but the second had to be a gunshot. The Brownshirt stopped in his tracks when he heard Mary's voice warn him, "That's far enough, isn't it? One more step will carry you right to the devil's door."

15

The Brownshirt's knees trembled, as if he required an effort to keep them from moving forward. His shoes seemed to be saying, *She wouldn't really shoot us in the back, would she?* What brains there were behind the shiny black hair plastered across his forehead answered, *Oh yes, she would. This was Irish Mary.*

The crowd stopped surging at the first gunshot and huddled down at the second, clutching their hats to their heads. When the Brownshirt halted at Mary's command, they started to rise. A rumor passed among them, which was at once debated—this being, after all, Tompkins Square. Two men in the front row started patting their chests, casting evil eyes at the thug cuffed to the fence.

Mary stood apart with one hand on the *tool*—the pickpocket in the headscarf—waving her revolver at the Brownshirt. A grin creased her face and softened her eyes. "Would anyone be kind enough to call Centre Street?"

When the black-coated men in the crowd realized that she was in fact a policewoman from the pickpocket squad, who had not only captured a gang of three professional *dips* but had nailed the Nazi as one of them...they could hardly believe their good fortune.

Like a hometown crowd at a football game, when the quarterback can't pass the ball and tucks it under his arm, ducking tackles and leaping over defenders to carry it safely to the end zone, they lifted their hands over their heads, clapping and stamping their feet on the fresh green grass of the park. Then they closed their fists, still in the air, and cheered in Yiddish for Mary.

Two. Exile on Centre Street

"That was good work, Mary, commendable work," said Captain Patrick McVeigh, whose calm voice and genial manner concealed his ability to punch as hard as any man in the Detective Bureau. The two of them sat in his office on the second floor of 240 Centre Street. The overhead bulb was out, as the Captain liked it, but a brass lamp glowed on the edge of his desk. Outside the window, buds were opening at the top of a sycamore, while the panes rattled softly in the afternoon light. "You know how Hizzoner feels about those bastards."

Everyone in Manhattan did, and everyone in Berlin. Fiorello La Guardia had told the American Jewish Congress in March that the 1939 World's Fair should have a chamber of horrors for "that brown-shirted fanatic menacing the peace of the world." News of his speech reached the Third Reich, who lodged a complaint with the State Department and received a formal apology from Secretary Cordell Hull. The President agreed to reprimand La Guardia, but when the Mayor visited the Oval Office, Roosevelt saluted and said, "Heil, Fiorello!" To which La Guardia replied, "Heil, Franklin!" The Nazis were not satisfied with this rebuke and vilified the Mayor in every fascist rag.

"Of course, yours weren't actual Brownshirts, were they?"

"No, sir. They were dips."

"And you're on the Pickpocket Squad. But you discharged your sidearm again, Mary, in a crowded park. Twice." The Captain held up two fingers, closed their vee, and aimed them at her like a double-barreled shotgun. "You know what they're calling you around the precinct, don't you?"

Mary couldn't suppress a grin. "I have an idea."

"Annie Agnes Oakley. And instead of feeling ashamed, you're proud of it, aren't you?"

McVeigh sighed and shook his close-cropped head. It wasn't an accusation, exactly, and the reception Mary received arriving at the precinct house with three members of the Dutch

Mob precluded disciplinary action. It was an *observation*, the Captain might have said, without observing further that firearms were rarely discharged by members of the Pickpocket Squad. Most of the squad were bare-knuckle men, who used their fists and blackjacks as standard equipment. Mary was one of only three female detectives, who were determined to prove themselves as tough as the men with far less body weight behind them.

"That's why they're issued to us, isn't it, Captain? To discharge when necessary? Both shots were necessary."

"Based on your experience?"

She raised her eyes to add, "Limited as it is."

McVeigh knew what that meant, and it wasn't humility. The Detective Bureau was the one place in the Police Department where a female cop could shine, and Mary had already made the most of her assignment. She had collared Chinatown Charlie working Fifth Avenue with a couple of *moll buzzers*, who would bump into ladies and then apologize extravagantly, while Charlie hooked the valuables from their handbags. Mary won a commendation for that arrest.

But the Pickpocket Squad was not the ticket to a big career on the force, and Mary's size and Irish brogue did not suit undercover work. If a case required a woman who could pass for a prostitute, Mary would never have been tapped, and what other undercover job called for a woman, instead of one of the bureau's two-fisted men? Patrol duty and promotional exams were available only to men. McVeigh knew that Mary wouldn't transfer off the squad to pat down females in the precinct house, but she couldn't chase *cannons* for the rest of her career, if she hoped to make Lieutenant someday.

"You want off the squad, Mary? Is that it?"

"I'd like to try my hand at something new, Captain. If you think Michael—God rest his soul—would have approved."

It was a card she played with care.

McVeigh had started with Michael Shanley as Arthur Carey's disciples. Both had protected Al Smith at Madison

Square Garden when the Governor lost his bid for the Democratic nomination for President of the United States, and then again in '28, when he won it. Those were the gravy days. But when Jimmy Walker took over the mayor's office and named Richard Enright his Commissioner, McVeigh had been sent to Siberia, also known as the Bronx.

Michael stood by him through those difficult times to help Pat keep his job on the force. When Judge Seabury's Commission forced Walker to resign, and Fiorello La Guardia was elected to clean up City Hall, the new mayor from the Greenwich Village Congressional district brought Lewis J. Valentine back to Centre Street, first as Chief Inspector then as Commissioner of the NYPD. Valentine recalled the old exiles, including Patrick McVeigh.

Now she had mentioned Michael again—said his name just once—and let the Captain's memory do the rest. In the silence McVeigh heard a twittering, high-pitched squeak he couldn't place but had been hearing off and on again all morning. It sounded like a phonograph after the record finished playing, when the needle kept bumping into the label.

The whole structure of the police department had been built on favors, on debts and expectations of payback. Not long before, a captaincy in the NYPD carried a price tag of twelve to fifteen thousand dollars. Most individuals couldn't afford that expense, so a sponsor was needed from the gambling halls or Tammany itself.

After the cash came the politics. Police officers were appointed by city aldermen, so a nod from the Manhattan Democratic Club was also necessary for a successful career on the force. But it was a good investment, considering the graft expected to flow to a captain. Some had racked up bank accounts of hundreds of thousands of dollars. La Guardia's election had returned to Centre Street reformers like Lewis Valentine and Patrick McVeigh, who took a dim view of bribery, but favors were still a currency recognized throughout the brotherhood in blue.

McVeigh was a man who remembered his debts. When Michael Shanley took a bullet on the job, Pat marched behind the casket, a step behind the widow. McVeigh owed Michael Shanley, and the debt was not canceled by his death. So McVeigh owed his widow a private survivor's benefit. He would rather have paid it off in cash and in visits to her parlor. But Mary refused to sit at home and showed up one day in McVeigh's office in her little white bowler with a black ribbon and black leather gloves, asking for a job.

Squeak, squeak. The Captain shifted in his chair, testing the springs, but that didn't help. It was more of a *chirping* sound than a phonograph needle. For a moment he listened to it as a welcome distraction. But when he looked up, Mary was still waiting for his answer.

McVeigh remembered Mary on her wedding day, a slender girl trembling on the arm of Michael Shanley. He remembered her serving him coffee in her kitchen two o'clock in the morning the day his own boy Donny died, when he wept on her table, wracked with the sobs he could not let Margaret see. And clearest of all he remembered Mary on the evening in February 1933, when he had gone to tell her that Michael had been shot in the Bronx, near Dutch Schultz's place on 149th Street. It turned out to be one of the last gun battles of Prohibition, and the fact that beer was pouring again by April hardly made Michael's death easier to forget.

When Schultz was gunned down the following year in Newark, New Jersey by Charles 'the Bug' Workman of Murder Incorporated, McVeigh sent a note to Mary. She responded with a visit and asked for a job, and he gave it to her. Now Mary sat across his desk again and kept her eyes on the battered baseball in McVeigh's ashtray, signed by the infield of the 1933 Giants after their victory over the Senators. She was asking for yet another dividend, but not one entirely outside the economy of favors.

"What are you looking for, Mary?"

She glanced at the photograph of La Guardia mounted on McVeigh's wall. "Something useful to somebody. Something to set right. Something *different*."

"A case of your own."

"Yes, sir."

McVeigh remembered Mary's first tour of duty—how her eyes had widened at what they saw and then narrowed, trying to fix it. She had picked up the language of the streets quickly, which now sounded like her native tongue. But she could still speak in the muted tones of the drawing room, which allowed her access to many places closed to a regulation dick.

At least it would keep her from firing her sidearm. A quiet investigation might be just what Mary needed and good for the bureau as well. Investigators talked to people and sifted through evidence. They never had to pull the trigger, did they? Johnny Cordes wouldn't even carry his gun. So how much trouble could Mary get into, assigned to the right case? She had brought in three dips on her own, hadn't she? Maybe she deserved a promotion. Or a rest.

He ran a hand over his buzz-cut. Mary waited.

"What is that twittering noise?"

"There's a nest outside your window. See it, in the tree?"

There was a pile of sticks in the crook of a branch. McVeigh didn't see a bird. "I've never heard it before."

"You wouldn't, Captain, would you? Since it's just spring."

He heard it now. *Twee twee, twee twee.* With all that racket at home, Mama must be out for worms.

McVeigh sighed. "The Dip Squad calls for an eagle eye, Mary. You've got two of those. But investigations require a detective to think—to put the pieces together in a logical way, to make sense of every little thing you see. Can you do that as well as Johnny Broderick?"

"I think so, sir. But if you need a second opinion, why don't you ask Margaret? Once she's back on her feet, I mean. Please send her my warmest regards. And wish her a speedy recovery."

"I will, Mary. Thank you. She'll appreciate that."

Mary waited. One. Two. Three.

McVeigh raised his eyes. "I never told you she was ailing, did I?"

"No, sir. But there's a bag from Ratner's in your wastepaper basket. Margaret usually packs your lunch."

McVeigh tilted his trashcan. Red-and-white striped wax paper under a crumpled report. "She could be out of town, couldn't she?"

"It's possible. But there's also your beard, Captain."

He stroked his cheek. "I shaved."

"Not particularly well, I'm afraid. Your left cheek is smoother than your right cheek today. You must've shaved this morning by the light from your bathroom window, without turning on the overhead bulb. But Meg is an early riser. She must be under the weather, if she was still asleep when you were up and about."

McVeigh rubbed both cheeks more vigorously, and the grizzle on his right felt rougher than the stubble on his left cheek. Below his right jaw-line he had missed a patch entirely. It was a shadow Johnny Broderick never would have noticed, or bothered to think about, even if he did.

"She went to bed with a migraine. But she's feeling better today."

"I'm glad to hear that, Captain."

The telephone sat on the edge of his desk. He could have called Margaret easily. But McVeigh already knew what his wife would say.

"I'll tell you what, Mary—we'll give you a turn at investigating and see where it leads. Okay?"

Mary held her breath. *Yes, that was just fine.*

"Nothing fancy, of course. You won't be after Willie Sutton or Legs Diamond. But a woman came in yesterday morning to report a girl missing from her boardinghouse, and she's come back today. Why don't you talk to her? If you find the girl, I'll see what else we can give you."

22

Mary knew the girl would probably be a pro who disappeared after a beating from her pimp. Or she had gone home to mother and would never have a kind word to say about New York. Yet it was a chance to take on a case of her own that would not come again.

"I'm game, sir," said Mary. And so she was.

Three. The Boarder Guard

The Detective Bureau was upstairs, on the second floor of the precinct house. Downstairs on the first floor were the beat patrols, the sergeants who sent them out, and the officers who took complaints from walk-in citizens. Mary tramped down the steps and found the boardinghouse manager waiting on a hard bench in the precinct's anteroom with a carbon of her missing persons form.

She was a white-haired woman in a knit sweater, who sat hunched over her cane. Her eyes were watery blue, squinting between pink, hairless lids at posters of the FBI's most wanted fugitives. Mary sat beside her, smelling German sausage and cabbage. The woman smoothed her skirt across her trembling knees. They sat for a moment in silence, two women on a bench, until Mary moved a little further away and cleared her throat. "Mrs. Teitlebaum?"

The old lady looked her over skeptically. "Tanenbaum. Like the Christmas tree. Unless you'd rather call me *Mrs. T*, the vay everybody else doss."

"Tanenbaum is fine, Mrs. Tanenbaum. My name is Mary Shanley. I understand you filed a report."

"Dot's right. Because von of my girls is missing. This is the place to come, is it not? For missing persons? Or am I barking at the wrong tree?"

By the woman's accent Mary knew she had been born in Europe, but by the way it slipped as she moved through her sentence, Mary guessed she had been here a while. The missing persons report form had been filled out with thick, deliberate pencil strokes, like a kindergarten child with a crayon, and the sevens in the phone number had crosses through the upright strokes.

"You reside at 228 West 21st Street?"

"For twenty-two years. An apartment three years before. Erich vas two when we first came, but when Eva was born, I needed a house."

"Where you now take in boarders."

"Girls only. No boys."

Mary put aside the report. "Tell me about the missing girl."

"Tell *you*?"

"Please."

Mrs. T looked past her. "I vant to see a detective."

"I *am* a detective. Officer Shanley. Just like any of the policemen here." The woman looked doubtful, but Mary refused to be offended by it. "Why don't you tell me about your establishment?"

Mary had noticed her use of *my girls*, which made Mrs. Tanenbaum notice it too. The old woman made a face that wrinkled her lips.

"Don't go getting the wrong idea about me or my girls. I run a decent house, for ladies who need one. No men are allowed in the private rooms, and none of the girls do anything they shouldn't, for cash on the barrelhead. I'm not saying every von's a virgin. Not in this day and age. When a girl has a fiancé and they feel like doing what they're going to be doing soon anyway, no one on earth can stop them. Just not in my house, is all I'm saying. No rooms for prossies."

Mary nodded. It was an important point among working class people, whose daughters were at risk of sliding into prostitution to cover the monthly bills. The dread of it kept every immigrant father at his labor, and every mother awake at night. The Depression had only made the danger tworse.

"Miss de Soto is a good girl, then."

"Rosetta is a working girl," Mrs. T said. "I mean, she has a *job*. More than one in the last four years." She shivered when the street door opened, but settled down again. "When she first arrived, she said she had a sales position at Wool-worth's," carefully pronouncing the two double-ues. "I don't think she did, at the time. Her friend Louisa, who brought her, she had a job lined up. But they took von look at Rosetta and hired her too. For the perfume counter." Mrs. Tanenbaum sniffed as if to suggest the scent.

Mary waited. "She's a nice looking girl?"

"Oh, yeah. She dresses nicely, always did, even right off the boat. Nothing frilly, you understand, just plain cotton dresses with a collar or a bow, but they always fit her figure in a flattering way. Of course, Rachel helps her take them in, who manages a sewing shop. But her dresses always fit nicer than Rachel's dresses, and she's the von with the needle."

Mary began taking notes. "Rachel --?"

"Lipinsky, another boarder. Her room is across the hall. Those are Rosetta's friends, Louisa and Rachel. Louisa I can understand -- a soft-spoken girl. Rachel, on the other hand -- when I gave her a key, I had no idea vat kind of girl she was."

"What kind is she?"

Mrs. T lowered her voice. "A Communist. Who spoke beautiful English, better than mine. She was a manager in a garment business, a dozen girls on machines sewing dresses during the day and taking in piecework for a few dollars more. That was her idea, to help them make ends meet."

"Thoughtful of her."

"Oh, she's always thinking! There's a sweet side to her, I've got to admit. Who knew a Jew spoke such perfect English? Only later, when she was already paying rent every month, I learned Rachel was mixed up in the unions. And worse than unions, if you know vhat I mean."

"Does Miss de Soto have anything to do with that?"

"Rosetta? She doesn't care about politics. She's Italian."

"Tell me about her other friend."

"Louisa? Vitanza."

Mrs. Tanenbaum watched Mary jot it down.

"Also Italian?"

"They met on the boat, crossing over. Rosetta had been sent for, you understand, by a cousin on her mother's side. Only the photograph he mailed to Italy must have been tventy years old. When she saw him waiting at the dock with a hat crumpled in his big red hands, she refused to go with him, and they sent her over to Ellis Island for a hearing. They could've sent her back to Sardinia, but she was healthy as an ox, and they always let the pretty ones stay. Rosetta had no place to go, but Louisa had a girlfriend who gave her my address, and the two of them showed up together. I felt sorry for her, when I heard her story. That's the reason I took her in, even though I knew she didn't have a job lined up at Woolworth's."

"Do you know the name of the man she was supposed to marry?"

"The first husband?"

"Did more than one man send for her?"

"Just the cousin. A butcher, Aboulafia. But the other is the man you should be asking about."

"Okay," said Mary, "I'm asking. Who was he?"

"Guiseppe Farinacci—Joey, she called him, when he came around. He owns a little grocery on Mulberry Street."

"Rosetta was supposed to marry him too?"

"She met him a just couple of weeks after she moved into my place, but he's a fast worker. Rosetta came home with a chunk of provolone or Genoa salami. And as fast as you could sing *O Sole Mio*, the two of them were engaged."

"But they didn't hit it off?"

"They hit it, all right!" Mrs. Tanenbaum sighed. "These Italians are always worried about their daughters' virginity— family honor, you know. But, like I said, once they're making wedding plans, there's not a lot anybody can say to keep a girl from doing something she might regret later."

"Did Rosetta regret it?"

"What else? Some of these guys will promise the moon on a Kaiser roll. But when it comes to making good, all you get is a handful of seeds."

"Joey refused to marry her?"

"Should he buy the cow, when he had the milk for free?"

"Is that what he said?"

"No. I don't know. They never got married. She didn't tell me why. But Rosetta would have told me—she always told me—if she was planning to go away for three days." Her eyes

27

filled suddenly and Mrs. Tanenbaum wiped them with her fingers. "Something happened to her. I feel it in my bones. If you don't find her, I'll never see her again."

Mary knew what any other detective working the bureau would have concluded: her complainant didn't know that a crime had been committed. According to her report, all Mrs. T actually knew was that one of her tenants had failed to come home three nights in a row, whose belongings were still in her room. Any other dick in the bureau would have said to her, "Thanks for coming in and filing the report. These things take some time, but we'll get back to ya."

And that would have been the end of it.

But Mary was not like any other detective, and in her opinion the fear in Mrs. T's pink-rimmed eyes counted as evidence. The NYPD did not set a priority on the anxiety of a woman like Gertrude Tanenbaum, or even on Miss de Soto. But Mary Shanley did. She knew that all over the city women were wiping away tears no one knew had fallen. Rosetta de Soto was a working class girl who had left her family in Europe. The only one who cared enough to notice she was missing was a landlady who stuck her nose into the business of her boarders. But this was Mary's case. Now there were two of them who cared what happened when a girl off the boat disappeared.

Four. Salami and Yeggs

Joey's American Grocery had a green awning with the name printed in white letters along the forward edge. Beneath that, a hand-lettered cardboard sign in the plate glass window read *drogheria.* The tiny store was crammed between a dress shop and *fioraria,* whose windows offered bouquets of bluebells, irises, and sunflowers, and half a dozen wilting roses. The dress shop was larger than the florist and twice as large as Joey's, with a large black Chrysler parked at the curb in front.

Joey Farinacci's grocery was much more modest, with no car parked in front of it. But the groceries had been carefully arranged to look fresh and inviting. On the sidewalk outside, creating an aisle to the open door, were slanted bins of potatoes, onions, and plum tomatoes, and a proud display of red and green apples. Another hand-lettered sign between the crates read, *Try Our Recipe For Apple Pie!*

A bell jingled over the door as Mary stepped inside. She found bare floorboards swept clean, shelves lined with canned artichokes and olive oil, whole tomatoes and tomato paste, and a stack of jars of peanut butter and jam. Along the right side of the store a refrigerated case offered three wheels of cheese, four kinds of salami, proscuitto, cappacola, and rising circle of linked grey sausages behind a sign that read *Hot Dogs!* Hanging over a chopping block at the back of the store were more sausages and cheeses in loose-knit casings and a pile of freshly baked breads. On the left side near the door was the cash register, and behind the register stood Guiseppe Farinucci, a slender young man in a red-checked shirt under a white apron. In front of the register stood a rack of newspapers, four New York dailies and *Il Progresso Italo-Americano*, a copy of which lay beside the register open to the sports page.

It had taken Mary until three o'clock to locate Farinacci's grocery, but there was no one else in the store when he looked up and asked, "Yes? Can I help you?"

His face was long and pale with a cleft chin and a dimple in his cheek that appeared and disappeared as he worked his jaw. One curl of black hair had worked itself free and flopped onto his forehead, so that Mary had to resist the impulse to push it back up.

"Guiseppe Farinacci?"

Her Irish brogue and fox-fur collar must have stood out in the neighborhood, because Joey replied, "Are you police?"

"How did you know?"

"Because you are here. I am waiting all day!"

"For me?"

"*Per la polizia.* You're a policeman, no?"

"A policewoman, yes. From the detective bureau."

"So!" Joey pointed toward the door.

Inviting her out? Mary hesitated. "I just have a few questions."

He moved to the door and swung it open, rattling the knob back and forth. "Picked, no?"

Mary examined the lock, which on close inspection did show scratches of a professional jimmy. It was a cheap lock, which probably took two minutes to spring.

"You really need something stronger than this."

"A cage," he said. "*Andiamo.*"

He turned and she followed him down the length of the store, behind the breads and through a door that stuck, into a tiny room at the back of the store. It had a running toilet, a stained sink, a metal locker cabinet, and beside the lockers an iron safe squatting in the corner. The door of the safe was ajar, and Joey swung it wide.

"You see?" he said. "Robbed!"

"Burglarized," Mary corrected, seeing no evidence of violence in the theft. But she didn't give him a chance to ask about the difference. "What did they get?"

"Everything." He gave her a mournful, tight-lipped smile. "Two hundred dollars." He spoke with a slight hesitation before each phrase, which could have been his difficulty with the language or the thought he was giving to his words. Despite his efforts at self-control, Mary read the emotion pressed between his lips.

"I'm sorry," she said. "It must be a terrible loss. But that's not why I'm here."

His dimple vanished. "No?"

"I'm investigating a missing person—Rosetta de Soto. I understand from her landlady you were seeing each other. Socially."

"Rosetta?"

"De Soto. That you even asked to marry her."

"*Si.* Rosetta was my *fidanzata.*"

"Your fiancée?"

"Yes."

"Why did you break it off?"

"Why did I ...? *Non caspisco.* I didn't break it off."

"You didn't?"

"Me? No. She did."

"Rosetta broke your engagement?"

He nodded. "She wanted to go out all the time, to movie houses and dance halls. I was always saving my money for this grocery store—first to rent the storefront, second to fix it up, and then to stock the shelves. I was saving every penny. But Rosetta, she wanted somebody to treat her to a night on the town or maybe a pair of stockings. Should I buy a store, or a pair of stockings?"

Mary peered into the safe, which was certainly empty. "How did you meet?"

"Here, on Mulberry Street. A cousin on her mother's side sent for her from Sardinia. He was a butcher on Mott Street, *un maiale*, you understand? A fat pig. When she saw him, she refused him. I met her a couple of weeks later, at the church. She was living with her friend Louisa at a boardinghouse on Twenty-first Street."

"At Mrs. Tanenbaum's."

31

"When I asked her to marry me, Rosetta said, '*Si*, Guiseppe, *grazie.*' We walked through the park like a couple in Italy, without the aunts. Then she started asking me to take her dancing, to the movies, every place. When I said, 'No,' she said, '*Arrivederci.*'"

"She left you? After she...?"

"Made love with me? You think I abandoned her? No, no. I would never do a thing like that to a good Italian girl."

"Was she a good girl?"

"Rosetta? Of course she was, when we were together."

"You were never intimate?"

"Intimate?"

"Did you always treat her like a gentleman?"

"Ah. Intimate. In Italy, you can only see a girl with her family, but here everything is freer. Once you're engaged to be married, girls will come to your room. Rosetta is a girl who enjoys herself, but she never did anything to make me think less of her, the whole time we were together."

"And after?"

He looked at the floorboards. "I don't know."

"What?"

He looked up and shrugged. "American boyfriends."

Mary nodded. "*Capisco*," she said, sympathizing with the struggle against the attractions of American life.

Michael had first noticed her at picnic and then came courting at her parent's apartment. But how many times had he called her his *girl from the old country* or *wild Irish rose*, poking gentle fun at her traditional manners? She had learned to be an American afterwards, as a police officer's wife. How much harder must it have been for Guiseppe Farinacci and Rosetta de Soto, when both of them were greenhorns, fresh off the boat?

"Thank you for your time," she said and stood up to leave.

"What about this?" He waved at the safe.

"They ought to send somebody to look into it," Mary said.

"When? Today?"

32

"I don't know if they can make it today," she admitted, knowing that the Detective Bureau had more pressing business on their agenda. The celebrity cops of the squad spent their days chasing gangsters like Arnold Rothstein, whose murder made page one of all the papers. How much time would they give a burglarized grocery on Mulberry Street, without clues or reward or headline ink?

She took a quick look around the scene of the crime. "You haven't touched anything in this room, have you?"

"Nothing," Joey swore, both hands on his heart. "But for how long? This is a grocery, a cash business, and now I have another reason to lock my receipts in the safe."

Mary pointed to, but did not touch, a square of wax paper with a few crumbs still in the crease, sitting on top of the toilet tank. "Then this isn't yours?"

Joey held out his hand. "*Mi scusi!* I'll throw it away."

Mary pushed his palm away. "No you won't. If it doesn't belong to you, who do you think left it here?"

He paused. "The robber?"

"One of them," Mary said. "There were two. One sat here, on the edge of the porcelain, eating a sandwich of cold cuts, while his partner opened the safe. Smell it on the wax paper? Ham and cheese."

Joey sniffed. "Prosciutto."

"Do you have something we can use to wrap it up?"

Joey left the room and returned a moment later with a torn page of newsprint. Mary took a black leather glove from her purse, fit it on her right hand, and used a gloved forefinger to slide the wax paper onto the newsprint. Joey folded it around the wax paper as if it were a quarter pound of Genoa salami fresh off the scale.

"Okay," said Mary. "We might be able to get a print off the wax—a fingerprint of the man who sat on the toilet seat and watched his partner work. Maybe even the one who picked the lock on your door."

It was a faint hope. Mary wasn't even sure that wax paper would hold a print, but it suggested that New York's Finest were doing something to catch the yeggs who had cracked Joey's safe and run off with all the money he had in the world. From the care with which he handed over the square of newsprint Mary could tell how much sacrifice had gone into the stolen two hundred dollars. Its earning had cost him a wife at least already.

"When should I call to find out?" Guiseppe asked.

"Let's see what they can do with it," Mary blustered, as she carried the square of newsprint carefully through the store. The bell jingled overhead as she opened the door with her elbow. "We'll get back to ya."

Five. Charity

Erich Tanenbaum had been the first man in his brickyard to volunteer to fight the war to end all wars, and the first man in his platoon to be wounded at the Somme. A mortar shell deafened him as he struggled over the wire, and when he could hear again, they told him they had to cut off his left leg below the knee. When he arrived home at his mother's house on West 21st Street, three female boarders had occupied the upstairs, including the bedroom that had been his own. Erich decided to moving downstairs when he realized he could no longer reach the second story without hugging the handrail and risking a fall. The brickyard had already hired their share of veterans, and no one else was eager to hire a one-legged construction worker, even for federal projects, so Erich spent his afternoons in his mother's first-floor parlor, listening to the radio and writing to the newspapers about whatever provoked his consternation and made his thigh itch.

La Guardia's reluctance to act against a threatened subway strike was the topic of the day's obsession, when Gertrude Tanenbaum admitted Mary Shanley into the foyer of her boardinghouse. Mary could not see Erich from there, but she could hear his voice as he shouted through the rooms. "You see, Mother? What did I tell you? What do you get, when you elect a labor lawyer to the mayor's office? The same old business, for the same old clients. While the tax-payers pony up to pay the piper."

"Since vhen have you been paying taxes?" Mrs. Tanenbaum replied, in a voice too quiet to carry through the rooms.

But Erich evidently heard her, because he roared back, louder, "And what vould you call my left leg?"

"Missing in action," said his mother, in a wistful tone that suggested it might have been better for everyone if Erich had gone with it. Then she turned to Mary and smiled. "My son doesn't get out much."

He spoke English without an accent, Mary noticed, until he got excited, when a bubble of his first language surfaced. Hadn't Gertrude said that Erich was two years old when he was brought to this country?

"Does your daughter live with you too?"

Mrs. T sighed. "Eva's gone to Spain, after her no-goodnik husband. Have you found Rosetta?"

"Not yet," said Mary. "Her former fiancé claims he doesn't know where she is, and I think he's telling the truth. You said you had a picture?"

"Yes, of course, right here," said Mrs. Tanenbaum, moving to the foot of the staircase. On the wall, rising with the steps to the second floor, were photographs of the family and of all the women who had boarded with them. Among the lowest on the wall was a framed photo of a slim young woman with rolling curls and fetching eyes. "You can't tell from black and white," Mrs. T said, wiping fingerprints from the glass, "but she's a redhead. With green eyes."

Rosetta wore a checkered dress with puffy half sleeves and a smart little hat tilted to the right, with a feather in the brim. Around her neck hung two gold chains, with a cross at the end of each one. She was smiling at the photographer, as if they shared a secret. This was not the picture her husband-to-be would have seen of her in Italy, but something else, taken of Rosetta in New York one night on the town.

"This is recent?"

"I had to ask Rosetta, again and again. But she finally took a picture and gave it to me, three months ago."

"I'd like to hold onto this for a while, if I can."

"Will you return it?"

"It might also help if I talked to her friend, Louisa."

"I don't think she's home," said Mrs. T. But she limped over to the staircase and called, "Miss Vi-TAN-za! You have a caller!" She waited a second before she said to Mary, "It's not so easy as it used to be for me to get upstairs. And ever since Erich came home without a leg—"

"I have a leg, Mother," he shouted from the parlor.

"Without two legs, we've been forced to give up certain niceties we used to enjoy here. A girl goes up to clean on Mondays and Thursdays, but when it comes to knocking on a door ..."

"Of course," said Mary. They waited another minute, listening, before she said, "Would you mind if I went up and knocked on her door myself?"

Mrs. Tanenbaum pointed her cane at the third step. "Watch that von. It's loose. I've asked Erich to fix it, and it's right here by the ground floor, where he can reach it. But he's glued to the couch by the radio." She shook her head.

"I'll be careful," promised Mary, stepping from the second to the fourth riser under Mrs. T's scrutiny. "Thanks."

From the parlor Erich called out, "First door on the left."

When Mary reached the top of the stairs and turned to her left, she found the first door closed but the second door open. Standing in the light from a window behind her was a figure wearing a blue cotton dress printed with red-and-white flowers large enough for Mary to distinguish the stamens from the pistils in the blossoms. The silhouette stood with one hand on her hip, which made her look provocative for a girl in her twenties, and her generous bosom stretched the fabric in a way the boys must have found attractive.

"She's not home," said the girl in the doorway.

"Louisa Vitanza?" said Mary, pausing to catch her breath from the climb.

"Right," said the girl. "She's out."

"And you are—"

"Her friend," said the girl. "Who are you?"

"Detective Shanley," said Mary, raising her hand to block the light from the window.

The girl made no move to accommodate her. "From your brogue and your sensible shoes, I would have guessed you were a cop, Miss Shanley. But I didn't know they had lady cops in plainclothes."

"They do."

"So enlightened. And enlightening."

"Don't you care for officers of the law, Miss --?"

"I don't care for anybody who beats innocent people over the head with a stick. Have you ever done that, Officer Shanley?"

"No."

"Not once? At some hardly-worth-mentioning police riot?"

"I work the Pickpocket Squad."

"Then you can come in. I'm Rachel Lipinsky." She turned into her own room without looking back.

Mary followed her.

After the hallway Rachel's room was stunningly bright. Its southern exposure once belonged to the master bedroom, with a view of a sweet-gum tree whose branches wore the setting sun like debutantes decked for a ball. When Mary's eyes adjusted to the light, she saw a bed made with hospital corners, a bureau without makeup or perfume bottles, a writing desk piled with papers, and a bookcase so stuffed with books, some had sacrificed their paper covers to make room on their shelves for new comrades. Unframed posters covered the walls, arranged as carefully as paintings in a museum, so that the red of one advertising Emma Goldman's magazine, *Mother Earth*, matched the trail of blood in another that showed a Pinkerton beating a coal miner. One poster publicized an exhibit in February 1908 by Robert Henri, John Sloan, and six other artists who painted ordinary people doing ordinary things on ordinary New York streets. Another poster publicized the June premiere of a musical called *The Cradle Will Rock*, produced by Unit 891 of the Federal Theater Project. By the brightness of its paper stock and the freshness of its ink, that poster was plainly newer than the rest, the only one advertising an event yet to occur.

"Do you like musicals, Officer Shanley?" asked Rachel, dropping on the edge of her bed without mussing its folds.

Mary was not a musical fan. Shortly before his death Michael purchased two of the three thousand seats in the Center Theater and took her to see "The Great Waltz." Backed by John D. Rockefeller, it had a cast of 180 wearing five hundred costumes while dancing to the music of Johann Strauss. For the "Blue Danube" finale, a fifty-piece orchestra rose from below stage, while eight crystal chandeliers descended from above. The only other time Mary had seen a live stage musical was when she had followed a "seat-tipper" into a Broadway theatre. As she led him out in handcuffs, Mary saw Bea Lillie struggling to order "a dozen double damask dinner napkins" in the Shuberts' revue, *At Home Abroad*. The routine left the crowd in stitches but it did not inspire Mary to buy a ticket.

"I don't have time for the theater," she said.

"Too bad," replied Rachel. "My boyfriend's working on a musical that's going to be a sensation. If you're interested, I can probably get you a ticket."

The playwright's name was emblazoned on the new poster. "Is your boyfriend Marc Blitzstein?"

Rachel laughed. "No, but I wouldn't chase him out of bed, either. My boyfriend's in the cast."

"Does your roommate have a boyfriend?" Mary asked.

"My roommate?"

"Across the hall."

"You mean Louisa, next door?"

"No," said Mary. "I mean Rosetta de Soto."

"Rosetta *is* across the hall," Rachel conceded, "when she's home. But I thought you were here to see Louisa. I distinctly heard Gertrude calling her name."

"I wanted to see her about Rosetta."

"Why?"

"She's been missing, for three days. Hasn't she?"

Rachel sat on her bed and leaned against the wallpaper. "She's been gone for three days, it's true. But that doesn't mean she's *missing*."

39

"What else could it mean?"

Rachel looked her over again. "What kind of cop are you, exactly?"

Mary shrugged. "Like any other officer."

"Only female."

"That's right. For whatever difference that makes."

"But it does," insisted Rachel. "It should. For one thing, you're here, aren't you? Mrs. T would never have let a male cop upstairs. Besides, how many cops do you think would be worried about a missing charity girl?"

"A charity girl?"

"Don't you know what that means? How did you get on the force, anyway?"

"I asked for a place."

"It must be a lovely world, for ladies like you."

Mary could have argued with that. Instead, she said, "What makes Miss de Soto a *charity girl*?"

"That's a complicated question," said Rachel. "But I'll tell you what it signifies. There are lots of working-class girls in this city, with underpaid, respectable jobs. They work telephone exchanges, sell lingerie, and do all the things you can't get a man to do for such low wages. Their families need the money to make ends meet, so they take the paychecks these girls bring home, but they don't give them back any spending money, like they do for their brothers. So how is a girl supposed to see a movie or go dancing, since all those places cost money?"

"A guy asks them out on a date."

"Sometimes, if they're lucky and belong to the middle class. Otherwise, they have to make some other arrangement."

"Like what?"

"Not what you're thinking. They're not doxies. They're very clear on that. They don't accept money for sex, and that distinction is incredibly important to a charity girl. They just trade favors for treating."

"What kind of favors?" asked Mary.

"That depends on the guy and the treat. If he takes you to a dance hall and buys you something nice, like a pair of stockings or shoes, you might be really nice to him. If not, maybe all he gets is a kiss or a hand job. One girl I know asked the man who treated her to pay her butcher bill. The butcher was closed for the night, but she would not take the money herself and pay off the butcher in the morning. That, you see, is what a whore would do, and she was not a prostitute."

"Is this a new thing?"

"The idea is as old as men and women," said Rachel. "What did your basic Neanderthal want for a seat at his fire? But the American version, of men treating girls in exchange for a little sex has been going on since the turn of the century, when dance halls and movie theaters first opened in New York. Before then, any woman out in public was presumed to be for sale. You found good girls at home, in their mama's parlors, waiting for suitors to drop by."

That was where Michael came for Mary. But she said, "You're telling me that Rosetta de Soto is—"

"A working-class girl in a Depression, who does what she has to do to get by. And to have a little fun, while she's trying. Do men want to treat her? Yes, they do. She's a pretty girl. Does she show them any charity in return?" Rachel made a face and shrugged extravagantly. "Who can say?"

Mary had the distinct feeling that Rachel could say, but she didn't want to press her or the girl stop might stop talking altogether. Mary touched her hand to her cheek, and it was hot. Despite all she had seen on the Pickpocket Squad, Mary discovered that she was still capable of being shocked by her fellow citizens.

"Isn't it dangerous? This 'treating' exchange?"

"It can be. Rosetta came home with a black eye, after one night out. I guess somebody didn't get what he expected. Rosetta said she would never see that guy again, and she stuck to it. But there are always new movies coming out and new guys willing to take you to see them."

41

"But why can't Miss De Soto pay for her own movie seat? I thought she landed a job at Woolworth's."

"She did, with Louisa's help. But Rosetta sends most of her salary home to Italy. I think she has a brother, who also wants to come over. Who knows how long that'll last? You might not have noticed, but people are losing their jobs every day."

"What about you?"

"Me? I'm in the *shmata* business—the garment industry. Our union gives us a little protection in the market."

"And in your personal life? Do you let strange men treat you to the town?"

"Officer Shanley! Are you asking me if I'm a charity girl?" Rachel laughed. "No, I'm not. I only sleep with dreamy-eyed socialists."

"While Rosetta's friends—"

"Are certainly not socialists. Treating is an exchange of the capitalist economy."

"Do you happen to know who they are? These men who treat Rosetta?" Mary remembered Joey Farinacci talking about *American boyfriends*, and only now understood what he meant by it. In his reluctance to explain, or even to meet her eyes, he had been acting like a gentleman after all.

"I don't know their names. Louisa might. But the heat cut out the other night, and Rosetta lent me a sweater when she saw my teeth chattering. I washed it out and have it here, somewhere." She opened the bottom drawer of her dresser, where Mary saw clean skirts and sweaters neatly folded and stacked. From one pile Rachel took a college sweater, close-knit white wool with blue-and-gold piping around the neckline and wrists. Rachel spread it across her bed so they could read the bold blue letters across the chest.

CHOATE.

"Now where do you think Rosetta got a thing like that?"

Six. The Midtown Tube

The Choate School in Wallingford, Connecticut, was founded in 1896 for young gentlemen, when Mary Atwater Choate and her husband, Judge William G. Choate, hired Mark Pitman as the first headmaster. In 1908, George St. John was named as successor, who was still serving as headmaster in the spring of 1937, when Mary Shanley tried to contact him by phone. The operator who picked up would not put her through, however, no matter how clearly Mary tried to state her name and business.

"Shanley, yes. With the New York City Police Department. As I told you, this is police business. That's right—I'm a detective. No, I'm not calling *for* a detective. Can you please put the call through to Mr. St. John?"

Apparently the operator could not or would not disturb the school's headmaster, who was teaching a class.

"At this time of night?" Mary inquired. "What sort of class is taught at ten o'clock in the evening? How to lay one's head on a pillow?"

But the operator did not have an ear for sarcasm and was not permitted to reveal any information concerning the school's curriculum by day or night.

"Would you ask the headmaster, please," said Mary, feigning patience, "to call me back at the number I just gave you? The call concerns a missing girl, who might have seen one of your boys on the night she disappeared. Would you ask him to check and see which of the boys might have caught a train from New Haven to New York City three nights ago? That would be very helpful. Thank you."

And Mary went to make herself a cup of tea in her kitchen. It was her favorite room in the apartment, just the right size for a woman of forty-four living alone. She had a Kelvinator made of steel and porcelain, and a two-tap sink with the new Marel finish that hardly left a stain. Michael had refinished the cabinets for her, and she had made the chintz curtains herself, with a delicate pattern of roses and lilacs over the small, rosewood table. The mahogany table in the dining room was too large for her, alone. The silence from the other chairs kept rushing into her ears.

Both bedrooms had become shrines to the two men in her life. Eddie's bedroom had been left the way it was when he went off to Notre Dame, Loyola Law, and Tammany Hall. Michael's spirit was still present in every corner of their room. The living room and dining room were the scenes of family occasions, birthdays and holidays, and Mary found the floating dust intolerable. No, the kitchen was the room where she spent her hours at home, as few as possible. But tonight, as she brewed her tea with her shoes off, Mary felt as pleased to be home as she could remember feeling in a very long time.

It had everything to do with Miss de Soto. For the first day on her own case, Mary had done rather well. She had spoken to several people who knew the missing girl, and from their accounts she began to get a sense of her character. She had a lead on a young man who might know where Rosetta was—who might even have gone for a joyride with her. Mary felt sure that another day of snooping would turn up the girl, or at least an explanation for her absence. Gertrude Tanenbaum would be reassured and Captain McVeigh would be satisfied, perhaps relieved, but either way willing to give her another shot at investigative work. All in all, Mary felt she had made a good start and sipped her chamomile, sweetened by a blend of fatigue and contentment.

An hour later, she dimmed the lights and looked out over Forty-Seventh Street. People were passing beneath the pin oaks at the curbside, and Mary heard the traffic on Second Avenue. Beyond that, the elevated trains rumbled on Third. She left the window open, so the sounds of the city could lull her to sleep. She did not need the silence that summoned Michael's ghost to kiss her eyelids closed for the day.

But she was not the only person awake that night.

*   *   *

The Lincoln Tunnel had first been planned in 1930, when the Port of New York Authority announced its intention to construct a Midtown Hudson Tunnel between 38th Street in Manhattan and Weehawken, New Jersey. Three years later, Governor Herbert Lehman appointed Robert Moses chairman of the New York State Emergency Public Works Commission, and the tunnel project was re-imagined by the man who served also as the Parks Commissioner of New York for Mayor Fiorello La Guardia.

Lehman had served as Lieutenant Governor under then Governor of New York State Franklin Delano Roosevelt. Lehman, La Guardia, and Moses had little trouble obtaining from President Roosevelt's Public Works Administration the money needed to construct the tunnel—seventy-five million dollars worth. Ole Singstad, who had built the Holland Tunnel at Canal Street, was hired to design a second tunnel to the north, and Othmar Ammann of the Port Authority was named chief engineer.

Workmen were hired to dig the tunnel from both ends and meet in the middle. Crews of "sandhogs" entered a series of air locks, which were sealed behind them as compressed air was piped into each lock, preparing them for the pressure in the next lock, deeper under the Hudson River. The inside seal would open and the crew moved to the next lock, where their ears would pop again from the increasing pressure. Each sandhog worked half an hour in the morning, rested for five hours, and worked half an hour again in the afternoon. Working in this way not a single life was lost by the time the crews met under the Hudson, when an engineer working the Jersey side was pushed by his feet through a hole in the earth to the New York crew in August, 1935.

Since that day, crews had worked in relative safety to complete the tunnel, which was scheduled to open to traffic in December, 1937. By day the walls echoed with picks and concrete mixers, with massive machines driving and the voices of men at several levels shouting instructions and warnings. By night the tunnel echoed only with the footsteps of security guards assigned to protect the equipment left on the site. The tunnel itself was beyond the need for protection. It was a grand project of the city as a whole, a hallmark of national renewal, as far beyond the ability of any man to destroy as it was for any individual to create.

But it was not the only project of its magnitude Robert Moses was working, the night Mary Shanley called Choate. At the same time, his crews were constructing the East Side Drive. The first section slated for completion ran from the Triborough Bridge at 125th Street south to 92nd Street. His original plan required the city to condemn properties owned by Con Edison and the Washburn Wire Works, at a cost of a million dollars and twelve hundred jobs. Moses was consumed with the problems of redesigning both facilities to accommodate his parkway, and had left the finishing of the Lincoln Tunnel to the senior members of his staff. For that reason, the call went to Deputy Parks Commissioner Lowell Handley, rather than to Moses himself, when one of the crew in the Lincoln Tunnel discovered something buried in the tube.

Lowell Handley was a plump man with a bald head who usually dressed in the vest and trousers of a three-piece suit. His heart doctor had forbidden him from smoking but not from chewing on an unlit cigar, which he did whenever he needed to focus his thinking. It made him look like a contractor rather than the Deputy Commissioner of Parks and Recreation, since Moses had plucked him from a contracting firm as "a man who could get things done." Moses gave him the title because it was available and because he needed someone on whom he could rely to finish the blasted tunnel. Lowell Handley's actual job had nothing to do with the parks of New York City, but he did know whose number to dial, when a night watchman turned up something awkward in a pile of fresh earth.

Handley called Commissioner Lewis Valentine, who called Patrick McVeigh, who called Detective, Johnny Broderick, who was drinking in a gambling hall with a couple of reporters when he got the ring. Always sociable to the press, Broderick invited his two drinking partners to accompany him to the Lincoln Tunnel for a bit of excitement. The morning papers carried the story beneath the headline:

DEAD GIRL FOUND UNDER THE HUDSON

A night watchman patrolling the site of the Midtown Lincoln Tunnel last night saw a glint reflect off his flashlight and found a cross of gold in a pile of earth waiting to be carted out of the tube. Digging deeper, Martin Yarazslavsky, 44, discovered the body of an unfortunate young woman, whose remains showed signs of a beating.

Detective John Broderick was called to the scene, who promised to "bring the perpetrator of this homicide to justice before he can wipe the dirt from his hands." Readers of this paper are familiar enough with the resourceful detective to know he intends to keep his word, "by any means necessary." Det. Broderick wasted no time in finding a clue: a second gold chain around the neck of the victim, which prompted a series of provocative questions from the experienced officer.

"If the girl is still wearing her gold cross, who does the second one belong to? Did the killer leave his own cross to mark her secret grave? Are we looking for a religious fanatic? Just another Catholic with a crime to cover up? Or someone with a grudge to avenge?"

The public is asked to call NYPD Headquarters on Centre Street with any information that might help identify the pretty young victim or solve her grisly murder.

Mary nearly spit up her canned peaches and sour cream when she read the story over breakfast. Could that be anyone other than Rosetta de Soto, buried beneath the river?

If both crosses had been found around the poor girl's neck, Mary would have had no doubt, and no alternative but to call Pat McVeigh immediately. Since the corpse had been wearing only one cross and the other had been left in the dirt, Mary had enough cause for uncertainty to finish her coffee and think about what it might mean for her own missing-persons investigation.

Johnny Broderick was a celebrity cop, a ham-fisted detective who insisted that criminal types tip their hat when they passed him on the street. If a junior officer brought in a suspect for questioning who walked with a swagger, Broderick would teach him to blacken the mug's eyes just to uphold the bureau's reputation. They called him "the Boff," since his tough guy days in the Gaslight District, when he copied his left hook from Jack Dempsey. The Boff would stroll down Broadway with a lead pipe wrapped in a newspaper and swing it at the first hoodlum he saw. If he took a shine to a working girl, he would stuff her pimp in a garbage can. The legend around Centre Street was that Broderick once played the same trick on Legs Diamond. Only the year before, Edward G. Robinson had played Broderick in a movie called *Bullets or Ballots*. Only the Boff was bigger than Edward G.

If Broderick found a body, and the press was around, the case was his, no question. But that was a case about an unknown girl in the midtown tube. The case of Rosetta de Soto was still Mary's and would remain hers only if she could turn up enough information to stake her claim to it. That would require more than telling McVeigh or Broderick himself, "I think I know her name."

Mary needed more time. She dialed McVeigh's office, knowing he wouldn't be in yet, and left a message for the Captain to call. Then she dressed in the new frock she had saved for a special occasion, because Eddie had warned her to look her best. He was coming by this morning in his car to drive her to City Hall.

The dress was a floral print with a white lace collar, and she set it off with a beige feathered hat. She tilted it to the left, tried it to the right, and before she decided which she liked best, the telephone rang, startling her.

For a moment she worried it might be McVeigh, returning her call. No—still too early for the Captain. Or Edward, calling to cancel, because something had come up at Tammany Hall that needed a personal fixer. It turned out to be Gertrude Tanenbaum whispering into the phone mounted on the wall at the bottom of the stairs in her boardinghouse.

"She's home," Mrs. Tanenbaum seemed to be saying.

Mary was confused. She imagined the dead girl in the earth turning over, who turned out not to be …

"Rosetta?"

"No, no! The other one. Didn't you vant to see Louisa Vitanza?"

Seven. City Hall

"No, Mother, absolutely not," said Edward Shanley, when Mary climbed into his 1936 Packard and he reached across her lap to close the door behind her. The front seat felt like a throne to Mary, overstuffed and covered in a crisscross weave. The padded dashboard was intended to buffer the passenger from a sudden shock, if she were thrown forward in a crash. Sunlight hit the windshield as Eddie pulled away from the curb into a stream of vehicles as ponderous as his own.

"No," he said again, as if she had insisted. "We do not have time to stop off—where did you say?"

"A boardinghouse. At 228 West 21st Street."

"At a boardinghouse? Why would you want that?"

"It's my job," Mary said quietly, anticipating his reaction, which was to flare his nostrils, flush his cheeks, and breathe more rapidly. He forced the shift in and out of gear, negotiating the traffic.

"Your job is to spot pickpockets. Are you expecting a rash of picked pockets at the boardinghouse?"

"Not exactly."

Edward shook his head. He did not like his mother working. He would have preferred she sit at home, knitting patterns from the Ladies Home Journal. If she had to get out, as she insisted, why on earth did she have to prowl the murkiest streets of New York?

"I'm trying something new," Mary told him.

"Houses of ill repute?"

"Missing persons," Mary said. "A missing young girl."

"Aha," said Eddie, as if he had tricked out a confession. "Something we need to discuss."

They were moving at a nice clip down Second Avenue, where the morning traffic could be awful.

"There's nothing to talk about," Mary said, "unless you want to discuss your work for Tammany. It's my job, Eddie. I'm a policewoman."

Mary's son made a face as if the gutter had just reached his nose. "You know how I feel about that, Mother."

Mary did, though she suspected he didn't himself, actually. Edward imagined he disapproved of his mother taking on any paid employment, let alone a job with the police that required her to visit a boardinghouse. He thought he was protecting her, keeping her from the reality of New York's streets. In fact he was ashamed of her, embarrassed by her public display, with no way to explain why his mother was not in her kitchen, like the mothers of his friends. Some of their fathers were dead too. But none of their mothers were Mary.

"I can't help how you feel, Eddie. But I'm not a thief. I'm the lady who catches a thief and locks him away."

Edward nodded. He had heard that before. He had heard it the day she took the job, and on many days after. "Do you have to catch one now, Mother? This very morning? Or could you possibly wait until the service is over?"

Ever since his father's death, Edward spoke like a parent to Mary. The pressure to become the man of the family had pushed him all the way to a disapproving dad. It seemed odd to her, because Michael had earned his son's respect with an easy manner that suggested he never needed to prove anything.

"It's practically on the way," Mary said.

"No, it's not, Mother. Not to City Hall." She was silent for a minute, and so was he, concentrating on the road as a big Chevy nearly cut them off.

When Eddie spoke again, it came out a whisper. "Remember what it was like for us? Do you really want Hizzonor and the rest of the brass waiting on Mary Shanley, while Sheila MacFarlane weeps silently on stage?"

Mary felt a pang of memory and pushed it away. She forgot sometimes that Michael's death was not her loss alone. Eddie had lost a father, and the anger she seemed to provoke in him was his own way of dealing with it—of not having to deal with it. She had to admit, she didn't relish the prospect of remembering it either.

51

With a flush she settled back against the woven seat, relieved that it was not her husband receiving a posthumous medal. Eddie cursed the traffic.

"Are you fighting with Liz again?"

"No. We're doing fine."

"You had better learn to get along, or how to use an iron. Look at your collar." She reached over to smooth it down.

"Please don't fuss, Mother! Sit back in your seat. I don't want you flying through the windshield, if I have to brake again for this idiot."

When they arrived at City Hall, Mary refused Eddie's offer to drop her out front but rode with him to the parking lot and walked back to the building. She loathed the idea of walking into that airless room without his arm to lean upon. But when they did, when they entered and found seats in the third row, when she took off her overcoat, folded it in her lap, and set her hat upon it, Mary discovered that she hardly remembered it at all. The room was larger than she thought, with high windows that allowed the crisp morning sunlight to pour in, marking off hazy trapezoids on the chair-legs and floor.

She found she could draw a breath, and there was enough air between the motes of dust floating in the sunlight from the windows. The relief enabled her to take a look around and notice what she had missed when Michael had been the officer they gathered to memorialize.

Most of the audience were police officers, the brass in uniform in the front row, detectives in suits and patrolmen in uniform scattered in the seats behind them. Mary recognized Commissioner Lewis Valentine in the first row, his long, narrow head rising above the others, even without his hat. She scanned the close-cropped haircuts and to her relief didn't see Captain McVeigh or Sergeant Broderick, who would have been sitting near Johnny Cordes in the second row of chairs.

There were a few women in the crowd, friends perhaps of the deceased or the widow, with here and there a suit among women dressed like widows themselves.

Mary only dimly recalled how it had felt, to sit at the front of the wood-paneled room in her widow's weeds, looking over the sea of faces who could not meet her eyes—or did not meet them, with a sad expression of pity and relief that whispered, *Better you than me, honey, better yours than mine.*

No, that was unkind. Mary knew their sympathy for her loss was genuine as their admiration for Michael's courage. But what good did sympathy do, if it could not bring him back? It could not dull the throbbing in her ears, or draw her mind away from the spot on her cheek where Michael had kissed her. She heard shuffling feet on the floorboards and saw the dyes of their clothing bleed together—blues, grays, white and black. Yards and yards of black.

Was that for her benefit? Or were they assembled not for her or even Michael but for themselves, to assure themselves they would not be forgotten if they fell in the line of duty?

"Fell" was the word the Mayor used, as if Michael had tripped on a banana peel, instead of standing up to Dutch Shultz in a gunfight in the Bronx, tracking a murderer to his hole. It was such a gentle word, really, almost graceful in the way you imagined he went down. Instead of bullet-ridden, bleeding from the holes in his chest and arms and even from his face.

The spot on her cheek still tingled, but more like a caress than a wound now. She set her fingers over it and it felt warm to her touch. Imagine.

Mary had to push that out of her memory, because Fiorello La Guardia had entered through a door in the rear of the room. Mary hadn't noticed it the last time. The mayor just seemed to appear in front of her, like an angel floating in the motes of dust and sunlight. He wore a dark jacket and pin-striped pants, a white shirt and pale gray tie, which gave him the look of a funeral director. But you couldn't help sensing the strength in the man, in his broad chest and the confidence of his movements. Mary could still feel the dry palms as he took her hands between his own—so much larger than she expected in a man of his size. He cupped her elbow, guiding her from her seat, while his gravelly voice murmured in her ear.

"Mrs. MacFarlane," he was saying now, as he walked the widow to the rostrum, where Commissioner Lewis Valentine was waiting. "You have our sympathy for your terrible loss. And our gratitude for the service of your husband. Scottie was a first-class officer, and even better a man."

Was that what he said to her? Mary couldn't remember. But it had calmed her, allowed her to breathe, to stand beside him at the rostrum, accepting the slippery ribbons that should have been pinned to Michael's chest instead of lying in a velvet box. Like the box in which they put Michael himself.

LaGuardia was shorter than Sheila MacFarlane, who bent her head at the rostrum to minimize the difference. He was solidly built, with black eyebrows that seemed darker than usual in a face composed for grief. New York's first Italian-American mayor had a background as mixed as the city itself. Catholic on his father's side and Jewish on his mother's, His Honor had been raised a Protestant. He spoke six languages well enough to work as an interpreter at Ellis Island. His first wife and daughter had both died of tuberculosis in 1921, when he devoted himself to public life, representing Greenwich Village in Congress from 1922 to 1932, heading the Board of Alderman, and winning the Mayor's office in 1934. He was up for re-election in 1937, but he knew how to control his feelings and when to explode them. He had controlled them pretty well on stage, while Mary's exploded beside him.

Now it was her turn to sit on a hard wooden chair holding her hat in her lap and watching Sheila MacFarlane weep beside the Mayor. But Eddie was right—it was better to sit in the crowd making foolish faces than to sit on the stage trying to stanch the hole where your heart used to be.

Valentine's long, narrow face did not change expression as he unclasped the box and held it open to the mayor. Hizzoner lifted the thing by its ribbon and caught the medal of honor in his free hand. He seemed to admire it for a moment and then turned to Sheila MacFarlane almost reluctantly.

"It's not much," he said to her, "to replace the man you lost. But it's all we can do to honor his memory. Please accept this medal, Mrs. MacFarlane, on behalf of Scott. And know that it means more to us who knew him than we can possibly say. The City of New York is a safer place today because Officer MacFarlane lay down his life to protect it. We won't forget his sacrifice, or yours, in the days to come."

"Stop fidgeting, Mother." Eddie leaned forward and picked a nit from the crease of his trousers.

Mary sat back, squaring her shoulders.

"Officer MacFarlane responded to a burglary alarm," La Guardia said. "From the description provided by the druggist, he recognized the robber, who shot a clerk on his way out of the pharmacy. Scottie knew where his man would go to brag about his crime. Without a thought for his own safety, Officer MacFarlane drove to a gambling room on the Bowery. He walked right up to the second floor and collared the burglar in front of his laughing friends. Except one of them wasn't laughing. He shot Scot MacFarlane in the back, as he dragged his suspect downstairs by the scruff of his neck.

"Scottie had called the precinct on his way over, so we got the drugstore burglar and the coward who shot him in the back. They both got what they deserved, thanks to Commissioner Valentine and his boys. They're good men in a pinch. But how many officers have the courage to do what Scot MacFarlane did? We all know bad guys. We even know where they are. But how many of us would walk right into the middle of them, to haul out a murderer?

"It wasn't long ago in this city that the average citizen had no place to turn for protection. The police weren't interested in a robbery unless the store's proprietor could post a private reward. But those days are over. Officer MacFarlane took the call, knew his man, and went to get him, without asking for a handout from the citizens he served.

"That's the kind of police force we need in this city, and that's the kind we have, thanks to men like Lewis Valentine and Scott MacFarlane, whose heroism has cost a terrible price. Mrs. MacFarlane, I can only say thank you again from all of your fellow citizens, for the price you personally have paid. I can only promise you this: we will not forget your husband. We must all work together to build a city that deserves men like Scott MacFarlane to defend it."

He put the Medal of Honor back in its velvet and handed the box over to Sheila MacFarlane as if it were the key to the city. The audience clapped politely and stood at their seats, and Sheila MacFarlane started weeping again. La Guardia gave her his hankie and urged her to blow her nose, which she did, twice, discreetly. Mary had to wonder how a grieving widow left the house without a hankie of her own.

And that was all of it. The ceremony had seemed so much longer to Mary, when she had stood there, unable to control her weeping, feeling exposed to all the pity and fear she found in the eyes around her. She had wanted to apologize, not merely for her own outbursts but for Michael's awkwardness in getting killed in the first place. They all had places they would rather be. None of the officers liked to be reminded of the danger he faced on the job. None of their wives needed to be reminded that the doorbell might ring late one afternoon and the precinct captain might be standing on the other side with a grim-faced pastor beside him. Now Sheila MacFarlane was looking out with the same apologetic face. But she couldn't say *Sorry*, so what could she say?

She nodded at La Guardia in thanks or acknowledgement, which is just what Mary had done. Only now, Mary hoped, she could do more. She thought of the girl in the Lincoln Tunnel half buried in the dirt and set a hand on her pocketbook to feel the revolver inside it.

Eddie leaned closer to murmur, "What did you think of the speech, Mother? What do you think of Hizzoner?"

"He seems to care about law and order."

56

"He needs to seem that way. He hasn't secured his party's nomination yet. An incumbent mayor."

"I thought he was very popular."

"He could win in a New York minute. But La Guardia is a Republican—not one of ours. And his party is unconvinced he has a Republican heart."

"Will he get it?"

"Sure. But first they'll make him sweat."

He did seem to be sweating already, but it was hot in the room. People were scraping chairs, filing out, and talking—cheerfully, it seemed. While the new Widow MacFarlane still stood at the front, blinking in the sunlight.

Afterwards, when the mayor had left with the uniformed brass, some suits and patrol officers lingered in the hall, drinking coffee from a percolator on a folding table by the door. On the wall above the coffee was a mural of New York in the eighteen-twenties, when the city hardly reached above Fourteenth Street. The New York Police Department didn't exist until twenty years later, in 1845, when 800 men started patrolling the streets under its first Chief, George Matsell. Edward knew some lieutenants from his work at Tammany Hall, whose political and financial support had secured their promotions. They stood in a circle, murmuring through tight lips, clamming up whenever anyone else came by to refill their cup at the pot. Mary thought she saw Eddie passing out cigars, but none of the looeys would light up in City Hall, in the morning, with ladies present.

Mary did not see Johnny Broderick or Pat McVeigh in the hall but she recognized Izzy Einstein and Moe Smith—two middle-aged, Jewish federal agents who made nearly a thousand arrests a year in the 'twenties and would have closed down the breweries all by themselves, if the United States Justice Department hadn't shut them down instead. They were talking to two ladies in feathered hats and gingham frocks with black ribbons pinned to their lapels. Mary remembered them from Michael's memorial service. They must have lost men of

57

their own and turned out to pay respects. Mary was a member now of the widows-of-heroes brigade, but she was the only one of that corps who carried a badge of her own.

On the ride home, she sat for a while in silence. So did Eddie, who seemed to concentrate on the road more than he had on the way down. There was more traffic, later in the morning, but his mood had changed more than the number of cars on the road. He glanced at Mary a couple of times, as if he had something to say to her but never managed to get it out. He unbuttoned his jacket, tugged on his checkered vest, and raised his chin as he peered through the windshield.

When they approached 20th Street Mary said, "Drop me at the boardinghouse," and Eddie didn't object. He turned down 21st Street and rolled to a stop at a fire hydrant in front of 228. Leaning across his mother, he unlocked the passenger door and pushed it so that it swung open wide.

"Good luck, Mother," he sighed. "You can go get the bad guys now."

Eight. Frozen Roses

Louisa Vitanza was sitting at the kitchen table in a bathrobe when Mary Shanley came in from the street. The bathrobe was pink chenille, ragged at the cuffs, with a faded orchid stitched over the heart. She had cheekbones, with big brown eyes and pouty lips sipping coffee from a chipped cup. Her hair was black as India ink, cut short, and pinned in tight curls along her neckline. In front of her sat a piece of burnt toast on the saucer, scraped with gobs of jelly.

Mary accepted a cup and allowed Mrs. Tanenbaum to fill it halfway with coffee. From the parlor came the radio, tuned to a broadcast from the Jarama Valley, where the Abraham Lincoln Brigade were fighting to keep the roads open between Madrid and Valencia. With her free hand Mary waved the landlady out of the kitchen and occupied a yellow chair at the table.

As Mary settled herself, Louisa crunched her toast. "You're the lady cop, aren't you?"

"Rachel told you about me?"

"Mrs. T said something. But I can always tell. By the way you sit. Like you're squeezing something between your knees."

"I'll try to stay loose."

Louisa shrugged. "Don't go to any trouble on my account."

"I'm here on Rosetta's, actually," Mary said.

"She's not home," said Louisa, sipping her coffee and making a face.

"You're friends, aren't you?" asked Mary. "You met on the ship from Italy."

"It's a long trip. I talked to lots of people."

"It *is* a long trip. So you must have had time to get to know one another."

"I guess. She told me her story and I told her mine."

"But that wasn't the end, was it? When she met Aboulafia and refused to marry him, you came to her rescue, by helping her find a place to stay in the city."

Louisa broke a sugar cube in her coffee. When it dissolved, she said, "I wouldn't call it a *rescue*. Somebody told me Mrs. T ran a cheap and decent place. I wasn't sent for, so I had to make my own way in America. Rosetta had no place to go either, so I let her tag along."

"And then found her a job at Woolworth's."

"They needed a girl on the soda counter. She needed a job. Big deal."

"It was a big deal to her, wasn't it? A life-saver, I'll bet."

"Okay, you got me—I helped her out. Anybody decent would have. If she's in trouble with the law, that doesn't make it my problem."

"She's not in trouble. At least none that we know of."

"Then why are we having this conversation?"

"She's been missing for the last few days. Mrs. Tanenbaum is concerned."

"I already told her she shouldn't be. Rosetta went off for a few days, that's all. She needed a little vacation."

"She told you about it?"

"Not the details—just asked to borrow my suitcase."

"Did you see her carry it out?"

Louisa frowned. "You think I sit around, watching people? We all come and go. And have to work sometimes."

"We can find out if she used it."

"How?"

Mary glanced upstairs. "Let's take a look."

"In her room?"

"It shouldn't take very long."

Louisa shook her head. "Rosetta...went on a trip, okay? She told me she was going away. If Gertrude had asked me first, I could've told her that, and she never would have gone to the precinct house."

"Have you any idea where she went?"

"Rosetta? Not exactly."

"And you wouldn't tell me, anyway. But if you don't know where exactly, you can't be certain she went. So let's make sure she's all right." Mary stood up and waited.

"This is ridiculous," said Louisa, settling her cup as if she planned to get up. But she just sat there, staring at the puddle of coffee at its bottom.

Mary brought her face close to Louisa's. "You want to get rid of me, don't you? It's that easy. Just a few steps up the stairs and down the hall. Then I'll be satisfied. I can finish my report, and you can drink your coffee in peace."

Louisa put her palms on the table and lifted herself to her feet. "It's cold already, full of grounds, and way too sweet. Let's get this over with."

It didn't take them long to reach the second floor, even with Louisa dragging her slippers over each riser on the staircase. Mary tried the knob of Rosetta's door, which turned easily, but she had to use Mrs. Tanenbaum's key to open the lock. Inside, Mary saw a bed neatly made with a plaid blanket and a suitcase lying on top of it. Open.

"Is that yours?"

Louisa nodded. "She must've had something to add."

"And left it behind," said Mary.

Louisa stepped forward and pressed down the clothing. A lacy nightgown nearly floated out, clinging to her palm. She stuffed it back inside and smoothed down some lingerie and casual wear, a fancier frock and a sweater. Too many things for a weekend.

Louisa snapped the suitcase shut and turned a worried face to Mary. "Well? Do you know where she is?"

"I have an idea."

"You can tell me, can't you? After all those questions?"

"I could show you," said, Mary, "if you're willing to come with me."

"Where?"

Mary shook her head. "I'd hate to get it wrong. It won't be pleasant, but it could be helpful."

"I have to be at work in a couple of hours."
"We'll be done by then."
"Is there anything I should bring?"
"Just a coat."

*   *   *

Bellevue Hospital was founded in 1736 as the first public hospital in the future United States. Bellevue was the site of the country's first maternity ward, ambulance service, and nursing school, on the principles of Florence Nightingale. The hospital building in 1937 resembled the Biltmore Hotel in Los Angeles, with two big rectangles connected by a short central section, where Bellevue's main entrance was located.

As they headed downstairs to the basement, Mary chatted with Louisa, whose growing awareness of their destination drained the blood from her cheeks.

"Mary Nolan is here," said Mary, glancing at the ceiling and the psychiatric ward above them.

"Who?" said Louisa, stumbling on a step.

"Mary Nolan, the movie star. She played in *Shanghai Lady* and *The Foreign Legion*. She danced in the Ziegfeld Follies, too, as Imogene Wilson. The papers called her Bubbles. But that must've been before your time."

"Uh huh."

"Are you all right?"

"I guess." But Louisa was shivering, and they hadn't even reached the Morgue.

When they did, they found a young man with a bird's nest of red hair. He was sitting on a stool beside a dissecting table, leafing through an illustrated anatomy book. His white coat was stained on both sleeves from his cuffs to his elbows.

Louisa whispered, "Is that the coroner?"

"The Chief Medical Examiner for the City of New York? I doubt it."

The young man looked up. "Can I help you?"

62

"We'd like to see a body," Mary said, fishing a badge from her purse. "A new arrival."

He peered at it doubtfully, and she scribbled a name in the margin of his book, which he turned and tilted to read.

"Just a minute," he said, shoving a tangle of hair off his forehead.

Ten minutes later he returned with a corpse under a thin white sheet. The gurney was steel, and one of its wheels kept turning toward the others, so he had to pull it from the front to prevent it from swerving.

"Couldn't find her at first," he said. "We still had some sewing to do."

Louisa's face lost even more color. She reached her hand toward the thin sheet but couldn't bring herself to lift it.

"Let me get that for you," he said and rolled the sheet back from the face. He did it with surprising delicacy, as if the cadaver might complain.

"You're a medical student," Mary said.

"Pathology," admitted the redhead, extending his hand. "Warren Wexler. They opened a program in forensic medicine five years ago. Best place in the world to learn it. I'm only in my third year, but they let us work on the…patients."

"Did you work on this one?"

"Assisted. She came with a lot of noise, you know? From the tunnel they're digging to Jersey. They don't give us the high-profile cases. Just the drunks and whores."

He glanced at Louisa, who was blinking at the corpse.

"Is it her?" asked Mary.

Louisa shook her head. "It could be. I can't tell for sure."

"Because of her face? Or the damage?"

Louisa shook her head. "What happened to her?"

"She was autopsied," said Wexler. "Standard procedure."

"Is that what caused…all this?"

"Bruising? No, she came with most of that. You see the stitches, here?"

He pushed back her hairline to reveal a jagged line.

63

"Those are post-mortem—where we cut to see her brains. We don't beat them black and blue."

Mary smoothed down the hair. "You think she was beaten to death?"

"That's what the M.E. decided. These marks usually come from fists."

"And the square ones?"

"A belt. We found traces of leather where the skin was broken. But the interesting thing is, no buckle marks. Whoever did this was angry enough to take the belt off his trousers but considerate enough to hold the metal end."

"They look wide for a belt."

"Some belts are skinnier. They make 'em wide, too."

"Anything else you can tell us?"

Wexler looked at Mary, then at Louisa, and flushed. He shook his head.

Mary had an inkling what that might mean. She stepped behind Louisa, who was still staring at the corpse, and crooked a finger at Warren.

He followed her, growing redder.

"Pretend you're not talking to a lady," Mary said, out of Louisa's earshot. "Imagine I'm just a cop with a moustache and beer belly. What could you tell me about the deceased?"

He looked at the ground and mumbled, she had something or other.

"What?"

"Sex," he blurted. "She had sexual relations. Not long before she died."

Now it was Mary's turn to blush. She looked at Louisa, who didn't seem to hear, while the moment gave her a chance to collect herself.

"Can you tell with who?"

Warren shook his head. "It's not like he left his fingerprints. All I can tell you is, I typed the, uh, evidence, and he's AB positive."

64

Warren flushed again, and Mary knew that was all he was going to say. She gave him a curt nod and returned to the body on the gurney.

Louisa was bent over the dead girl's head now. She cupped her chin in one hand, and held her scalp with the other, as if it might fall off. The eyes were closed, but there were still traces of shadow on her eyelids and dabs of lipstick on her mouth. The skin looked flabby, pale, and glazed over, as if they had pulled it from a lake in the winter.

"She looks cold," said Louisa, touching the flaky lipstick. "Petrified. Like rose petals in the freezer."

Mary said, "She's Rosetta de Soto, isn't she?"

Louisa bit her own lip, to stop it from trembling. "Yes, I think she is. Or was."

Afterwards they sat outside, and she cried on a bench.

"I know it's hard, Louisa," Mary said, "and you don't want to think about it now. But if we're going to get him—if we're going to catch the guy who did this to Rosetta—we can't afford to waste any time. If we let it slip away, so will he."

"All right," said Louisa. She wiped her eyes with her hands and her nose on her sleeve. "What's going to happen to her? When they're done with her body?"

"They'll keep her here a while. Then bury her."

"In a pauper's grave?"

"Unless somebody claims her. Did she have any family?"

"Not in New York. Somewhere In Italy, but I don't know where, exactly."

"You talked on the ship, didn't you?"

"We boarded together in Palermo. But she didn't come from there. One of the other islands—I got that impression. Sardinia, maybe, or Corfu."

"Does her last name tell you anything?"

"De Soto? I don't think it was her family's name, in Italy. She changed it when she got here. She wanted to sound more American."

Louisa smiled bitterly and then fell silent.

Mary waited a few minutes to allow her to continue, before prompting her with a question. "When was the last time you saw her alive?"

"On Thursday," said Louisa, "when she asked to borrow my suitcase. I gave it to her and left her to pack. Then she called me back, to close it. We both had to sit on top."

"But we found it open."

"I guess she must've opened it."

"She never said where she was going?"

"No."

"Weren't you curious?"

"I knew. Somewhere with one of her boyfriends."

"Tell me about them."

Louisa hesitated. "Rosetta was a pretty girl. She had a few boyfriends."

"Did you two talk about them?"

"Sometimes. She joked about them. Like, there was one that worked for the city, in construction, I think. An older guy. Mr. Stubs."

"Stubbs? One B or two?"

"That wasn't his actual name. That's what she called him, because he chewed these smelly cigars right down to the last half inch."

"Can you remember anything else? Anything she told you about him?"

"I can't think too clearly right now."

"Whatever you can recall."

"He likes jazz. At least, he likes going to clubs in Harlem. She saw Chick Webb at the Savoy. Count Basie at the Apollo, too, with Billie Holiday."

"All with the same guy?"

"I'm not sure. I thought so."

"Did he hit her?"

"With his fists? Not that she ever told me."

"Miss Lipinsky told me about a date who gave Rosetta a black eye. Could that be the same one?"

"No. I remember him. Guillermo. He was only a couple of years older than us, but already going bald. Skinny, with big hands, like lumps of coal. She promised me she'd never see him again."

"She called him Guillermo?"

"Rosetta called him *Paisano*. Guillermo was his name. La Motte or Ciotti, something like that. I can't remember exactly."

"You met him?"

"Once, but I know the type. The way they do it in the old country." She balled her fist.

"Do you know where we can find him?"

"I know where she met him. At the marionette theatre. *Orlando Furioso*. She told me he goes all the time."

"Who else?"

"Boys who took her out, bought her drinks and things. She never took money from them. Even when they offered."

"Just gifts."

"Right. Stockings, say, or shoes, nothing bigger than that."

"Except a little get-away?"

"A vacation? Maybe. I'd call that a gift for both of them, wouldn't you?"

Mary felt the color rise in her cheeks. This was not the way she spoke to her own lady-friends. "Any idea who could afford to take her away for the weekend?"

Louisa shrugged. "Her college boy could. She called him Mr. Darling. His family owns a place on the vineyard."

"Martha's Vineyard? In Massachusetts?"

"I don't know. A vineyard."

"Did she ever mention which school he attended? Are you sure it was a college?"

"He could be in reform school, for all I know. Boys lie. It had a funny name—Choke, or Shoat. Like killing a cat. "

"Choate?"

"Yeah. That sounds like him." Louisa made a face. "It's not a college, huh? Silly old Rosetta should've known."

67

Nine. Connecticut Corners

The following morning Mary did a regular tour of duty on the Pickpocket Squad. The Captain had explained that her "special assignment" would take her off the rotation, but when the squad was short-handed, Lieutenant McPherson could reach out and call her in for a tour. One brisk Wednesday morning, Mary found herself again on Broadway, following two ladies into a theatre lobby, where an usher wearing crimson and gold braid reached for her ticket and touched the cool metal of her badge instead.

"There are seats still open on the floor today, Ma'am." And he opened the drape to the orchestra seats, where the best-dressed guests were assembling. Mary smoothed the fur of her fox collar and undid the buttons of her coat.

Her target this morning was a gentleman with his overcoat turned up against the weather. Except he didn't fold it down again in the over-heated lobby, and stood in the shadow of the first balcony while the lights were still lit in the orchestra section. Once the lights went down, however, he strolled to a seat one row behind two ladies in feathered hats. He sank into a seat diagonally behind one of them, where he watched her feather bob up and down as she gestured to her neighbor. Her coat was already on the seat beside her, her handbag tucked behind it, and as she spoke, she undid the pin and set her hat on top of her coat.

The gentleman behind her unbuttoned his overcoat but never removed it, so the collar rode up, obscuring the line of his jaw. And yet, as the lights dimmed and the overture began, he settled back in his seat and stretched out his legs before him, preparing to enjoy the show.

Or so it seemed. But as the first act moved to its climax and the heroine on stage wrung her hands, the gentleman's foot was nervously active behind the seat in front of him. The toes of his leather boot found the bottom of the seat and tipped it carefully forward.

One row ahead, both ladies were staring at the unfolding scene, caught up in the angst of the moment. While their focus was fixed in the proscenium arch, the seat beside one of them raised silently, until the handbag tucked against the back of the seat fell through the opening, onto the floor. When it did, the gentleman behind them leaned forward discreetly and reached under the seat. But he did not rush to return the bag to the lady who had lost it. Instead, he allowed her to continue enjoying the drama, while he nestled her handbag in his arms and sidled out of his row.

He reached the aisle at the very crescendo of the scene. While the ladies dabbed their cheeks and kept their eyes on the stage, the gentleman behind them left the last seat and crept up the aisle toward the exit. But just before he slipped through the soundproof drapes that led to the theatre lobby, he felt an iron grip seize his wrist and heard an Irish brogue in his ear.

"This is a pinch, honey," Mary whispered, as she tightened the cuff around the thief's left wrist and then bent it upward, where she snapped the second handcuff around his right wrist. "You're busted."

It felt good to be using the argot of the street again, which in the last three years had become Mary's natural language. She wondered what Michael would think if he heard her now. He had avoided using the language of the street in her kitchen, but a lot had changed since he last drew his chair up to their table. Now Mary was trying to change, to enter the fraternity of Homicide detectives like Johnny Cordes and Broderick, where the talk was bound to be different. Yet compared to the change she had already made, it was hardly a leap—just a baby step from the Pickpocket Squad. "C'mon, pally," she said. "There's a nice, warm cell waiting for you."

He was a big lug, but with both hands cuffed behind his back there was only so much trouble he could make, as Mary dragged him back to the precinct house, shoved him into a cage, and typed up the paperwork. He stood in a corner of the cell and mumbled to the uniforms passing by, until they struck the bars with their nightsticks. He complained about the bust, his entrapment and the violation of his civil rights, but no one paid him any attention, and he finally sat down on the bench in his cell and settled into a funk.

But Mary wasted no time in booking this "seat tipper," as pickpockets working the matinee crowds were called by the plainclothes dicks. She had bigger fish to fry. And as soon as the wagon came to haul him away, she clocked out, completing her tour of duty and heading uptown to Grand Central Station, back to her own case. The very words, *her case*, thrilled and troubled Mary, who would only have cases of her own in the future if she made good on this one.

Grand Central Terminal had been built in the nineteenth century by the shipping magnate Commodore Cornelius Vanderbilt as part of a planned railroad empire. The renovated station opened one minute past midnight on February 2, 1913. More than 150,000 people stopped by on opening day. Its success stimulated the building of hotels and skyscrapers on Park Avenue, over the original tracks, and on 42nd Street, which by the 1920s included the Chanin Building, the Lincoln Building, and the Chrysler Building, each over fifty stories high. In 1937, Grand Central was the busiest train station in the United States, having housed at various times a changing suite of shops and restaurants, an art gallery and art school, a newsreel theatre, and a museum of railroad history. It was grand in all senses, from its clocks and ornamental eagles to the glittering chandeliers hung from its vaulted ceilings.

Mary needed the New Haven line. She was forced to quicken her step to take her place among the serious men in business suits and women in leather coats and silk skirts, sophisticated sheaths, or linen suits that flared smartly, concealing their hips. She bought a ticket at a window like the betting cage at Belmont and made her way to the track off the lower Suburban Concourse where the train to Connecticut lay waiting like a rodeo bull for its rider. The train was hardly full at that time of the afternoon, so she had little trouble in finding a seat by a window, where she watched her fellow travelers move more and more quickly down the broad steps and along the platform, until they were actually running and the train had left them behind.

It was a pleasant ride along the north coast of the Long Island Sound, through the Bronx, Pelham, New Rochelle, Mamaroneck and Port Chester, then over the state line to Greenwich, Connecticut, for the ride through Fairfield County. Mary rode past Westport, Southport, and Bridgeport, where the glittering blue sea reappeared in the window, as the coastline snaked in and out. The train rocked on its tracks, rattling on steel wheels as it sped from the cramped blocks of the brick city through the tall grass of the suburbs to the comforting stability of Union Station in the outpost city New Haven. It was not the last stop on the line, but Mary knew enough to gather up her things and disembark before the doors closed again for the last stretch of track to State Street.

There was a bus on South Main Street in the center of town, but Mary didn't know the route, so she hailed a cab and asked the driver to take her to the Choate School for boys. She was relieved to see that the cabbie needed no more address than that, since the school had been open for nearly forty years. Mary Atwater Choate and her husband, Judge William Choate, had founded the place in 1896, with four students under the care of its headmaster, Mark Pitman. The current headmaster, George St. John, had been running the school for the past twenty-nine years and was nowhere near stepping down. He was a keeper, no doubt about that, who bought dozens of houses and hundreds of acres of land, built eight Georgian buildings, and increased the enrollment to nearly five hundred students. All this Mary learned as her taxi bumped over lumpy New Haven streets and turned onto the boulevard that led to the campus. By the time they pulled into the curving driveway, she considered her fare very well spent on the information that accompanied her ride.

It was more than she learned from her visit to the school.

71

The headmaster's office was on the ground floor of one of the Georgian buildings, but George St. John wasn't in it. Instead, Mary found workmen cleaning the flue in the office chimney and refinishing the wood on the built-in bookcases. While his office was being refurbished, the headmaster had relocated to a small cottage on a hill, where two large collies lay in the grass outside the picket fence. Inside the fence were rosebushes with the buds of early spring starting to sprout and flowerbeds of exotic specimens lining the walk to the door. Mary lifted a brass knocker from the whitewashed door and let it fall against the brass plaque, twice.

A woman's voice responded, "Come in, please," and Mary did as she was told.

Inside the cottage, a tiny entrance hall opened on the reception room, where a woman in pince-nez glasses sat behind a writing desk. She was younger than the style of her glasses might suggest, and her hair was arranged in ringlets around her narrow face. She wore a white, ruffled shirt with a rounded collar, a big pink bow in place of a necktie, and a suit of pale green linen. The hues of her suit and tie matched the rose in a crystal vase on the left front corner of her desk. The right corner nearly touched the wallpaper beneath her window, through which Mary heard bees in the garden.

"Yes? Can I help you?"

"Is this the headmaster's office?"

"For the time being. Mr. St. George has been receiving here. But you don't have an appointment to see him, do you?" She turned the page of a ledger, screwed up her face, and turned the page back.

"I tried," Mary said. "But he hasn't returned my calls."

"He's a very busy man."

"So am I—busy, I mean. My business is rather urgent." When the woman looked doubtful, Mary leaned closer to add, "A homicide."

The woman closed her big ledger and held it against her shirtfront like a shield. "Are you with the police?"

"Yes."

"Detective Mary Shanley, is it?"

"That's right."

"We've spoken on the phone. I took your messages. But I haven't had a chance to share them with headmaster."

"You haven't even told him I called?"

"Not yet, no. He is—"

"A busy man. I understand. But now that I'm here, having made the trip from New York, is there any chance of telling him now?"

"He's with a student right now."

"He might appreciate the interruption, in this case. Because one of your young gentlemen may be connected to the death of a young lady."

The woman's jaw set resolutely. "I seriously doubt that."

"I'd rather discuss it with him."

"I told you, he's with a student. In conference."

"'I'll wait."

"It may take some time. His conferences do go on."

"Perhaps you have a magazine, or a book I could read." Mary glanced over the bookcases built into the wall behind a loveseat and Queen Anne armchair. The shelves buckled under enough reading material to keep Mary engrossed for several weeks of waiting.

The receptionist made a face. "Take a seat, please."

Mary found a collection of Edith Wharton's ghost stories to entertain herself, but an hour later, the door to the headmaster's inner sanctum had still not opened, and the woman in front of it was no more willing to disturb him.

Mary said, "Do you mind if I stretch my legs? And admire your grounds?"

"I told you he was busy today."

"I won't lose my place in line, if I do?"

The woman consulted her ledger. But the chairs were conspicuously empty.

Mary stepped outside the cottage and stood on the front porch for a few minutes. The two collies were still in the grass outside the picket fence. The bigger one picked up his head and looked Mary over, then resettled on his front paws, exhausted by the effort. Mary unlatched the gate to the picket fence and whistled under her breath, until the larger collie sat up on his haunches.

The smaller dog curiously followed her companion.

When Mary returned to the cottage interior, the receptionist was hard at work, printing addresses on envelopes in a florid calligraphy. She did not look up, until Mary said, "That can't be good for them, can it?"

The receptionist followed Mary's gaze to the window. Outside, one of the collies was standing beside a rosebush with his huge rear leg lifted. The smaller one was squatting behind him. The receptionist leaped to her feet. "You left the garden gate open? Miss Shanley! How could you?"

"Shouldn't I have?"

The receptionist didn't give her the courtesy of a reply, but rushed out of the door, shouting, "Bad dog! Bad dog! Get away from those roses, you bitch!"

Mary took advantage of the moment to push her way through the door that led to St. John's private office.

On the far side, the headmaster sat behind an ornate desk, while a skinny young man in shorts and a polo shirt slouched in a wing chair. George St. John had the build of a football player, with thinning white hair and a thoughtful face. His lips were pressed together and his eyes attentive as he listened to his guest's recitation.

"You know, headmaster, that Frederick Arlington was my only real competition. Now that's he's withdrawn, I don't see why you can't simply count up the votes."

"Has he withdrawn? Formally?"

"He told me that he would, sir. I'm sure he has."

"Why?"

"He thought better of his candidacy and went home."

"How fortunate for you, Jack."

"I enjoyed the give-and-take, of course. But now that Freddie's out—"

"We can cut short the voting? Is that what you want?"

The young man shifted his legs uneasily, and ran a hand through his tousled hair. He had a charming grin and turned its full wattage on St. George.

"I normally wouldn't ask, headmaster. But I think you know that Franklin has named my father to the Court of St. James. And it would mean so much to him if I were named Most Likely to Succeed before he sailed. To the whole family, really. And there are lots of us."

"I'm aware of your father's distinction," St. John said, "and the size of your family. But we have a process here at Choate. What would be the lesson, if we failed to follow it through? That one can play fast and loose with the rules? I'd hate to see you doing so, in the future. You know our philosophy. We save a boy's soul at the same time we are saving his algebra."

"My soul has been secured, sir, count on it. By all my years at Choate."

The headmaster looked heavenward and seemed to notice Mary for the first time. "Yes? Can we help you?"

Young Jack glanced at Mary and quickly lost interest. He crossed his arms in front of his chest and inspected his fingernails.

"My name is Mary Shanley," she announced. "Detective Mary Shanley, of the New York City police."

The headmaster listened with courtesy. "And—?"

"I'm investigating the death of a young lady who might have spent her last night with one of your students."

"Jack," said St. John, "would you mind stepping outside for a moment? I'll be right with you."

The young man looked at Mary with keener interest but left the room, nearly closing the door behind him.

When he was gone, Mary lowered her voice. "This might take more that a moment, sir. Since Rosetta de Soto spent the last night of her life with a Choate boy."

"She might have. Isn't that what you said?"

"I think she did."

St. John set his fingertips together. "I see. You *think* this unfortunate girl *might* have known one of our young men. Do I have that right?"

"It sounds tentative," Mary conceded, "but we could establish the truth with your assistance, headmaster. One way or the other."

"What sort of help did you have in mind?"

"You must keep track of the comings and goings of your students, I imagine. Who called a taxi to New Haven, who returned after hours. If you were willing to share those records, we could clear your students of the poor girl's murder."

"Or make a case against them."

"If they're involved."

"Not every case that seems convincing reveals an underlying truth," said St. John, "as any Platonist could tell you. Socrates was convicted by his fellow Athenians on the basis of a flawed argument. We at Choate would rather not contribute to false allegations against our own young men. I'm sure you understand."

"Not entirely."

"But enough to take my meaning."

"You won't cooperate."

"I thought you would understand, Miss Shanley. You might not like it, but you understood."

"What if they're guilty? Or involved in any way?"

"They're not."

"How can you be so sure? Before we start to investigate?"

"The gentlemen who enroll at Choate are not the sort to involve themselves in the kind of activity you are investigating. I have had sufficient experience of their integrity to say that with confidence."

"But what if you're wrong about one of them?"

"Then we will take care of it. If we have a problem of any kind—and I'm sure it will not include homicide—we will address it quietly at Choate, without assistance from the New York City police department. Thank you for your offer to inquire, but we who live in academic seclusion prefer to handle our own affairs."

His language was polite, even clerical, but George St. John meant that Mary had no jurisdiction in rural Connecticut, of which she was only too aware. He could refuse to share any information he chose, and Mary had to accept it. The only thing she could do was write her name and telephone on a slip of his creamy paper and set it on the edge of his desk. "If you change your mind," she said, and left the second half of her conditional hanging. The headmaster looked past it without touching the paper.

"Would you mind asking Jack to step in, please? On your way out?"

The young man in the polo shirt did not wait to be asked, but strode into the room and fell back into the chair as if nothing very serious had interrupted their conversation. Mary disappeared again into the Persian carpet.

"So, then, if you're ready, sir. To decide the contest."

"I'm sorry, Jack. But rules are rules."

"Is that your last word, headmaster? The best that Choate can do?"

George St. John shook his leonine head. "That's the wrong question, my boy. Ask not what Choate can do for you. Ask what you can do for Choate."

Jack broke into his million-dollar grin. "That's good, sir," he said. "*Ask not* ... I like that. Do you mind if I use it myself, someday?"

Ten. Pinball Politics

Whenever Fiorello La Guardia heard a certain kind of coughing, a pain ran from his left shoulder to his right hip, like a javelin through his heart. Since 1921, when he lost his first wife Thea and their daughter to tuberculosis, he could never stand the sound of a child coughing or heaving or gasping for breath. That meant he could barely tolerate tenements for their desperate poverty, the maiden aunt of malnutrition and illness. He liked to keep his windows open, even in the winter, so the chill in the air this spring morning was hardly a reason to shiver. As he sipped espresso in his underwear and robe, he listened to the traffic on his city's streets and wondered where he had left his trusty sledgehammer.

He would have asked Marie, who always knew where everything was. But she and the children were in Westport, Connecticut, opening the summer house they rented to escape the heat of Italian East Harlem. Without them the apartment was uncomfortably silent. The walls did not answer when he spoke to them. That was no reason not to brew his morning coffee or tie the sash on his red silk robe, but it did mean he would have to find the sledge for himself.

La Guardia had been raised in Arizona, on the army base where his father served as a bandleader. Though his mother was Jewish and father Catholic, Fiorello had been brought up Protestant, which meant attending church on Sundays with uniformed soldiers in the dry desert air. Having learned to speak six languages qualified him to work as an interpreter at Ellis Island, where he got a first-hand look at the immigrants of New York. He marched with strikers as a labor lawyer, and when he was elected to Congress in 1922 from Italian Greenwich Village, he spoke for "116th Street and Avenue A, instead of Broad and Wall." He could rouse a crowd as well as Hitler, Mussolini, or any of them, and won election in 1934 as New York's first Italian-American mayor.

Sure, he had made some mistakes, such as ordering the police to lay off striking taxi drivers rioting in Times Square. But he had also kept the price of milk at city health facilities at eight cents a quart, instead of nine. He did the same for public utilities and subway fares, refused to charge tuition at municipal colleges, and built new schools in the Bronx, Brooklyn, and Queens. He appointed Robert Moses as the Parks Commissioner, brought in Lewis Valentine to clean up the cops, and opened city jobs to Italians, Jews, and Negroes—or to *dagos, yids*, and *spades*, as his critics complained, under their breath or over a beer. But the voters of the city were on his side, and Fiorello's re-election in 1937 was a sucker bet, if only he could win his party's nomination.

The story in the paper was all about the resistance of Republican party bosses. Yes, they knew he could win the popular election. But no, they weren't sure they should nominate him, even if it meant backing a loser instead. After all, the party had to stand for something, didn't it? A political philosophy, fiscal policy—something. But whatever it stood for wasn't La Guardia.

His chief obstacle was Kenneth Simpson, the Republican Party leader with his name in the Social Register. Simpson was a Yalie who had belonged to Skull and Bones. He wore a moustache and parted his hair in the middle. Simpson would insist that the rest of the ticket be approved party stalwarts—most likely Newbold Morris for Council President and Joseph McGoldrick for Comptroller. La Guardia wanted Adolph Berle for the City Council job, but worried that even turning those posts into patronage positions might not be enough to satisfy high-minded Simpson.

The problem was he didn't *look* like a Republican, at just over five feet tall and nearly as wide. His political opponents called him *swarthy*, a champion of immigrants and worst of all, a favorite of Franklin D. Roosevelt. How could any self-respecting Republican support him for a second term as mayor of New York?

It was pure foolishness on their part. He was certainly no Democrat. He had crusaded against influence peddling by Tammany Hall, the Manhattan Democratic Club, for ten years in Congress. He had even been invited to speak at Yale. But what did he have in common with the bankers in their three-piece suits who controlled his own party? Not much, except a public aversion to vice, and gambling in particular.

La Guardia had opposed Prohibition. He had published his own recipe for beer, to demonstrate that it could be made with legally available ingredients, as was done all over New York in speakeasies and private bathtubs. The repeal in 1933 had been widely celebrated in the city. The first keg was tapped by Jimmy Durante, who served the first beer to Jack Dempsey at the Paradise Restaurant on Broadway and 48th Street. It was just after midnight on April seventh, four days after repeal. Ruppert's Brewery in Yorkville hired a thousand men on that day, an event worth celebrating for its own sake during the Great Depression.

But gambling was different. Gambling took money out of the pockets of the poor and lined the pockets of the Mob. LaGuardia had seen the costs of gambling extracted from too many working-class husbands and inflicted on too many wives. His Republican colleagues might have their own religious reasons for assailing gambling in public, but the Mayor didn't care why. They had that in common.

The gambling halls had protection from Tammany or higher. There were hidden pockets of politics everywhere. But there were other gambling spots spread across the city that no public official could protect. La Guardia hated going after the little fish, just because the sharks swam too deep. But his party's nomination was at stake.

Ergo, his sledgehammer. It might be in the front hall closet, standing beside his umbrella and Veteran's Day flag. Hizzoner sighed and set down his cup, tasting the bitter grounds of espresso ringing the bottom. He had some calls to make.

*   *   *

Mary Shanley returned to New York City without much to show for her trip to Connecticut. Still, she felt she had better report to the Captain, before he heard the story twisted by somebody else. Tired as she was, she made the trip from Grand Central to Centre Street and did not have to wait before McVeigh called her into his office. Where Johnny Broderick sat in the Captain's own chair.

"Mary," he said, swiveling back and forth.

McVeigh was standing at the window, trying to shut it evenly to keep out the late afternoon.

"Captain," said Mary crisply, ignoring Broderick.

"Mary, is it true," McVeigh asked, "that you have some information about the girl we found in the tunnel? That should have been shared with the detective?"

Mary hesitated. "I do have some ideas about the case, sir. Nothing definite."

"Except a positive I.D.?" Broderick said.

"I took Rosetta De Soto's roommate down to the morgue," Mary told the Captain, "in case she turned out to be my missing person. Louisa couldn't be sure it was Rosetta, though she did think she saw a resemblance."

"Taking into account the condition of the body," Broderick said, addressing his remarks to the Captain now as well, "the beating she suffered, not to mention the damage to the corpse from a quickie burial in a construction site—"

"We don't need to mention any of that, Johnny," McVeigh said slowly, "because Officer Shanley is aware of it."

"Then what the hell, Captain?" Broderick rose from the chair. "This is my damn homicide."

"The homicide may be his," Mary insisted calmly, "but the missing persons case is mine, isn't it? You gave that to me, didn't you, sir?"

Broderick shook his head.

81

"It's the same case, Captain. You might have given Mary some girl to find, but this is serious police work, now. The newshounds are onto it. Do you really want reporters following Annie Agnes Oakley?"

Mary glared. "Instead of Boffo Broderick?"

"Pat," said Johnny, "you gave her a missing persons. That was very big of you, very up-to-date. A lady investigator on your detective bureau. But she's found her missing girl now, hasn't she? The rest of this is mine."

Mary shook her head. "Oh, no. You can't ask me to leave her where I found her, Captain. Stone-cold on the slab."

McVeigh put his weight against the corner of the window-frame, which gave way suddenly. The thump on the sill made them both look up.

"You're right," he said.

The two detectives looked at each other.

"Which one?" said Broderick.

"Both of you," said the Captain. "This is a serious case now, Mary. You've never handled a homicide. And the beat reporters and gossip columnists have always treated Johnny with kid gloves."

"Captain --"

"Don't interrupt, Mary. I'm not finished. We don't want the papers chasing you the way they chase Johnny, but if you're right about the girl's I.D., you've given us the first clue we've had in this case. I'm not going to take that away from her, Johnny. The only thing I can do, as a wise commanding officer, is assign you both to the case."

"Captain—" said Johnny and Mary at once.

"If anybody has a problem with that, there are other open cases. Not with a crowd of reporters on their tail, but cases that need careful police work."

Johnny looked at Mary, to suggest her for that assignment, and she looked at Johnny with just the same expression.

"That's what I thought," said McVeigh.

Broderick snorted and opened his mouth, but the Captain's face made him close it again. He looked at Mary as if he wanted to beat a confession out of her, but all he said was, "You didn't by any chance get a picture, did you? A snapshot of your missing person?"

"As a matter of fact," replied Mary, fishing out of her purse the photograph she had from Gertrude Tanenbaum.

Johnny Broderick took the snap and looked it over. The scowl on his face said it would hardly do. But he stuck it in his vest pocket anyway. "All right, then, " he told her, "just button your lip and keep out of my way."

Mary shot him a glance that should have frozen his blood, but Broderick didn't notice. He was a senior investigator with a track record of homicides, while she had only the pickpocket squad on her jacket. When he did look up, she gave Johnny the briefest smile that ever creased her lips. But it was apparently enough to please Patrick McVeigh.

"That's a beginning," he said. "We're all one bureau. Let's see what we can do, working together."

Broderick studied the ceiling. Mary didn't object. But she didn't mention Choate, or Mr. Stubs either.

*   *   *

Leon Catalan spent most of his time in Poppy's Candy Store on the corner of 22nd Street and Seventh Avenue. His father was in Spain, fighting the fascists as a soldier in the Abraham Lincoln Brigade. When he was shot in the gut on the outskirts of Malaga, Leon's mother sailed after him. She left Leon in the care of her mother, his grandmother, who loved him with an unstinting heart but had very little idea how he passed his days. Leon told her he got a job, and that three-letter word was all she needed to hear for him to spend as much time away from home as he wanted.

Poppy's was not the worst place he might have chosen to hang out, which he did after three o'clock on weekdays, all day on Saturdays, and whenever he cut school. There were fountain drinks at the counter, comic books on the racks, and pinball machines in the back of the store, where the older guys gathered.

Bing! Bing! Ga-jing-a-jing!

Leon was pretty good with a pair of flippers. He had no quarters to feed the machines, but when there was money involved, some of the guys would stake him to a game and bet on his score. To keep him off the machines, Poppy gave him a job. Not during school hours—he could hang out then on his own dime, but Poppy wouldn't pay for that. It wasn't much of a job and it wasn't for much money, but Leon earned a couple of dollars a week sweeping up the place, stacking the comic books and Life magazines, stocking the counter display with Chiclets, Sen Sen and Lifesavers, and making deliveries when the occasions arose. They didn't come up often, so Leon spent most of his time sweeping or stocking or watching the games of pinball in the back.

Which is where he was the day Mayor LaGuardia strode into the candy store, followed by cops in uniforms and men in suits with flash cameras, who popped gumballs and snapped photographs of Hizzoner swinging his sledgehammer into the glass covers and wooden bases of the pinball machines.

Crash. Smash. Splinter. Bulbs flashed and cameras clicked. The noise sounded almost like a pinball game itself.

"Awright," said an officer with stripes on his sleeve, shoulders like an ox, and a clipped walrus moustache. "You all get out! This is a raid."

A bluecoat caught Poppy by the old man's slender arm and turned to the Walrus. "What do we do with this one, Sarge? Take him in?"

Sergeant Walrus looked over at Hizzoner, who shook his stocky head. And that was the end of the raid.

The regulars scattered as soon as they saw the blues coming through the door. They left Leon and Poppy to clean up the mess, watching through the plate glass window as the Mayor stood outside on the sidewalk, talking to reporters about the blow he just struck against the mobsters, who, as everyone knew, collected the lion's share of receipts from those jingle-jangle slots and pinball machines.

Leon pushed the broom while Poppy picked up chunks of shredded wood and jagged glass from the floor. When Poppy had rounded up all he could and carried out the trash to the cans in the alley, he took the broom from Leon, but instead of pushing it, he leaned on the handle and watched the Mayor waggle his pointer finger.

"New York's little flower," he said.

"Who?" Leon unwrapped a one-cent Bazooka and stuck it in his mouth.

"That's the mayor out there," Poppy said. "Fighting crime wherever he finds it."

"In here?"

"Wherever the Mob puts its gambling machines."

Leon blew a bubble with his chewing gum and popped it.

"The only thing is," Poppy went on, while flashes still lit up the street, "this hurts the Mob a whole lot less than it hurts a schmoe like me. You know how much I make on a handful of Chiclets? Or even a pack of Luckies? I was making more on those damn machines than papers and candy."

The Mayor left first in his limousine, then the cops, and then the press. When they had all gone, the street was scattered with scraps of paper and seemed even darker than usual. Leon spit his gum in a trashcan gleaming with shards of glass.

"All right, Pops," he said. "See you tomorrow."

The old man looked at the door and his face grew as long as the shadows. "I'm sorry, son," he said, "but without the quarters from those pin-ball machines, things are going to be tight around here. Looks like I'll have to push my own broom for a while." And that was the end of his job.

Leon sympathized with Poppy, as he did with the folks living in Hoovervilles and the Loyalists fighting for the Republic in Spain. Not to mention the girls working sewing

85

machines for pennies an hour. The world was full of injustice, Rachel said, and all you had to do was turn your head to see it. As he walked home, kicking the cap of a soda bottle, Leon did turn his head and felt something hit him hard on the cheek. It nearly knocked his head off his shoulders. His hand came away bloody, and Leon saw a couple of kids across the street with their fists in their pockets, bulging with rocks. *Irish*, Rachel would have called them. *Micks* to anybody else. Leon didn't care who was after him, particularly. He took off and didn't stop running until he rounded a corner and couldn't hear feet on the pavement behind him—

But ran into a faceful of camelhair.

Wham! Leon looked up and saw, beyond the collar of the coat, two frog's eyes staring down between a square jaw and broad-brimmed hat. At first Leon thought the man must be drunk, because his face was red. Then the frog-man shook his head, and Leon noticed that the second side of his face was splotched even redder than the first.

"Watch where you're going, boy. You could get hurt that way."

Leon felt thick fingers dig into his shoulder and push his away. But he didn't say a word, because the man's free hand reached into his coat pocket, where Leon's face had bumped into something through the camelhair. It felt hard and leathery, like a blackjack or a shillelagh. He didn't wait to find out which, but slipped out under the man's grip and loped off toward the porch-light of the boardinghouse.

It was dark now. Dinner-time. His grandma would start to worry. And his uncle would start talking about the creepy night crawlers. Leon caught his breath as he trotted the last half block to home. He kept an eagle eye out for the big Packard with city plates, but it was nowhere in sight. Leon sighed and accepted that, as he did the loss of his job at the candy store. Just when he needed his second source of income, it too had fled.

In his ten years on earth Leon had seen enough rocks and blackjacks to last him a lifetime. What he wanted to see was something entirely new. As he climbed the steps to his grandmother's house at 228 West 21st Street, Leon imagined what life might be like without flashbulbs, marching songs, or fists raised in the air. Passing a day in the park with a kite, maybe, or seeing the Babe in the Bronx swatting horsehair. Doing something calm and untroubled—forgettable even. Something fun.

Eleven. Boffo's Beat

"What makes you think," Mary Shanley asked Johnny Broderick, "Rosetta de Soto would ever see the inside of a place like this?"

They were sitting in a nightclub on 52nd Street, where Joe Bushkin was at the piano playing *We Minus You,* low and solo, between numbers with Bunny Berigan. Their waitress was young, with slim limbs, short sleeves, and a pleated skirt skimpy enough to get her arrested on the sidewalk.

"She was a good-looking doll, in the city. She had to work somewhere."

"She worked at Woolworth's department store."

"They all say that. Or the telephone company. She didn't work the switchboard, by any chance, did she?"

"No. The perfume counter."

"Uh huh. Rye for me," he told the waitress, who wobbled on her heels, blinking at them through wide green eyes, heavily lashed in mascara. "And a whiskey sour for the lady."

"Make that Irish whiskey," Mary said. "Straight up."

Broderick tried to pinch the waitress, who neatly sidestepped his reach. He watched her pick her way between the tables and then said, "She was charity, wasn't she? Your Miss de Soto. So even if she worked at Woolworth's by day, where do you think her gentlemen callers took her in the evenings?"

The trumpet stood up for an unconvincing solo. Mary said, "Not here."

"Then some place like it. We've got all night."

Johnny called over the *maitre d'* and showed him the photo of Rosetta de Soto. The man was a bruiser, who stuck out his boxer's chin as if he were daring you to take a swing at it. He might have been a bouncer in a speakeasy five years before. The *maitre d'* stroked his grizzled cheek thoughtfully and shook his sleek head, but he whispered something into Johnny's ear, which made the detective laugh. When he slipped a folded bill into the man's huge paw, he said, "Thanks again, Sergeant Broderick," with just the note of respect Johnny deserved.

They didn't stay at the first club long, but worked their way up Eighth Avenue and then down Seventh, spending hardly more time in each joint than it took to pinch another waitress and down another rye. But Johnny didn't really hit his stride until they reached Broadway. Mary noticed his spine straightening, his shoulders settling back, and his pace quickening as they crossed the Great White Way.

Suddenly, it was *Mister Broderick* wherever they went. Hat-check girls took his hat without giving him a ticket. He was led to a table ahead of the line at the hottest spots in town: El Morocco, the Trocadero, everywhere. Walter Winchell sent over a magnum of champagne, and cigarette girls winked at Johnny, offering Cubans. Each time he passed a criminal type, Broderick stared until the hard case tipped his hat. Everywhere they went, Johnny showed the photo of Rosetta de Soto and got the same reaction—eyes rolling with a sorrowful shrug.

When they had worked enough midtown clubs, Broderick headed north to Harlem. Count Basie and his band were playing the Apollo with his new vocalist, Billie Holiday. At the Savoy Ballroom, Benny Goodman was taking on the house band, the Chick Webb Orchestra, in a battle of the bands that drew crowds of nine thousand over the weekend. Fewer than half could squeeze inside. On a Wednesday night the place was crowded, but there was just enough room to fit a table for Johnny and Mary right in front of the stage. Webb was a small man with a big face and broad shoulders, hunched over his drums on a platform. He noticed Johnny from the stage, smiled, and broke into a three-minute solo. When it ended, the crowd jumped to its feet, Johnny nodded thanks, and Webb pointed his drumstick at Ella Fitzgerald, who took the microphone and sang "T'aint What You Do (It's the Way That You Do It)," also, it seemed, for Johnny.

When they left the Savoy, Mary asked, "How old could that girl be?"

"Ella?" Johnny said. "Nineteen, I think, with a birthday coming up. But don't worry—Chick adopted her. Signed the papers and everything."

Mary gave him a suspicious look and stuck a finger in her ear to stop it ringing. It was the volume, not the music that strained her eardrums, but Broderick only noticed her pinkie wiggling around.

"So what do you like to hear?" he asked. "A polka or something?"

"I enjoy a Chopin mazurka," Mary admitted, "but prefer a Strauss waltz."

"Well, you won't hear a lot of those either," Johnny said.

What they heard was jazz—from Saint Louis and Chicago, New Orleans and the Bronx. What they did not hear was a single word about Rosetta de Soto. Not that Johnny quit trying. When the last clubs closed in the morning, he was still talking, still pinching, winking and drinking. And driving. He managed to keep his tires near the yellow line, though sometimes to the left of it and sometimes to the right.

Mary yawned and settled back against the vinyl seat. "That was exhausting."

"You're done for the night?" Johnny asked. "I'm just getting started."

"Johnny," said Mary. "Sergeant Broderick. It's now almost three in the morning. What club in the city limits would let two cops in now?"

"Who said anything about a nightclub?" A smirk curled his mouth. "Look, Mary—do you mind if I call you Mary?"

"A fine time to ask."

"I know you think Rosetta was a good Italian girl. But I'm not so sure. To tell you the truth, I'm never really sure about a thing like that."

"You're not. So—"

"So my next step might be difficult for you to take. A well brought up Irish lady like yourself. If you say the word, I can drop you off right now, and we'll say nothing further about it. Or you can come with me"—that smirk again—"and say nothing about it to anyone else."

Mary had some idea what he might mean, and it unsettled her, because Broderick had a point. Four years before, she had been an Irish housewife, safe in her middle-class home. Since then, she had seen enough on the Pickpocket Squad to teach her that people were capable of anything. But she hadn't been forced to witness them doing it. Mary's wifely sensibility had been calloused enough by police work. She wasn't sure she wanted it thickened any more by whatever Johnny planned to show her.

"It's getting late," Mary said.

Then she saw by the quickening of his breath that was just what Broderick had been waiting for. In her moment of uncertainty his eyes grew narrower, as a cop's eyes will when a suspect starts to break. That had been his point all along—that Mary wasn't up to the challenges of a homicide, of seeing their case through to its grisly conclusion. But the very idea that he might be right provoked her to prove him wrong.

"So where are we going next?"

They were heading down Second Avenue at eighty miles an hour. The car hit a bump in the road and jumped, but Johnny hung onto the wheel.

"I thought you were going home."

"Wherever you go, I go, Johnny. That's why they call us partners."

The gears ground together as he shifted out of third. "Right," he said finally, as the engine roared, slipping out of gear into neutral until he forced it back into fourth. "Let's get down to business." His shrug implied he had given her fair warning. But his smirk had vanished completely.

Johnny drove to a nicely kept whorehouse on 97th Street, a few doors west of the park. It was a townhouse with a clean brick face and drapes in the windows. There was a yellow light over a green wooden door, a brass bell and a knocker. Johnny rang the bell, since no one heard the knocker.

The door was opened by a colored woman who said, "Mr. Broderick," in a sweet, professional voice. Inside, music issued from a parlor on the left—a piano, where Mary saw a girl in a nightgown at the keys playing a song about a boy who loved a girl he couldn't afford. When she finished, she bowed her head and accepted the applause of three other women in various states of undress, two gentlemen in shirtsleeves, and an older woman in a high-buttoned collar. This lady had golden curls fixed in place, as if they had been sculpted out of bronze. Her wrinkled face was shocking beneath that blonde coiffure. She nodded; the piano girl smiled; and they all noticed Johnny watching from the hall.

The two gents in their shirtsleeves stood, buttoning their vests, until the madam in the collar waved them back to their seats. "Sergeant Broderick," she said with a stiff-lipped smile, "is an old friend of the house."

Johnny entered the room, taking the woman's offered hand as if he might kiss it. But he turned as Mary followed him, and the madam folded both her hands in her lap. "Who's your friend, Johnny?" Half the welcome leaked out of her voice, replaced by a Lower East Side accent in her sinuses.

Mary Agnes Shanley of the New York City Police," Broderick said. "This dazzling dame goes by Gloria Bea."

Gloria's hand was not offered to Mary, who did not offer her own. "Is there a Gloria A?"

The two gentlemen mumbled their excuses and left. The piano girl remembered something she had to do. Clutching sheet music to her chest, she retreated upstairs, dropping loose pages behind her.

"B-E-A," explained Gloria. "As in Beatrice, from Dante's Paradise."

"I thought this house was closer to the other place."

"Gloria is our hostess, Mary," Broderick said, "proprietor of this establishment and somebody you should know as a homicide investigator."

"Are you often involved with homicides, Miss Bea?"

"None, recently. Though I know some gentlemen willing to do the honors, if they hear I've been disrespected."

"Does that come up frequently?"

"Now, ladies," Johnny broke in, "there's no percentage in getting off to a bad start. Why don't you give one another a chance? Gloria is a successful businesswoman, Mary, who moved into a managerial position when her darling Danny-boy met the wrong end of a shovel. Miss Shanley is a detective, Miss Bea. You two should have lots in common, both being professional women."

Mary looked at him. "Are you going somewhere?"

"Upstairs," he said, glancing after the pianist's negligee. "Where our informants will be. Why don't you see what you can learn from Miss Bea, down here? Unless you'd rather come with me?"

The steps looked steep indeed. The curtains at the top were pink chenille, two large swirls of fabric with a fold between them. Mary's cheeks flushed at the idea of pushing those curtains aside. "You go up," she said, "if you think you might learn something useful. But don't be long, Johnny, or we might have to send a squad after you."

Broderick grinned, but he took the steps two at a time.

When he disappeared through the curtains, Gloria said, "He won't find many girls lolling about tonight."

Mary sat up straight. "Then he won't be long. We wouldn't want to interrupt your business."

"Johnny never does," said Gloria. "But you're the curiosity, if I may say so, Miss. You're not the kind of sidekick he usually brings along."

Mary smiled, despite herself. "I'm not the kind of audience he prefers. Sergeant Broderick is a one-man show, but I'm not the man to clap for him."

"Are you really a detective?"

"I am."

"What does that mean? Frisking prostitutes in the precinct house?"

"It usually means the Pickpocket Squad."

"Dips," said Gloria, with a nod. "Nasty bastards. A woman works the streets an entire evening, giving her all. Then she'll bump into some degenerate, and what will she have to show for her sacrifice?"

"An empty purse."

"You might suppose we resent the police, in this house. We don't like to be raided or threatened, of course. But that's a cost of doing business. Me and my girls, like most women in our line, support the police in ninety percent of their duties. We raise a cop's spirits when he starts to sag, and help support his family at home. When you see a sergeant's wife with a rock on her finger, or a chinchilla coat to her ankles, you know he didn't pay for it on a city salary."

Mary thought of her own engagement ring and wondered where Michael found the funds. "What do you get in return? Protection?"

Gloria laughed. "They're not protecting us anymore."

"What do you mean?"

Gloria's looked up, and her eyes studied Mary's. "I've been in this business for a long time," she said. "First as a whore myself, and then as a madam. Ten years ago, even five years ago, it was a whole different racket. Prohibition was good for business, ours and theirs." She fell silent, though the muscles in her jaw continue working.

Mary said, "Whose? The police?"

"Theirs too," said Gloria. "But don't forget the mobsters. Luciano and Schultz organized private armies to keep their beer flowing in the speaks. Then, all of a sudden, on April seventh, it ended. Bang! You could buy legal beer from any vendor, cheaper than the mob offered it. Worst of all, the cops would back you up, so long as you paid your monthly pad. So what were Dutch and Lucky supposed to do for revenue? What were they supposed to do with their tough guys? You can't just turn an army loose on the streets of the city. They needed another business to run. Booze was legal as soda pop, so what other vice could they sell?"

"Yours?"

Gloria shrugged. "My Henry tried to stand up to them."

"Your husband?"

"He might as well have been. But Lucky had his methods, and they worked just as well in the brothels as they did in the speaks."

"They murdered Henry?"

"You tell me. You're the police. One night Henry says he's going to brush off Luciano, and he never comes home again. Coincidence?"

"And you never heard—"

"I heard enough, loud and clear," Gloria said. "When Lucky's men came back again, I agreed to pay them off. But they didn't want to be paid, you see. They wanted to own the joint. And there was no Henry to object."

"So this—"

"Is Luciano's place, since Dutch is dead. People still call it Gloria's, for old time's sake. You've got to have a name people trust, in business. Lucky knows that and doesn't mind, so long as we understand one another."

Gloria Bea lit a cigarette, puffing energetically, and the two women sat in silence, until Mary said, "That stinks."

Gloria shrugged. "Now you understand, too, Officer."

They heard the tramp of Johnny's steel-toe shoes on the stairs. "Does Sergeant Broderick know all this?"

"Course he does, honey! It's not exactly a secret, the mob's in this business. They like to be anywhere a John goes to do what he shouldn't be doing."

95

"I meant about your place."

"I'd tell him, if he asked. Not that he ever did."

When he entered the parlor, Johnny's tie was loose and his hair disheveled, but his eyes glinted with an ardor more thrilling than sex. "I think we got something," he said. "One of the Johns upstairs—the gent with April—"

"Fu Manchu," said Gloria.

"Thought he might have seen her at a club in Brooklyn. I gave him the photo and asked him to look closer. He studied it a long time and then said, yeah, he was almost sure of it. He danced with De Soto."

"In Brooklyn?"

"At a shithole called the Shanghai Ballroom."

"What would Rosetta be doing in Brooklyn? Dancing with Fu Manchu?"

"Earning a living," said Broderick.

"Johnny, I told you," said Mary, "Rosetta wasn't a pro. Begging your pardon, Gloria, but our girl wasn't a prostitute, a doxie or a—"

"Dancer? That's what the John said. He gave her a ticket he bought for a dime, and squeezed her for thirty-two bars of *Flat Foot Floogie with the Floy Floy.*"

"I don't believe it."

"Not Rosetta, huh? Well, maybe she's the same girl and maybe she isn't. There's only one way to find out."

"You want to drive out to Brooklyn? At this hour?"

"Those dance halls are open all night."

"Not me," said Mary. "I'm sorry. If you feel like dancing, Johnny, go right ahead. I'm going home to bed. In the morning you can drive out to Timbuktu to track down Fu Manchu. But I've got my own leads. Why don't you work your case your way, and I'll work my end mine?"

Broderick's smirk was back. "If that's the way you want it, Mare." His eyes met Gloria's impassive gaze. The madam didn't like what she was witnessing here, but the arrangement suited him fine.

Twelve. Mother Sara's Seesaw

In the morning Mary took a cab to 21st Street to see Louisa Vitanza. Louisa wasn't home, but Mary found Rachel Lipinsky instead.

"Where's Louisa?"

Rachel shrugged. "She was supposed to be home an hour ago. Why? Did you find something?"

For a moment, Mary considered telling Rachel what she and Louisa had found in the basement of Bellevue. But the morning was bright, Louisa hadn't been sure it was Rosetta's cadaver, and Mary saw no reason to rush the awful news. There were also two people waiting in Rachel's room. The first was a young man in a pilot's leather jacket, lying across the bedspread on his back. His arms reached out like a crucified martyr and he was groaning through his nose.

"Uhhh-hnnn. Uhhhhhnn. Uh-ah-uhnnnnnn."

"Sit up, Mark," said Rachel, sitting down hard on the mattress. "Officer Shanley thinks you're strangling."

Mark sat up in a blink. He had black curly hair, deep blue eyes, and a cleft chin, which he scratched with two fingers. "No problem." He looked around for a cop and only slowly focused on Mary. "Hello there."

Mary thought him dopey but cute, with a bad-little-boy charm. He glanced at Rachel as if they had a secret he enjoyed keeping from grown-ups. "You're the copper, are you?"

"That's right," said Mary. "Detective Shanley."

He stuck out a hand with dirty fingernails. "Mark Gamble."

"An actor," said Rachel, as if it were an arsonist. "I told him the name was too close to Gable, but did he listen to me?"

Mary guessed not. "Have I seen you in anything?"

"Probably not," he said cheerfully. "Unless you spend a lot of time off Broadway."

"Off off Broadway," Rachel said. "And then off that."

"Are you acting in anything now?"

"As a matter of fact, I am," said Mark, scowling at Rachel. It only made him look more fetching. "At the Maxine Elliott on West 39th Street. We're having an open rehearsal on Friday, if you want to check it out."

Rachel frowned. "I doubt if Mary would be interested in *The Cradle*."

"Doubt is a thing without feathers," he told her.

"That must be one of your lines."

"It's Emily Dickinson," said Mary. "Only backwards."

"You see? She reads." He nodded. "If you want to know what the people are thinking, that's the place to find out."

"It's a musical," snorted Rachel. "Can you imagine him singing?"

"Is that why you were—"

"Exercising my vocal cords. Exactly. Demonstrating a training technique for my young friend, here." He turned toward a straight-backed chair in the corner of the room, but no one was sitting in it.

"Leon?"

On the far side of the bed a boy sat up, who must have been crouching behind it. He looked to be about ten years old with moist brown eyes in a dark complexion. He held up a red rubber ball. "It rolled underneath."

"This is Leon Catalan," Rachel said. "Mrs. T's grandson. Leon—this is Mary. His mother sailed for Spain, when his father caught a bullet in Mallorca."

"Malaga," said Leon.

"In the leg," said Rachel. "He almost lost it, to the knee. But Maddy showed up in time and wouldn't let them near him with a saw."

"Maddy?"

"Eva Catalan. Mrs. T's daughter. She asked me to keep an eye on Leon, so I'm showing him the city."

Leon said, "We're going to see Mrs. Roosevelt."

"Eleanor Roosevelt?"

"Are you a fan too?" asked Rachel. "So am I. But she's still out of the country, somewhere in the African bush. We'll have to settle for Sara."

"You mean the President's mother?"

"She's in town. Didn't you know? Don't they tell the police anything?"

"Her protective detail needs to know. I don't."

"They rebuilt a playground in her honor. Franklin came to dedicate it in October. It used to go by the name of the Christie-Forsythe Park. Poor Christie and Forsythe! Will anyone remember them, now that their park is a Roosevelt's?"

"Mother Sara is coming to see it?"

"Today. There should be all sorts of mucky-mucks, don't you think? So we're planning a little reception of our own."

"We are? Who are *we*?"

"Oh, just some of us. A few of our friends, who would like to send a message to her sonny-boy in Washington. Want to come along?"

Mary had no interest in joining a political protest but did have a lively interest in Mrs. Roosevelt. With Eleanor traveling to the four corners of the earth, the President's mother had assumed by default the pinnacle of polite society. Still, Mary shook her head. "I need to talk to Louisa."

"Why?"

"Is there any chance Rosetta took a second job?"

"Maybe," said Rachel. "She wouldn't tell me, but she might've told Louisa. Who's going straight to the playground."

"Is that what she said?"

"She said she'd be home by now. But they sometimes keep her working at the store. Without a union, there's not much she can do about it, is there?"

Mary took the bus along with Rachel, Mark, and Leon, a ride that turned into a party. Rachel packed a picnic lunch and started handing out sandwiches as soon as they got on the bus. It was crowded with folks on their way to the park. Mark stood at the back of the bus, trying to strike up the *Internationale*. A

99

couple of teenagers joined in, missing most of the words, until the driver came to a stop. He opened the doors to admit passengers and then turned to face the seats.

"Cut the noise, back there! No singing on the bus."

Mark bounded to the front to stand in solidarity with the teenagers. "What right do you have to silence us?"

The driver tilted back his cap and said, "This is a public vehicle."

"My point exactly."

But the new passengers had all boarded. The door closed with a hiss, and Mark opened a leather pouch of Spanish Loyalist wine. By the time they reached the playground on the Lower East Side, he was reciting snatches of the pep talk Henry the Fifth gave his troops on St. Crispin's Day. But even the Shakespearean king's words of inspiration were lost in the circus atmosphere at the playground.

The crowd was astounding. Unemployment had benefits, Mary thought, by the number of people who showed up at Sara Delano Roosevelt Park to see its namesake for themselves. There were mothers with strollers, retired civil servants, and plenty of job applicants. A saxophonist had opened a case and was wailing for nickels and dimes. At the eastern end of the basketball court, a platform had been erected out of plywood, with rows of folding chairs reaching back to the opposite basket. Most of the seats in the front section were occupied, while parents sat on benches toward the back and watched their kids on the swings, seesaws, and monkey bars.

Leon's eyes grew round as the sprinkler-heads built into the concrete wall that ran around the basketball court. He watched a girl climb to the top of the monkey bars and took off after her. Rachel watched him run across the park and crawl into the steel cage, hanging upside down from the third tier. Rachel started after him but stopped halfway across the park, when she saw a meandering line of students waving signs that read: JOBS ARE A RIGHT NOT A PRIVILEGE! and KEEP THE U.S. OUT OF WAR. The protesters were having a hard time staying focused as they tired of standing around. They sat on the seesaws and started to teeter or sat on the swings and started to sway.

Rachel ran over, calling, "Mark! Help me hold the line!"

But Mark had found a basketball and was shooting hoops between folding chairs at the far end of the court.

The playground had originally been built only three years before, but it had been enlarged and redesigned to be state-of-the-leisure-arts. Both FDR and LaGuardia were determined to fight revolutionary politics with a social compact that met the needs of the people, from public housing to amusements, and a park named after the President's mother cast that social policy in steel and concrete.

As she passed the plywood platform, Mary heard the *boom* of rubber balls on the handball courts. Above her, on the platform, the honored guests had already gathered. Sara Roosevelt sat in the first row. On her right was an empty seat waiting for the mayor. On her left sat Parks Commissioner Robert Moses, and squatting behind Moses was a plump man in a porkpie hat, chewing on an unlit cigar. To the right of La Guardia's seat, a svelte blonde twisted around in a sheath with a silk shawl slipping off her shoulders. She was trying to engage Mrs. Roosevelt over the din of the crowd. Mary heard her ask about Franklin's favorite dish, *Did the White House staff serve salted fish every day for lunch?* Mrs. Roosevelt mumbled a reply. Then Mary heard the blonde ask, "Is it true that Eleanor always carries a pistol?"

Mrs. Roosevelt turned her back and whispered to Mr. Moses.

The blonde shrugged her bare shoulders and pouted at the gentleman on her left, whose pinstriped wool suit marked him as a Very Important Person in his own right. And crouching behind him was Mary's own son, Edward.

When she caught his eye, Eddie stood and climbed down the steps from the stage. He crossed the basketball court without lifting his gaze from his mother and didn't stop until he stood directly in front of her chair.

"Mother," he said sternly, "have you been harassing the headmaster of Choate?"

Taken aback, Mary shook her head. "No, Eddie, I haven't. Who told you that I have?"

"It doesn't matter who told me, Mother. What matters is that you don't. Tell me the truth. Did you go to Connecticut?"

"Yes."

"Why? What could you possibly have to do there?"

"My job, Eddie, that's all."

"Your job? In Connecticut? You are assigned to the Pickpocket Squad. Was somebody picking pockets in Connecticut?"

"I've been given a new assignment, Edward."

"What assignment? To harass the next generation of world leaders? You have no idea who these people are, Mother. They are not degenerates who learned their trade in prison, or girls with missing buttons from the tenements. These people have to be treated with kid gloves, and you are not exactly the kid-glove type."

"What girls do you mean?"

"What girls have you been asking about?"

"I mean, who told you I've been asking questions about a missing girl?"

"As I said—it doesn't matter who told me, Mother."

"It does, Eddie. It does matter. How did you find out so quickly what I've been investigating? Has someone been pressuring Tammany Hall to shut me down? That's what you're trying to do, isn't it?"

Eddie stared at his mother. He opened his mouth to deny it, but couldn't quite. He turned on his heel and marched back to the platform, where he knelt down beside the pinstriped gentleman and whispered into his ear.

A moment later, Rachel returned, dropping into the chair beside Mary's. She crossed her legs, braced her elbow on one knee, and propped her chin on her elbow. On the far side of the park, the protest was dissolving. But Leon was doing nicely, moving among the bars as if he had been doing it all his life.

"This is lovely, isn't it?" Mary said.

"It's disgraceful," said Rachel.

Mary watched a swing fly by. "Leon seems to like it."

"That's the point," Rachel insisted. "It's patronizing. I should say *matronizing*—the President's mother treating us all like ten-year-olds! Do you read the papers, Mary? Do you know what's going on in this country?"

"Some of them," said Mary.

"Chrysler is on strike. So are taxi drivers in Chicago, coal miners in Pittsburgh, and who knows who else tomorrow? John L. Lewis is talking to U.S. Steel, trying to negotiate a five-day week for something like a livable wage. Governor Lehman tried to pass a Child Labor Law, and it lost in the state assembly by a landslide. Capitalism is failing all around us. So what are Franklin Roosevelt and his New Dealers doing about it? Building parks and playgrounds and swimming pools."

Mary didn't think that was fair. "Do you know how many playground directors this park employs? Twenty-six—plus nineteen maintenance men. And this is just one project of the Public Works Administration."

"They made up a few phony-baloney jobs, planting trees or cutting them down. But nobody wants to pay for the PWA anymore. Congress wants out, and the Governors can't afford it. The whole thing can't be fixed by s fireside chat. So what do you think our President will have to do next?"

"What?"

"Take us to war."

"I thought you people were in favor of war."

"Us people?"

Mary lowered her voice. "Radicals."

"To help out Mother Russia?" Rachel laughed. "I wonder which papers you've been reading? I'm worried about what's happening in Germany, of course—any sensible person is. But

103

I'm against war of any kind. You don't have to love Joe Stalin to give a girl who works a sewing machine two cents closer to the value of her labor. Since what's-good-for-General-Motors has put half the country on relief."

Rachel looked over hopefully toward the fence where the students had gathered, but even fewer of them stood there now. Two girls had found the seesaw and were going up and down, while the boys on the swings were pumping their legs, competing for who could sail highest. Some others had climbed onto the monkey bars, watching friends who had cleared enough folding chairs to start a game of basketball. The bright orange ball circled the rim and swished through the ropes of the new basket.

Two bare-chested protesters slapped their hands in the air.

Rachel sighed. "There goes the revolution."

But Mary's attention was fixed on the platform, where Eddie was squatting beside the gentleman in the first row. Even from her seat Mary could see that Eddie was sorry for something he couldn't control.

"Who is that?" she asked Rachel. "The man beside the glamour girl."

"Beside Gloria Swanson?"

"Is that who she is?"

Rachel laughed, sympathetically this time. "Everyone in the country knows who she is, Mary. Everyone in New York knows him. And everyone who reads the gossip columns knows what's going on between them."

"Who is he?"

"That's Joseph P. Kennedy. Who is married to Rose Fitzgerald, the daughter of Honey Fitz, a big wheel in Boston city politics. The Kennedys own a place in Riverdale, in the best part of the Bronx, but they spend most of the year in Washington."

"She doesn't seem to care for him, does she?"

"Gloria?"

"She keeps turning away."

"She's probably mad as a wet hen. The columnists say Roosevelt is about to appoint Joseph Kennedy our Ambassador to England—where he will no doubt bring his wife. So what is poor Gloria supposed to do, when FDR ships off her sugar daddy?"

"What?"

"She'll find another sugar daddy, that's what!"

"You mean she and Mr. Kennedy ... ?"

Rachel nodded, sagely.

"Poor Rose!"

"Irish housewives stick together, is that it? Because I can think of a lot of people poorer than Rose Kennedy. But I can't believe you're interested in Hollywood gossip, Mary. So why are you asking?"

Because Eddie kept scouring the public seats, his frown deepening as he found his mother. Shrugging to showing his regret. He was making excuses for her, Mary realized, to the next American Ambassador to the Court of St. James.

But what could Mary possibly have done to offend the great man—except her job? Which meant she now knew who dated Rosetta de Soto.

Thirteen. Most Likely

Mary was back on a train to Choate before the end of the working day. The train was much more crowded now, with commuters heading home for dinner, rustling through the evening papers, or shuffling to the bar car. These were working people too, but they ended the day with a sense of satisfaction as well as exhaustion in their bearing. They had made money today. Outside the window, the track-bed gravel was dark, and Mary saw her own grave face reflected in the glass.

But none of that made a difference now. She knew where she was going, and what she had to say.

She caught a cab on the same street corner of New Haven, but didn't ask for the Headmaster's office. Instead, she had the taxi driver drop her off at the residence hall. She caused a stir, making her way down the hall, as young gentlemen appeared in their doorways to see her pass. But Mary kept her eyes on her goal and the hallway carpet. By repeating the name, Mary was led to the second floor and then to the next to last room on the left side of the hall.

When she entered, the young man was leaning back in his desk chair with his ankles propped on the unmade bed. He wore a blue crew-neck sweater, charcoal slacks, no socks, and loafers. The slacks and sweater hung loosely on his lanky frame.

Mary said, "Mr. Kennedy?"

The young man smiled toothily. "Jack," he said, setting down his chair and rising to offer his hand. Mary felt her own palm disappear in his warm greeting.

"I don't know if you remember me. Officer Shanley."

"We met the other day, didn't we? In George's office."

"Mr. St. John's?"

"He prefers 'Headmaster.' But unless my memory fails me, you're a New York City detective. And this is the state of Connecticut."

"So I haven't any jurisdiction here. That's true. But your father is about to be named to the Court of St. James. So let's talk privately, you and I. Unless you think he would enjoy denying public allegations in the papers."

"I don't see any joy in that."

"I thought not."

"Then—what should we talk about?"

"Your father has been trying to stop my investigation, through Tammany Hall. Have you any idea why he might do something like that?"

Jack sat on the edge of his mattress and offered her the chair. "No. But I suspect you do, Miss Shanley."

"I have an idea."

"Then why don't you share it?"

"I think he was trying to protect you, Jack. He knows—or believes he knows—that you were involved with a pretty young lady in New York City, whose body was found a few nights ago in the tunnel to New Jersey."

"Rosetta de Soto."

"So you do know her."

"The Times carried the story. Just awful. Are you making any progress?"

"I think we're growing warm. White hot, in fact."

Jack blinked. "You don't think I killed her?"

"Didn't you?"

He shook his head. "No."

"Weren't you the Choate man who dated Rosetta de Soto on the night she died? If I canvas the taxis from here to New Haven, won't I find a cabbie who picked you up on campus and drove you to the station? If I talk to the conductors on the New York line, won't I find one who remembers punching your ticket that night?"

"No, no, and no," said Jack Kennedy.

"Then what were you doing on Thursday night?"

Playing poker. With friends."

"Close friends?"

107

"Close enough to take my chit. Not close enough to cover up a murder."

"Then tell me why your father is trying to stop my inquiry."

"Because I asked him to."

"You asked him to lean on Tammany? Why?"

"Because I'm running for Most Likely to Succeed," said Jack.

"And a dead girl might stand in your way?"

Jack hesitated. "You're close, Officer Shanley, I'll say that for you. But you've pinned the wrong Choate man."

"Have I?"

"The man you have in mind is named Freddie Arlington. He catches a taxi on Thursday nights, trains into Grand Central Station, and shows some working girl a night on the town. Then he comes back and tells us about it."

"Sounds like a charmer."

"Which is just what he did last Thursday night, after he saw Miss de Soto."

"He actually told you her name?"

"He did. He usually called her Rosie. But when the story came out in the paper about the dead girl in the tunnel, he turned to mint jelly and shut up like a clam."

"Where is he now?"

"Home in St. Louis. He wasn't feeling so well."

"Guilt?"

"I think nerves. You can go to Minnesota and ask him, if you like. His uncle is a judge in St. Paul."

Mary wasn't so sure how the Captain would feel about that, since Tammany must have called him too. "This Freddie Arlington—"

"Frederick," said Jack.

"You're sure that he saw her on Thursday night?"

"That's what he said. To everybody."

"And they made love?"

"They had sex. He said. On the second floor of the Edison Hotel."

108

"When did he drive her home?"

"He didn't. He gave her taxi fare and hailed a cab to the station. The trains don't run to New Haven all night."

"The story in the paper didn't supply any names. How did he know the dead girl was Rosetta de Soto?"

"By the two crosses of gold. She used to wear the first one, and he gave her the second. But instead of replacing it, she liked to wear both. Freddie thought you could track him down from the sales receipt at Tiffany's."

"He told you all that?"

"He was afraid his family name would get mixed up in the scandal. So he asked me if my father could do anything to prevent that."

"And you agreed to do that favor for him, because—?"

"He made me a tempting offer."

"Not cash? You wouldn't succumb to money."

"No. But not so far off. Freddie was my principal rival for Most Likely to Succeed. He offered to withdraw from the contest, if I helped him out."

"With a little obstruction of justice."

"Except it wouldn't be, in the end, because Freddie couldn't have killed her. Let's look at this logically," he said in a tone cultivated for the debating team. "First is the question of character. You don't know Freddie. He's incapable of taking any action so bold. I don't mean to minimize the tragedy here, but it takes determination to beat a girl to death. Freddie hasn't got it. He can hardly rush a quarterback."

Mary could picture the two boys tangled on a football field. "You'd be surprised what a person can do, under the wrong circumstances."

"Point taken," said Jack with an affable nod. "We don't always act on our best instincts. That's why I place such importance on the evidence I've already testified to—the fact that he told us about her."

"Bragging is not inconsistent with murder."

109

"Think about it for a moment, Officer Shanley. He came home and talked all about his conquest. Only when the story hit the paper did he blanch and ask me to help him keep the whole affair secret. Now if he had actually killed her on Thursday night, would he have come home boasting?"

"Perhaps."

"Perhaps not. More likely he would have come to me terrified, asking for Father's help sooner. He didn't know that she was dead until he read it in the paper."

And, Mary realized, *Mr. Arlington* could have become *Mr. Darling* in Miss de Soto's playful accent. Mr. Kennedy was awaiting her verdict with remarkable poise for such a young man. She couldn't help admiring his self-possession. "You're headed for law school, I presume."

"I haven't much choice about it," Jack said, with a rueful smile and squinting blue eyes. "Harvard Law is my family's finishing school."

*   *   *

Mary's entire mood changed on her ride back to the city. She no longer had a reason to believe Jack Kennedy was involved in the crime. Asking his father to interfere to help him win Most Likely to Succeed seemed just the sort of thing a rich boy would do, as Rachel Lipinsky might say. Mary noticed how often she thought of Rachel lately, and the idea was disconcerting.

The *toot* of the express train roaring through a station brought Mary back to her case. Frederick Arlington might have murdered Rosetta de Soto. He had seen her on the night of her death and tried to conceal his connection. But Kennedy had made a good case for his defense, and an expensive attorney could do just as well. She had no proof against him, no physical evidence, and the boy was enrolled in a school outside of Mary's jurisdiction. She couldn't even bring him in for questioning. If Mary really thought he had murdered Rosetta, she would have to find some evidence.

But the truth was Mary no longer suspected either boy of the crime. If Freddie had killed Rosetta accidentally, he would have returned to Choate terrified. Bragging was definitely the reaction of an innocent or a sociopath. The fear he exhibited afterwards, his willingness to withdraw from the contest in exchange for Joe Kennedy's help, did not indicate a sociopath. Frederick Arlington felt more like a dumb rich boy in the wrong place at the wrong time.

Which left Mary…where? If Frederick Arlington was not responsible, who was her most likely suspect? She ran through all the names she had heard the last few days and took a second look at Guillermo La Motte—or was it Ciotti? A man who beat a girl once on a date might do it again. Louisa said that Rosetta refused to see him again, but Rosetta seemed to be good at keeping secrets. What if she did see him again? Mary dug out of her purse the name and location of the theatre where Rosetta had met Guillermo. It was worth a visit now that her prep-school suspect seemed so unpromising.

The next day, Mary was scheduled for a tour of duty with the Pickpocket Squad. She set the alarm for six o'clock and went to find the theatre on Sixth Avenue. It was at the corner of 23rd Street, three blocks from Mrs. T's boardinghouse. The marquee read: *The Song of Roland*. A woman and a little boy stood underneath it, looking at the posters showing marionettes in armor with long wooden noses. But a bus rolled up the Avenue and stopped on the corner by the subway. The woman helped her boy climb on and followed him.

Mary tried the heavy door.

Inside, the theatre was dark, but there was a light in the wings of the stage and the sound of hammer. Mary picked her way through wooden folding chairs and climbed a stepladder to the stage. Behind the curtain on the left, a woman in a white shift was sitting on the floor, repairing the leg of a female marionette in a medieval gown. Leaning against the curtain

111

was a male marionette in silver-painted armor. The puppet's left hand was empty but shaped in a grip. On the floor beside him lay his sword, with patches of wood showing through the paint.

The woman in the shift drove a nail into the ankle of Roland's paramour, securing a slipper. She flexed the calf between the knee and the ankle, and both joints bent smoothly. She stood, brushed herself off, and saw Mary.

"I'm sorry, Ma'am," she said, "but we're closed right now. Obviously."

Mary said, "Ariosto?"

"*Orlando Furioso*," the woman said. She wore her hair brushed back, with a smudge of black eyeliner for make-up. "But we are in America now, so we speak English here."

"My name is Mary Shanley," the detective said, "with the New York City police. I'm looking for one of your customers. A theatre fan."

"In the audience?"

"A man who comes to see your show almost every night. Skinny, with thinning hair and the hands of a working man."

Two olive-brown eyes looked up. "Are you talking about Billy?"

"No. Guillermo—"

"*Si, si!* That's Billy in Italian. William."

"You know him?"

The woman laughed. "I should. He's going to be my husband."

"Guillermo? Is your fiancé?"

"That's why he comes all the time. He started as a fan of the theatre, who loved to hear the old stories. But he was still in his seat one night, when I came out to sweep up the stage, and we started to talk. He asked me out for a coffee, and..."

"You fell in love."

"Something like that. I'm Lucy Morelli."

"Lucia?"

"Once upon a time. Not any more."

"Miss Morelli," said Mary, "do you happen to remember if you saw Guillermo last Thursday night?"

"Of course. We had dinner together. We always do."

"This was not just any night. Think carefully before you answer. Are you sure you two were together this Thursday?"

"Yes. We were. Why?"

"Did you go out to eat at a restaurant?"

"No. I cooked for him myself. A nice piece of whitefish."

"Were you together all night?"

"That's hardly a proper question, Miss Shanley."

"It's important."

"You still haven't told me why."

"Because a young lady was murdered on Thursday night. You might have seen the story in the papers. We found her body brutalized in a tunnel."

"A prostitute?"

"No."

"But a woman on the street? Nobody stole her out of her parent's house?"

"Some people would call her a charity girl."

"A floozie."

"Not exactly. Not any more."

"And you think Guillermo had something to do with that?"

"Maybe not. But he took her out once, and we thought he might be able to tell us something useful."

"He took her out? Not on Thursday night."

"You're sure?"

"Somebody was eating fish in my kitchen. If that wasn't Guillermo, I don't know who it was. And I know Guillermo like the back of my hand."

Mary knew that feeling. "It sounds like you're very close."

"You said it yourself—we're in love. We're going to be married. He wouldn't be interested in any other women." She brushed a stray hair off her face.

"I can see why not."

"Thank you."

"Are you close enough to lie for him?"

Lucy Morelli paused. "Yes, I might lie for him, if he was accused of a murder he didn't commit. But I would never lie to cover up his running around with another woman—and a charity girl! If Guillermo was keeping company with a woman like that, I'd help you prove it. And when you did, I'd throw the switch myself."

She picked up Roland's sword as if to run the puppet through. But she knelt down beside the disarmed knight and fit the hilt into his fist. Then she picked up her hammer and drove a nail through the sword and hand.

Mary left the theatre convinced of Lucy's passion. Guillermo would have to be crazy to ask a fiancée like her to alibi his murder of another woman. But if Guillermo was eating fish in Lucy's kitchen, and Freddie Arlington was crowing about his conquest, who could have beaten Rosetta to death and dumped her body in the tunnel?

Her most likely suspects were dropping like flies when Mary reported for duty with the Pickpocket Squad. They would be working the Thirty-fourth Street shopping district that morning. Mary picked a Macy's shopping bag and filled it with a sweater from the Lost and Found. It felt like she would be working with them for a long time.

Fourteen. The Go-Between

"When the Nazis marched into the Ruhr Valley," Erich Tanenbaum told Mary, "they had no steel or oil. Nothing but *chutzpah*—although that was probably the last word they would've used to describe it." His chuckle forced air through his nose. "The French army could've popped a cork and chased them back to the Fatherland. But the French, being French, talked about it instead and pointed a finger at the British. So the Nazis got their steel from Essen."

Mary had no idea if he was right about that. She did not know the Ruhr Valley from the Rhine Valley, or Rudy Vallee. History had never been her strongest subject. But she knew it was passing as she sat in a Queen Anne chair covered with cat hair and waited for Gertrude Tanenbaum to join her in the parlor. For the first few minutes of her visit, Erich sat on the sofa under a blanket, listening to the radio in German. Suddenly, he leaned over and snapped it off.

"The French are committed by Locarno since 1925 not to mention a treaty they signed three years ago. But you know what Benes is saying?"

Mary didn't know who Benes was.

"Eduard Benes?" said Erich. "Leader of Czechoslavakia?"

She nodded, of course. "What's he saying?"

"That the French and English are scheming to sell the Czechs out."

Mrs. T entered just in time to catch her son's remark.

"Don't listen to him, Mary," Gertrude said. "He thinks if you serve in von war, you're an expert on all the others."

"No, but it helps if you listen to the news."

"I found another picture," Mrs. T told Mary. "It's not as good of Rosetta as my other. Not as pretty a smile. You see? That's her in the hat."

Standing beside Louisa outside Woolworth's. "Thank you, Gertrude."

"It's crazy," said Erich. "We can defend the Sudetenland. The Czechs are ready to fight, and they have mountains on their border. If we don't stand up to Hitler there, where are we planning to do it? In Poland?"

"The Fuhrer is not going to invade the Sudetenland," Mrs. T insisted. "He's just concerned about the treatment of the Germans living there. If the people here played the same nasty tricks, don't you think he would speak up for us?"

"Not for me."

"We are German by ancestry," Gertrude said.

"I'm American," Erich told her, "all the way. And I have the wounds to prove it." He slapped the top of his left thigh. The blanket slipped, and Mary suddenly remembered why he hadn't stood up when his mother entered the room.

*   *   *

"This is difficult," said Mary, when she and Gertrude were almost alone. Erich was hunched over the radio again, turned up loud, while the women sat across the room over a teapot. "There's something I have to tell you, Mrs. Tanenbaum."

"Gerty, please," said Mrs. T. "After all this time."

"Gertrude," said Mary, "we ran some tests with her dental records, and they came back this morning. Louisa must have told you about our trip the city morgue."

"No. She didn't say a word."

"Then I'll have to be the one to tell you. I'm sorry, Gertrude, really I am, knowing how you felt about her—"

Mrs. T watched her steadily. "Rosetta?"

"Yes. She's dead. Her body was found in the tunnel. We've got our best man on the job, tracking down her killer."

"Is that you?"

"Not just me. Johnny Broderick is working his own leads on this case, and you know the police will put resources wherever the papers do."

"You're sure? It's my Rosetta?"

116

Mary nodded, and Gertrude's pink eyes finally filled with tears. "*Ach du lieber*! I knew it," she said, wiping her cheeks with the cuff of her woolen sweater. "I felt it when I first came to see you."

Mary would have liked to leave her to her grief. But the trail grows cold quickly, and her leads were running out. "Do you mind," she said, "if I ask you just a few more questions? To help us find her murderer?"

Gertrude said nothing, but looked up expectantly.

"Was she working a second job?" Mary asked.

The old woman shook her head. "She never said anything to me about that."

"That's what everyone says."

Gertrude made a face. "What does it matter now?"

"It does, if it helps us find her killer. She was seeing several men."

"Okay."

"Her college boy is a bust. So is the man who hit her once before. The only one left on my list is the older gentleman, who might be in construction, or might work for the city. The one she called Mr. Stubs."

"Who told you that?"

"Louisa. Because he smoked cigars down to his fingertips."

Gertrude shook her head. "I never met him."

"But you heard about him? You knew she was seeing someone like that?"

"No."

"No? He must have picked her up, or dropped her off."

"If he must, he must. I don't see what difference that makes now."

"You don't?"

"You told me she's dead, right? That's vhat I needed to know. Thank you for taking my case. Thank you for looking into it. But I don't see any reason to sully a gentleman's name."

"What if he murdered her?"

117

"What if he didn't? Excuse me, Officer Shanley," Gertrude said, "but if Rosetta is not coming back, I have plenty of things to do."

She stood, bent slightly, and walked up the stairs.

For a moment Mary sat, while Erich sat across from her, listening to a game of the New York Knickerbockers. The announcer Marty Glickman was one of two Jewish track-stars bumped by American officials from the 400-meter relay team for the 1936 Berlin Olympics—at the Nazis' request. To accommodate Hitler, Glickman and Sam Stoller had been replaced by Ralph Metcalfe and Jesse Owens.

Erich lowered the volume on the radio and his own voice. "Mama asked you to excuse her, please, and that's what you should do."

"Did I say something wrong?"

Erich shook his head. "My mother has a healthy respect for authority," he said. "It's her German soul. And a consequence of zoning."

"Zoning?"

"This used to be our family home—a private residence," he said. "Now it's a public boardinghouse. Along the way there were some issues of classification. Mother was at her wits' end, when Rosetta thought her friend might be able to help."

"And was he?"

"Who knows? But no one asks about zoning, lately. Another time, they were doing some construction across the street. The noise of the cement mixer kept Mother up at night. Rosetta's friend made a call and chased the trucks away. No more work after her ten o'clock bedtime."

Mary understood. The parlor was comfortable, but none of the furniture was new. Gertrude must have been facing the loss of her home, until she began taking in boarders. What would Mary have done, without help from Michael's old colleagues? "Do you know the name of this helpful gentleman?"

"Mr. Stubs?" Erich shook his head. "From my post on the sofa, I hear a lot of things, over the radio and on the stairs.

118

But I only catch snatches of talk, in passing. As Mama likes to say, I don't get out much."

"Have you any idea who might know his name?"

Erich looked out the window and sighed. "*Der Vermittler*."

"Pardon?"

"The go-between," he said.

For a moment Mary showed her confusion.

"Talk to Leon," Erich said. "My sister's boy. If you can find him."

* * *

Leon Catalan was at that moment in the very last place on the island of Manhattan Mary Shanley would have looked for him. When Eva Catalan set sail for Spain, she left her son in the care of her mother Gertrude Tanenbaum. But she asked Rachel Lipinsky to keep an eye out for him and help him get a twentieth century education. Rachel made it her business to bring the boy along to protests, playgrounds, and street performances in New York, the world's most modern city.

At Park Avenue and 39th Street, William Van Alen had constructed a site not to be missed. The House of the Modern Age was an all-steel structure Van Alen designed as a model to be replicated, mass produced by manufacturing plants in New York, Cleveland, Pittsburgh, and Chicago and serviced by a hundred dealers. Van Alen was a Brooklynite, a night student at Pratt, who went off to study at the Ecole des Beaux-Arts in Paris. In 1924 he designed the Childs restaurant at Fifth Avenue and 49th Street, on the strength of which he was hired as the architect of the Chrysler Building.

That earned him the title, "the Ziegfeld of his profession." There was a photo of Van Alen dressed as the Chrysler Building in a costume made of silvery cloth, wood, and flame-colored silk, trimmed in patent leather. But Rachel was not impressed by him or his House. How many working-class families really dreamed of sleeping in a steel bedroom? Leon

119

liked the place, especially the noise it made when you kicked the walls. The pair were still discussing it when they returned to 21st Street and found Mary Shanley waiting, sitting on the curb across the street.

"What are you doing out here?" asked Rachel.

"Waiting for you and Leon."

"Wouldn't you rather wait for us in Mrs. T's parlor?"

"I thought I'd look around," said Mary. "I'm on the city clock. We can go inside now, if you're ready."

Mrs. T's parlor was empty when they entered. Mary invited Leon to sit and talk with her there. But Leon did not want to talk, and Rachel refused to leave him, so Mary invited Rachel to sit in while they visited.

Rachel plopped into the Queen Anne chair, while Mary sat on one end of the sofa. That left an empty seat on the opposite side of the cushion, where Erich usually sat, near the radio. But Erich wasn't there, and Leon wedged himself between the sofa arm and the seam on the edge of the cushion.

"Now, Leon," said Mary in her best maternal voice, "I don't want you to be afraid to say anything. I am a policewoman, but I'm not here to arrest you. You're not in any trouble. I'm only interesting in hearing what you know that might help us find a very bad man. Do you understand?"

Leon glanced at Rachel, who didn't know what to make of it either. The police were always the enemy, strike-breaking tools of the captains of industry. Even the union's friend, Mayor LaGuardia couldn't keep them from swinging their clubs at people they called "Commie unionists." Talking to the police was an act of foolishness if not betrayal in Rachel's circle of friends. But Mary was chasing Rosetta de Soto's murderer, and a friend who lived across the hall was a different degree of friend from the kind who lived in your circle.

Rachel leaned forward and asked, "Do you?"

"Uh huh," Leon told Rachel.

"Good," said Mary, as if he had responded to her.

Leon glanced at Rachel, who settled back in her chair.

"You know Miss de Soto, on the second floor, don't you?" Mary didn't wait for Leon's answer. "And you also know the men who come to visit her. I'd like to hear what you think about one of them."

Mary waited until Leon said, "Which one?"

"Mr. Stubs."

"Which one is that?" asked Leon.

Mary didn't know, so she turned around the question. "Which ones are there?"

"The young one, and the rich one." He ticked them off on his fingers.

That didn't help Mary much, since Freddie Arlington could have been either one. "What about the old one?"

"I said him already. The rich one."

Rachel asked the boy, "How do you know he's rich?"

"By his car," Leon said.

"He came by car? Not by taxi?"

The boy nodded.

Mary asked, "Did he ever give you money?"

Leon looked at his shoes. "Maybe."

"That's all right," she said. "You can keep it. All I want to know is, who is he? Do you know his name?"

"Herbie," said Leon with confidence.

"That's what he told you to call him?" Rachel asked. "Herbie?"

Leon shook his head. "He always told me to tell Miss Soto, 'Your friend is waiting outside.' She was the one who called him Herbie."

"Excellent, Leon," Mary said. "You're doing very well."

Leon exhaled audibly.

"It's hard work, huh?" asked Mary.

"Uh huh."

"Then let me make it easier. Herbie used to pull up outside the house and sit in his car. He sent you in to get Miss de Soto. Am I right?"

"Yeah."

"And she would come?"

"Sometimes."

"And other times she wouldn't?"

"Not right away."

"You went out to tell him what she said?"

"Uh huh."

"And what happened if she said 'No'?"

"Herbie said, 'You go tell her this,' or 'Promise her that,' or something."

"And then?"

"She went out to the car."

Mary nodded. "When was the last time, Leon? The last time you saw his car? Two days ago? A week, or more?"

"Tuesday," he said.

Rachel said, "Last Tuesday? Are you sure?"

"How do you know?" asked Mary.

"I remember, because she said, 'Tell him no. It's Tuesday. I can't stay out late.' But then she went anyway, and did. Stay out late."

"How do you know?"

"I waited up."

"To see that she came home safely?"

He looked at Rachel, who said, "Tell the truth."

"For the candy," Leon admitted.

"What candy?" she persisted.

"The cotton candy. He said he'd take her out for cotton candy."

Rachel looked to Mary for direction, as Leon climbed onto the sofa backwards and sat on the edge of the seat cushion, dangling his legs.

"But she didn't bring me any."

Mary was starting to doubt his whole story. A ten-year-old was hardly a reliable witness. The line between history and fantasy blurred too easily. She wondered if the boyfriend's name was really Herbie, or if that too was a lie.

"Leon," she said, "I want you to think before you answer this question. Try to remember what really happened. Are you saying that Mr. Herbie took Miss de Soto out to see the circus?"

As far as Mary knew, there was no circus in town. The circus had to be going on in the center ring of a ten-year-old imagination. But Leon felt certain of his story now and smacked a fringed throw pillow.

"No! He said to a club. The Cotton Candy Club."

Fifteen. Dutch Treat

In 1920, the World Heavyweight Champ Jack Johnson opened the Club Deluxe on the corner of Lennox Avenue and 142nd Street in Harlem. Three years later, the place was acquired by a bootlegger, Owney Madden, who changed its name to the Cotton Club.

Its customers were white, while its performers were not— Cotton Club chorus girls were expected to be "tall, tan, and terrific," which meant at least five-foot-six, light-skinned, and younger than twenty-one. Officially owned by a Broadway producer, Walter Brooks, the club's true owner for much of Prohibition was the notorious Dutch Schultz, whose death in Newark in 1935 provoked a round of drinks on the house, and a sigh of general relief from everyone in it.

The Cotton Club launched a galaxy of black stars. Duke Ellington led the house orchestra until 1931, when Cab Calloway picked up the baton. Lena Horne started in the chorus at sixteen. Coleman Hawkins played the sax and Dorothy Dandridge sang there. The Nicholas Brothers and Bill Robinson danced. By 1937, Owney Meany was in Sing Sing for his second stint, where his strippers dropped by to perform for him. A race riot in 1936 closed its Harlem location, but the Cotton Club reopened on Broadway and 48th Street, when Jimmie Lunceford led the house band, though Ellington, Calloway, and Louis Armstrong still dropped by now and then for old times' sake.

Johnny Broderick had skipped the Cotton Club on their trip up Broadway because he said it was "strictly for tourists" now. Maybe it was, but Rosetta de Soto, like most charity girls, was a tourist herself among men-about-town. And the man who took her out on Tuesday night just might prove to be a regular customer.

Before Mary visited, she called the Detective Bureau to see if Johnny wanted to come along. She learned he was out in Queens somewhere, at a garbage dump they were trying to reclaim as the site for the World's Fair. Mary didn't need to know what he was doing out there and didn't feel that she needed him at the Cotton Club either. Leon's memory was *her* lead. Mary was willing to share it if Johnny was available, but she wasn't going to wait for him to chase it down.

When Mary arrived at Broadway, the front entrance was locked, but she made her way around the corner and found the stage door. Inside, the staff was rushing around, setting up tables for the night. Mary took Mrs. T's second photo of Rosetta-in-a-hat out of her purse and caught the arm of a waiter.

"Have you ever seen this girl?" Mary demanded.

The waiter looked annoyed, but looked again at Mary and said, "No, Ma'am." Then he left with a handful of silverware.

Mary tried again with a skinny young woman vacuuming the rug, who couldn't have been older than fifteen. "Has this girl ever been here?"

The woman with the vacuum didn't glance up at the photograph. Perhaps she couldn't hear the question over the noise of her machine, or perhaps she didn't want to. She bent down and pulled her vacuum out from between the legs of a chair. Then she tracked a line of lint around Mary's feet and followed it out of the room.

Behind her, a busboy was polishing a champagne flute with a linen napkin, trying to remove a spot.

"Whyn't you ask *him*?"

Mary turned, but the busboy didn't seem to notice her. He was a colored man in his forties, who raised his chin as he lifted the flute into the light.

"Did you speak to me?"

He still didn't look at Mary when he said, "Why don't you ask the gentleman by the potted plant? Nobody's gonna talk to you before he does."

Standing beside a potted plant was a mug about four-foot-six. He looked like a jockey who had lost his nag. He was dressed in a white tuxedo jacket, which he must have bought in the Boys department at Brooks Brothers. But the arms inside his tuxedo strained its fabric, pulling the seams apart, as if the little man had filled up his sleeves with horseshoes.

"Him?" said Mary.

The busboy didn't answer, but moved on to wipe off the next flute. The jockey gave the busboy a nasty glance and then walked over to Mary.

"Scuse me, lady. Who let you in here?"

"I did myself," said Mary.

"I'm sorry, Ma'am," he shook his head, "but we ain't even opened yet."

"I'm not a customer," she said. "Are you the manager?"

"You can call me that. Most people call me Schmidt." His eyes were like two pebbles in his head. "The show starts at eight. For customers."

"I'm with the police."

"Bully for you. We're fixed for the month with the fire inspector."

"I'm not looking for a code violation, or a hand-out, Mr. Schmidt. I'm looking for a missing girl. Have you ever seen her?" She held up the photo of Rosetta.

Schmidt squinted. It took him too long to deny it, and he knew she noticed that, so he said, "Who wants to know?"

Mary sighed. "Sergeant Broderick."

And just as it did in the speakeasy era, Johnny's name opened the door. The short man yawned like Ali Baba's cave. "Sure, I recognize her. She was here Tuesday night. Ringside as usual, with Mr. Handley, Mr. Boone, and another chippy."

"With who?"

"Lemme show you," he said, friendly-like.

He led her backstage behind the curtain, to a hatbox filled with folded sleeves of cardboard. Schmidt took one out and handed it to Mary. On its front cover was the name of the Cotton Club, in its distinctive script. Inside, on the left, was a page for autographs, and on the right a three-by-five inch snapshot of a man and woman at a table on the dance floor.

"You've seen the cigarette girls moving through the tables, haven't you? We also have a camera girl, with a flash Graflex. When it's slow, she snaps a few pictures without waiting to be asked and offers to sell them for a dollar. The ones that people don't want go in here."

Mary opened another one, which showed two men with raised shot glasses. Their faces were flushed and they were sweating.

Schmidt picked up a handful. "These should be from last week, around Monday or Tuesday." He flipped through the stack. "Here we go," he said, turning one so that it faced Mary. "That's Mr. Handley on the left. Boone is on the right."

Mary recognized Hanley's face from someplace, though she couldn't remember where she had seen it.

"Quite a party, wasn't it?" Schmidt said. "They had bubbly, Beluga, the works—like they were sailing in the morning for Europe."

"Do they come here often?"

"Often enough. They're in the same business, you might say."

"What business is that? I thought that Mr. Handley worked for the city."

Schmidt's crooked grin revealed a chipped front tooth. "A course no one in the city does business," he said.

"What business is Mr. Boone in?"

"Construction. Concrete. Didn't you ever hear of Booligan Boots? Boone and Mulligan were partners, until Maxie Mulligan skipped out four months ago. With ninety thousand smackers from the Triboro Bridge account."

"In...fishing boots?"

Schmidt gave him the fisheye. "When the Dutchman wanted to lose a mug, he'd pour him a pair. Then drop him to the bottom of the Hudson."

Mary said, "You mean cement overshoes."

The little man grinned. "Dutch invented them, did you know that?"

"Creative guy."

"Oh, yeah. Nobody got past him. Until the end, a course. But the whole business was turning shit, wasn't it?"

*   *   *

Mary thought she needed to do some good, old-fashioned detective work—plodding systematic, and unglamorous. It was her favorite kind. Her first call was to Booligan Concrete, where the company operator told her Mr. Boone was out.

"For how long?"

"I couldn't say, Ma'am."

"Is he due in later?"

"I couldn't say that either."

"Can you ask somebody who could say?"

The line went dead, but three minutes later, the operator was back. "I am sorry, but the only thing anybody here can say is that Mr. Boone is out."

Mary then attempted to locate Mr. Handley, somewhere in the New York City bureaucracy. Her guidebook was a directory of city employees she lifted from the sergeant's desk at Centre Street.

Mary had two names—a first name and a last name—but not much faith in either one. The first name had come from a ten-year-old *Vermittler*, negotiating the terms of a charity girl. The second name came from a half-pint gangster-turned-floor-manager, with no cash motive to tell the truth. The resulting *Herbie Handley* did not show up in any directory of city employees. But Mary knew that Mr. Stubs or Handley, if that really was his name, must have some public influence. Hadn't he been able to help Mrs. T resolve her problem with the zoning commission? According to Leon, the mystery man drove a big black car with city plates. According to the Dutchman's jockey, he partied with Booligan Boots. What sort of municipal job offered those perks?

There were dozens of Herberts in the municipal directory, but only five Handleys in positions of authority exalted enough to call in a favor from the zoning commission. Mary called the first, H.G. Handley, in the Department of Motor Vehicles. Her call was put through immediately, and a female voice picked up. "Yes? Can I help you?"

"Can I speak to H.G. Handley, please?"

"Speaking."

Helen Georgina Handley. Mary hung up and dialed the second name on her list, Lowell Handley, in the Parks Department, with even less expectation. *Lowell* was a long way from *Herbert*. No one answered Lowell's line after seven rings, so Mary called the third name on her list.

She hit a lucky strike with Mortimer Handley, who audited the purchasing office for the Metropolitan Transit Authority. Mr. Handley was in and would be glad to see her. He was always happy to assist the members of the police force. No, he saw no problem, if she was free at the moment to run right over for a brief *tete-a-tete*.

The MTA bought trains. Their budget ran in the millions. As she passed over a subway stop, Mary felt the earth move below her feet. She clutched the snapshot from the Cotton Club and marched over to Handley Three.

She found the Inspector-General of Purchasing in a tiny office on the fourteenth floor, behind an old desk. The oak veneer had peeled off two of its corners, and the green leather visitor's chair was lumpy with springs. Mary sat on the very edge and studied the man at his desk. He wore a black jacket with worn elbows, and his wrists stuck out inches past his cuffs. His face was pale but seemed too wide for his frame, which looked as if he had skipped lunch every day for a year. His chin was clean-shaven and his eyebrows bushy. As he hunched over his blotter, the overhead fixture glistened through the wisps of hair crossing his head. Mary checked her photo souvenir, just to be sure, but there was no way this man had taken Rosetta de Soto to the Cotton Club.

129

"How can I help you?" he asked.

"You can't," Mary replied and left his office. Behind her, he closed his ledger and snapped off his desk lamp.

The fourth Handley, Mary discovered, had died six months before. He was still listed under personnel at the Hall of Records, because no one had noticed yet. Or rather, no one had reported his death to the proper authorities, which meant the necessary form had not been filed, which meant the man was not formally deceased, as far as their office was concerned. They had contacted a relative in Parkview, Ohio, who had asked to have the form mailed out to her. But it had not come back with a notary public's stamp, and until it did Norman Handley's name would remain where it was, over his mailbox and in the official directory.

Sixteen. Concrete Reality

Mary was running out of Handleys, but the fifth one looked like a candidate. He was still in his forties, for one thing, and even through the frosted glass at the Department of Water and Power, the cut of his suit suggested a man who might have a taste for jazz. Unfortunately, the woman sitting at the desk out front was protective of her superior. For the second time she asked, "Do you have an appointment, Miss Shanley?"

"I told you," said Mary, "I'm with the police."

"Officers make appointments, too," the woman replied. "I tried to see a detective once, about the couple who live upstairs. It sounds like he's strangling her, every night. I asked to see that cop in the papers. That Johnny—"

"Broderick?"

"No—Cordes. But you know what they asked me for?"

"Evidence?"

"They said, 'Do you have an appointment?'"

While Mary was talking to the woman outside his office, Theodore Handley opened his door to show out a slender woman in a jade green dress. "I'm sure we can see to your little problem," he said. "Is there a number I can reach you?"

She fished in her purse for a pencil, and he surveyed the room for his next guest. Before he could choose, Mary rose from her seat.

"Excuse me, Mr. Handley," she said, "but the New York Police Department needs a moment of your time."

"Of course." He looked around. "Where are they?"

"Right here." Mary raised her glove and preceded him into his office.

She sat in a tubular Art Deco chair with a thin gray pad on the seat. He followed and sat in a matching chair behind a steel desk. The standing lamp in the corner reflected off the desktop, making Mary blink wherever she shifted her head. It gave him a subtle edge over his visitors.

"So you're a policewoman. In plainclothes."

"We do exist," said Mary.

"I'm happy to hear it," Handley said, tilting back his chair. "Why can't a woman swing a rubber hose?"

Was that supposed to be a compliment? "We do all right."

"I'll watch my answers, then." He crossed one leg over the other and tugged his trouser knee. "So, what crime are we here to solve?"

He was trying to charm her, Mary knew. There must have been women who fell for it, but she wasn't among them.

"I'm investigating a homicide. You're a suspect."

He sat upright. "I am? Heavens, why?"

As he moved into the light, Mary got a closer look at Theodore Handley, Jr., who did not look too much like the man in the souvenir photo. The face across the desk was longer and narrower, though Mary had heard that the camera could add ten pounds. The man in the snapshot was chewing on a stogie, and there was a cigarette butt in Theodore Handley's ashtray. Both men wore cuff links and both had pasty complexions, but those weren't enough points in common for the D.A. to hang a murder rap.

"I'll ask the questions, if you don't mind. Where were you Tuesday night?"

"Tuesday? At 21. Having dinner."

"Alone?"

"With my mother. She loves their lamb chops in mint jelly."

"How about Wednesday night?"

"Again, I think, with Mother. She's going through a rough patch."

"And Thursday?"

He glared at Mary. "With Mother, all right? What can I say? She likes to keep an eye on me. I happen to digest better, when she cuts my chop."

Mary held up the photo in its sleeve and studied it. Then she looked at the live Handley, sitting in his metal chair, blinking back a tear. The resemblance was definitely fading.

Mary stuck the viewer in her coat pocket. "That explains it," she told Handley.

He sniffed. "It does?"

She patted his hand. "Don't worry your handsome head."

He wiped his eyes and with the same hand brushed back the hair at his temple. "All right. I won't."

*   *   *

From a phone booth on the corner, Mary tried to reach Lowell Handley again. His office phone rang eight times, nine times, ten…and Mary decided to see for herself. But when she got to his office in the Parks Department, everyone had left for the day. The entire floor was empty, a great open space filled with desks in the center, surrounded by private executive offices. Each door was locked, with a keyhole in the doorknob, until she reached the office in the far corner.

A brass nameplate by the door read: Lowell H. Handley.

It was locked, with a huge, iron padlock. The door was taped shut with black and yellow tape, to make sure nobody opened it.

Mary sat on the corner of a desk outside and lifted a telephone receiver from its cradle. The line rang twice, before the company operator picked it up.

"Booligan."

"I'd like to speak to Mr. Boone," Mary said.

"I'm sorry, Ma'am," said the operator, "but he's still unavailable."

"Not available *out*, or *in* but occupied?"

"Just a moment, please."

The silence was longer this time. When the operator returned she said, "They told me just to tell you again, 'Mr. Boone is not available.' But I heard him roar, so he must be back there someplace."

"Thanks. I think I'll take a look."

"Good luck, honey. You'll need it."

133

The Booligan Concrete Company sat over the East River near the northern end of the freshly paved East Side Drive. When Mary arrived, the gate was open with a lock dangling from its chain. Mary gave the fence a shove, and the gate swung wide. The yard inside was deserted, but lights burned in a ground-floor window. Mary peered through the dust and tried the door. Unlatched. Inside was a switchboard, with two blinking lights. But no one in the swivel chair to make the connection.

Mary said, "Hello?" and got no answer.

But she heard a thump on the ceiling and noticed a wooden staircase running up the exterior to an office that overlooked the yard. Mary began to climb the wooden steps. Halfway up, she was nearly toppled off the stairs by a skinny young woman with red-blonde hair, who came clumping down the steps with a large handbag over her shoulder. She did not slow down as she passed Mary, but muttered "Asshole" under her breath as she turned slightly and pushed her way through.

"Excuse me!" said Mary rather sharply, but the woman never turned to face her again. Mary's scalp tingled. She couldn't place the face, but definitely felt something familiar about her. It was only when she reached the top of the stairs that Mary realized where she had seen her. She was the second girl in the photo snapped at the Cotton Club, sitting between Handley and Boone.

Mary's foot tripped on the unfinished step.

Below her, a car screeched out of the yard. In front of her was a wooden door with a pane of frosted glass above the knob. The lettering on the glass read BOONE, but Mary could still read the outline of an old stencil poorly scraped off: & MULLIGAN. The door jammed against the floorboards, but Mary used her shoulder to shove it open. Inside, the floor was covered with scraps of paper.

"What about this one?" a woman's voice asked quietly.

"Toss it," boomed a bear of a man, with his broad back to the door. "Anything you see you're not sure about—toss."

Mary turned and saw a woman in a telephone headset talking to the second man in the Cotton Club's photograph. No question, it was him, grizzled cheeks and all.

"Mr. Boone?"

He turned and saw her. "Yeah? Ah, great. Who are you, now?"

"Mary Agnes Shanley. With the Detective Bureau."

"Good for you," said Boone, opening a shoebox of documents. He rifled through them and turned the box upside down, scattering papers everywhere. He picked up one sheet, squinted at it, and tore it to bits.

"I need to ask you a couple of questions."

Boone didn't bother looking up. "I'm sure you do, sweetheart. Get in line."

"Where does it start?"

He didn't answer. "Irene! Get in here! What is this?"

The woman in the headset said, "She left."

"Irene did?" he bellowed. "Walked? The *cunt*."

Mary made a face at the word. "I think I might have passed her on the stairs. Irene is a strawberry blonde, isn't she?"

"Excuse me," said Boone, staring at her for an instant before returning to the papers from the shoebox. "Shit," he said, running a hand through his thinning hair. "Crap, I mean. Crapola."

The telephone operator looked at Mary. "You're the cop, aren't you?"

"Does it matter?"

"A woman like you? Sure as shooting."

"It seems to mean more to you than it does to him."

The operator waved toward a chair. "Would you like a seat, Detective? As you can see, Mr. Boone is occupied at the moment."

"Thank you," said Mary, perching on the edge of a stylish chair and gripping both arms for support.

"Watch your fingernails on that leather," said Boone. "It's Italian. From a little shop in Florence."

135

Mary wore no polish. "I am always careful with my nails," she said, "as I am with furniture."

Boone did not notice the tone of her reply but fell to his knees again, crawling through the scattered scraps of paper. He snatched one off the floor and sat back on his haunches to read it. With every line he scanned, his spine sank lower and face fell further.

"God-damned Mother of Christ," he groaned.

Blasphemy chasing profanity. Mary was not particularly religious but found that cocktail distasteful.

"Charming."

"Cut him a little slack," the operator murmured, clucking in sympathy. "Reality is sinking in. It isn't every day a man's indicted."

*　　　　*　　　　*

Mary got the story from a law clerk she knew in the Manhattan D.A.'s office. Bertram Boone, Jr., was about to be indicted for misappropriating federal funds, together with Lowell H. Handley, the Deputy Parks Commissioner who oversaw construction of public facilities. Plenty of concrete went into those playgrounds, but the parks were only a small piece of a much more profitable scam. Handley was also involved in a tangled skein of Robert Moses projects.

That was where she first saw him, Mary realized— squatting behind Moses on the platform of honor at the Sara Roosevelt playground. A plump man in a porkpie hat, chewing on an unlit cigar. He had the same cigar in the corner of his mouth in the shot snapped by the camera-toting girl at the Cotton Club.

At issue in the indictment was the purchase of concrete, yards and yards of the stuff. Moses was building highways on the East Side and the West Side, paving the New York waterfront mile after mile. A man like Bertie Boone had everything to gain from a secret partnership with Herbie

Handley—inside information, even a contract above the lowest bid—until their sweetheart deals were made public, by a Federal indictment. Then their relationship had to go by the book. Parties at the Cotton Club were strictly off limits or had to stay hearsay, at worst.

But two young women had been with the conspirators, partying at the Cotton Club. One of them was Rosetta de Soto, whose body had turned up dead. Was there a connection? Had Herbie Handley killed Rosetta to keep her from testifying? Mary couldn't help wondering. Was Handley the sort who might turn to murder in order to escape a scandal? And what kind of scandal were they talking about, exactly? There was only one man who would know for sure.

Seventeen. The Books of Moses

Robert Moses, master builder of New York's parks, pools, bridges, and highways, never learned to drive a car. He kept a squad of chauffeurs at his disposal to drive him from one construction site to the next. Mary's challenge was where to find him. Moses's principal office as Parks Commissioner was in the Arsenal Building in Central Park, but he maintained several office suites throughout the city, each fully staffed including a chef on call. The papers reported that Moses worked fifteen-hour days and left piles of work for his assistants in the mornings. Mary started at dawn and went from office to office, talking to the great man's assistants. She finally caught up with him back in Central Park, where he stood above a grassy field that once been a reservoir and was now home to the forest of tents comprising New York's largest Hooverville.

He was standing at the top of an asphalt path that curved up a hill. A small group of other suits circled around him, but it wasn't hard to pick him out. Moses was almost fifty but looked younger than that and surrounded himself with the best minds of the next generation. His large forehead and prominent ears stuck out over a blue wool suit, dark blue tie, and light blue cotton shirt, with cuff links. The other suits were of similar blues, but Moses stood upright with his shoulders back, while the rest seemed to crouch so as not to impede his vision.

Only the cut and fabric of his suit showed his taste and upbringing. His father, Emanuel Moses, owned a department store. His mother, Bella Silverman, moved the family from New Haven to a townhouse on East 46th Street, where Robert grew up. He entered Yale at seventeen, two years ahead of the rest of his class. He studied the British civil service system at Oxford in 1909, and earned his doctorate at Columbia in 1914, where his thesis argued that civil service jobs should go to the men who merited them, on the strength of their class and education.

Yet his construction projects used public resources to ennoble the experience of the man on the street—or rather, the man in his car. Moses put the common man into the driver's seat. His first project was the transformation of a sandbar on Long Island into Jones Beach, with two fabulous bathhouses of expensive bricks and mosaics, surrounded by signs, fountains, railings, and trashcans based on ship designs. It opened in 1930 to immediate popular success. In the years that followed, Moses built the Island's Northern and Southern Parkways, cutting through the estates of wealthy New Yorkers to put the verdant island within reach of a middle-class tank of gas.

Mary heard a story about one silk hat who complained to Al Smith that Moses and his Parks Commission were bringing in the rabble. The Governor said, "Rabble? That's me you're talking about." And Moses got the green light to acquire more parkland.

Smith brought Moses to Albany for the second time in 1922 as Secretary of State and Chairman of the New York State Council of Parks. In 1933 La Guardia asked Moses to become the first Parks Commissioner of New York City. Moses wrote the legislation uniting parks departments in five boroughs to create his new job. With no formal training in planning, law or architecture, he also wrote the legislation for the Triboro Bridge and Tunnel Authority and accepted the post of its first President.

When FDR became Governor, Moses resigned as Secretary of New York State, but no one could imagine the Bridge and Tunnel Authority without him at its helm. Only once did he throw his own hat into the political ring. In 1934, he ran for Governor of New York on the Republican ticket. Moses lost to Herbert Lehman in a landslide and never ran for elected office again. Yet by his positions on authorities and commissions, in 1937 Robert Moses held twelve separate titles. From most of them he drew no salary. These public-private entities floated bonds to raise the funds to build new bridges and tunnels and paid them back with quarter tolls—ringing up huge piles of cash for Robert Moses to spend on other public projects. The title he liked best, he often told journalists, was "a man who gets things done."

In 1934, Moses placed a notice in the newspapers, soliciting architects. By dawn a line two blocks long was waiting outside the Parks Department building on Fifth Avenue. In the first few months of that year, 1700 individual projects were done—park benches rebuilt, a new golf course constructed, and the Central Park Zoo redesigned.

Through the 'thirties Moses kept building swimming pools, playgrounds, public housing, the 79th Street Boat Basin, and the West Side Highway. He paved the Grand Central, Interborough, and Henry Hudson Parkways, and raised the Bronx-Whitestone Bridge. In 1936 he completed the Triboro Bridge, joining Manhattan to the Bronx, Brooklyn, and Queens in a seamless network of asphalt and macadam.

It was an open secret that Moses and La Guardia had screaming fights, with Moses calmly patronizing, Hizzoner hollering at the top of his lungs. But they made a potent team. After the Republican Mayor delivered New York City to the Democratic President during Roosevelt's 1936 campaign, La Guardia could waltz into the Oval Office and draw Federal resources into the City like no Mayor before him. And Moses had a purpose for every penny. Over La Guardia's first term of office, the two men rebuilt 119 dilapidated playgrounds into 400 modern facilities. They opened 200 tennis courts and swimming pool after swimming pool, in one stretch ten pools in ten days.

In 1936 Moses planned a special celebration for the Mayor's 54th birthday: the grand opening of the Henry Hudson Bridge, which connected the West Side Highway to Riverdale, the Sprain Brook Parkway, and the mainland United States. Unfortunately it rained on December 12th, and the party was forced inside a small administrative building. The ceremony was interrupted again by a radio announcement the Mayor insisted on hearing: Edward VIII, the sitting King of England, had abdicated to marry the woman he loved, the American divorcee, Wallis Warfield Simpson. A disaster for the British nobility, perhaps, but a triumph of American enterprise.

Moses's strategy was to use federal funds earmarked to fight unemployment to hire the labor he needed to pave New York. In 1937, Moses built, among other projects, the East Side Drive, the Ward's Island Water Pollution Control Plant, and the Lincoln Tunnel—where in a pile of fresh earth beneath the Hudson River they found the body of Rosetta de Soto.

Which led Mary to approach the great man on a hilltop in Central Park.

Moses lit a cigarette and surveyed the field below, smelling army tents and cold cooking fires. There were men in undershirts and women nursing babies in their arms. And there were children, more than Mary expected, running between the tents, knocking over water pots, and chasing one another around the lawn. Moses flicked his spent match into a clump of ailanthus.

"The problem," he said, "is that the people we need can't be hired with this fund, and the people who can be hired can't do what we need."

His colleagues mumbled agreement.

Mary climbed from the opposite direction and came upon the men unnoticed. "Excuse me, Mr. Moses—" she began.

One of the others intercepted her. Obviously the bravest of Moses's minions, he had a green stripe in his tie and an Elks Club pin on his lapel.

"Can I help you?"

Mary cast a glance at Robert Moses, who could hear every word that passed between them. "I'm a police officer."

"I'm sure you are," said the Elk smoothly. "Can I help you, officer?"

"I need to talk to Mr. Moses. It's important."

"I'm sorry. But perhaps if you told me what it's about—"

"It's about Lowell Handley."

Mary directed her last sentence to the man himself, who set his hand on the lesser suit's shoulder. "Thank you," he said, and to Mary, "Come with me." He turned on his heel and marched out of Central Park.

Mary started after him. It was hard keeping up, his strides were so long and each one followed so quickly on the last. Mary was out of breath when she found him curbside, sitting in a limousine, whose liveried chauffeur held the door. Inside, Moses wiggled his finger, motioning her to join him.

"Where are we going?"

"For a swim," said Moses. "Or I am. If you ride along, we can talk."

Mary settled back against the buttery leather. Through the rear window she saw a second limo follow them into traffic. Moses waited until she had turned around to face him.

"Tell me what you know about Herbert."

"Lowell Handley has been stealing from you. Or rather from the Triboro Bridge and Tunnel Authority and the people of New York."

"How?"

"By paying more for concrete than your office needs to pay, and sharing the difference with a contractor."

"Not exactly," he said, "but go on."

Their limo headed west on 34th Street. The second limo did the same. Mary said, "He conspired on insider bidding. With Thomas Berrigan."

"Theodore," said Moses.

"You know?"

"Of course I know. We have books, and from time to time we go through them. We have filed for indictments with the district attorneys of three out of five municipal boroughs. The question, Miss—"

"Shanley."

"The interesting question is, how do *you* know? The Authority is a special sort of entity, you see. Not quite private

142

but not public either. So how did our family problem come to your attention?"

"Accidentally," confessed Mary. "I'm usually with the Pickpocket Squad."

"And you spotted him picking my pocket?"

"I'm on a special assignment. It started out as a missing persons, but now it's become a homicide."

That caught his attention. For the first time, he met her eyes. "And you think…Mr. Handley may be involved in that?"

"Possibly."

"I doubt it." His gaze moved to the window, as they merged with other lanes entering the Queens Midtown tunnel.

"Nonetheless," Mary said. "Mr. Handley is a suspect."

"What makes you think so?" Moses inquired.

"The dead girl could have put him with Berrigan, in a place and time they shouldn't have been together, spending money they shouldn't have had, on women they shouldn't have been with."

He smiled indulgently. "Ah. I see."

"What makes you think not?"

His lips pursed while he marshaled his thoughts, as if he were making a case to the Planning Commission. "Herbert was an Eli, for one thing."

"A Yalie."

"We don't often murder young ladies. We swam together on the college team. He has what you might call an inclusive social policy."

"He likes women of all classes?"

"More than that. He's a jazz musician. Trombone. He trained for the orchestra, but likes to, you know, *blow*—as he says, without the direct object."

"That doesn't place him above suspicion."

"Like Caesar's wife? No. But consider: an indictment is about to be handed down. What does that tell you?"

"You already have enough to indict him."

143

"We have more than enough on Herbert Handley. We have his books, of course, and we have the expert testimony of Albert Sheffield."

Mary had never heard that name before.

"Mr. Sheffield is a Pinkerton—a private investigator in my employ. He saw Herbert pick up Miss de Soto at her boardinghouse. They drove to Berrigan Concrete, where they were joined by Mr. Berrigan and a red-haired woman. The four of them drove out to Rockaway Beach, to watch the tides come in. Then they went to dinner on Broadway and finished off the night with a party at the Cotton Club. Does that agree with your own information?"

It was more than Mary knew. "So far."

"Maybe these will help." Moses reached into his briefcase and drew out three sheets of stiff white cardboard. Then he flipped them over.

"You have pictures?"

The first was a grainy shot of Booligan Concrete, taken through the fence, of two people climbing into a coupe. The second photo had four people standing on a concrete pavilion overlooking a moonlit beach. Across the water, a wavy silhouette of the Empire State Building glittered through the fog. In the third, the shutterbug caught the same two couples under the awning of the Cotton Club.

Mary picked up the second print. "That's Rockaway?"

"Jacob Riis Park," said Moses. "On site of the Rockaway Naval Air Station. We're redesigning it now. Hell of a view, hasn't it?"

Mary studied the couples. Handley and the strawberry blonde stood at the rail with their backs to the camera. Herbert pointed over the sand. In the foreground, Boone seemed to be showing Rosetta his expensive Italian shoe. His foot looked smaller than Mary's own ladies' size ten.

"Tell me, whose testimony do you imagine would prove to be more credible—Mr. Sheffield's or Miss de Soto's?"

144

Mary drew a deep breath. "Both would be more credible than either alone, I imagine. But Rosetta is not going to testify, now."

"Rosetta was never going to testify. What possible motive could poor Herbert have to murder a young lady who refused to testify against him?"

Mary noticed that *poor Herbert*. "You don't seem to hold it against him, but he did cook your books. Don't you mind being cheated?"

"We did report the crime," Moses said carefully, "and we are pressing charges. But it's never easy to understand why another man acts as he does. Herbert was a decent schoolmate and a reliable deputy…until the day he wasn't. Like Brutus, poor Herbert was *an honorable man*."

Mary said, "Do you know where he is now?"

"Haven't the foggiest. But isn't that your job? To find him?"

They pulled up in front of the municipal swimming center in Astoria, Queens, a huge facility built by Moses himself. Behind them, the second limo pulled into a parking spot and waited.

"I'm going for a swim," he said. "If you like, you can join me. I'm sure we can find you a suit. Or, if you feel that duty calls, you can get in the car behind us. Its driver will take you any place you want to go."

Mary thanked him but passed on the swimsuit. The driver opened the door, and Moses climbed out. He helped Mary out and then loped off in long strides toward the municipal pool. The chauffeur of the second limousine was standing beside his car, with its passenger door open. Mary sat and the driver took the wheel.

"Where to, Ma'am?"

Mary hesitated. "Does Mr. Moses like to hold meetings in his limo?"

"Yes, Ma'am. All the time."

"He's often met with Mr. Handley this way?"

"That's right."

"And when they're done, you drive Mr. Handley wherever he wants to go?"

"Any place he tells me."

"Then take me wherever you usually drop him off."

She sat back against the leather seat. The driver put the limo in gear and pulled away from the curb with no further directions.

He drove back through the tunnel, turned right, and then headed cross-town on 42nd Street. When he pulled up at the curb, Mary saw they were sitting outside a movie theatre. "This is Handley's favorite destination?" she asked the chauffeur.

"One of them," he said.

The marquee overhead read, *The Awful Truth*. The poster showed Cary Grant and Irene Dunne.

Climbing out, Mary told the driver to keep his engine running and headed for the entrance. She found her badge in her purse and showed it to the usher at the door, whose flashlight she used to move up and down the aisles, searching for her man. From the first theatre they drove to a second, and then to a third. In a hour they had covered the theatres on Broadway and began to work the side-streets.

She found him in a theatre on 47th Street. The marquee read *Swing Time*. Inside, the house was dark, with a black-and-white film on the screen. Fred Astaire was waltzing Ginger Rogers around an Art Deco set. As her eyes adjusted to the dim light, Mary spotted a man in shirtsleeves, on the aisle, chewing on an unlit cigar. She checked the souvenir photo from the Cotton Club. The man in the third row wasn't dressed in evening clothes, but he had the same plump cheeks, flushed color, and earnest expression on his upturned face.

She sat down behind him, just as she would have done if she were trailing a dip. When the dance on the screen was done, Mary whispered, "Mr. Handley?"

He didn't even look up at the sound of his name.

For ten minutes Mary wasn't sure he was the same man. He stared at the screen, as if the only question that mattered was if Fred would be forced to marry his previous fiancée, or if he were free for Ginger. Fred sang the Jerome Kern song, "The Way You Look Tonight," and Mary began to care too. But once the song ended, the man in the row ahead of her stuck a porkpie hat on his head and ambled up the aisle.

"Mr. Handley!" Mary said, loud enough to draw *shushes*.

This time he looked at her.

"I've seen enough *Swing*," she said, "if you have."

"Lovely tune, isn't it?"

"Yes, it is. I'd like you to come with me."

She took his elbow firmly, but Handley offered no resistance. They walked up the aisle like Fred and Ginger, arm in arm.

When she led him past the front desk at Centre Street, the sergeant on duty was amazed. "Good Lord, Mary," he said, "I'd tip my hat, if I was wearing one. How did you manage to snag the man so quickly? The bench warrant couldn't have been issued more than twenty minutes ago."

"That warrant is for embezzlement, Sergeant. I'm bringing him in on a different charge. Suspicion of homicide."

The sergeant opened his ledger. "Who was the vic?"

"De Soto."

"Not the girl they found in the tunnel?"

"That's the one."

"You haven't heard, then," the sergeant said. "Johnny Broderick busted that case wide open. He booked the Tunnel Killer a couple of hours ago."

Eighteen. Bone China

Broderick was upstairs in the squad room, slouching on the corner of his desk, surrounded by reporters. He kept nothing on the desk but a telephone—no papers, baskets, even a typewriter—because Johnny never used it except to park his rear end while he entertained admirers. The circle around him now was laughing loud enough for Mary to hear from the landing at the top of the stairs.

"Ming-Lu Lin, not Rin-Tin-Tin," Johnny said. "It's not even close. He goes by Mickey among regular Americans. We picked him up at ten this morning, at 10462 Queens Boulevard."

"Nice private home?"

"What do *you* think? You had to see this dump. Chicken feet hanging over the kitchen sink. Not the whole chicken. Just the wrinkled feet."

"Has he confessed yet, Johnny?"

"He denies it, of course. They always do. Denies he even knew the girl. But the other dancer tipped me off, and we found his right palm print on the poor thing's belt." He held up a patent leather strap and waited for the photographer's flash. "According to the bandleader, she wore it every night."

"And not much else, eh, Johnny?" one of the reporters asked.

The others all smirked, except Broderick.

"Now, fellahs, show some respect for the departed." His eyes twinkled and they saw it coming. "But when you look at this, you can't help wondering. Where do you suppose his left hand was?"

His timing was excellent—the laugh that followed Johnny's quip was deeper and more sincere. He coiled the belt on his desk and reached in his jacket for a cigarette. That's when he noticed the new arrival.

"Here's Mary Shanley, boys," Johnny said. "She's been working another angle on the case. How's that coming, Mary?"

148

"Slowly but surely," she said. No one wrote it down.

"Tell us about Shanghai," a reporter said.

"I shouldn't," Broderick said with a sidelong glance at Mary to remind everyone there was a lady in the room.

"Please do," Mary said. "Don't be shy on my account."

"Let's just say it's a *ball*-room only in a certain sense of the word."

His fan club snickered.

"The clientele are mostly yellow. Japs and Chinese. You know how they like to snuggle American girls."

Mary was pretty through the hips, but she didn't recall a lot of Asian men whistling as she passed on the street.

"How'd it happen, Johnny?" asked one muck-raking journalist.

"It's a little early to know the details," said Broderick, slapping his closed fist into his open palm. "We'll know for sure when he starts talking. But we'll probably find out it went like this. He bought a few tickets, to start. He must've liked dancing up close and personal with a pretty young Italian. Did you boys gets a gander at her profile?"

The reporters craned their necks to see Mrs. T's photo. They seemed to know just what he meant.

"Then he started getting jealous, watching other men swirl his girl around. The manager at the Shanghai told me he bought up all her dances, after a while. But that wouldn't hold him off for long. A man can get frustrated, on a dance floor, and you know what sort of short fuse these yellow types have."

They scribbled that down, too.

"He was waiting for her, when she came out of the dance hall that night." He paused, and the gentlemen of the press leaned in closer. "My guess is, he tailed her. Then drugged her with opium or something like that, dragged her into the empty tunnel, and raped the poor thing."

The reporters shook their head, making clucking noises, as they wrote down the whole grisly story.

It was Mary who asked, "Was there any evidence of sexual assault?"

Johnny flushed. "Fluids and stuff? The M.E. will tell us, in good time. Like I said, we don't have all the details."

"We have some," said Mary. "Wasn't the body beaten?"

Johnny remembered that. "She must have fought back. So he killed her."

"Before he raped her?"

"Or after. To keep her from talking."

"Most women fight back," Mary said, "before they're raped."

"But she was drugged," said Johnny, "with opium. Let's say she woke up and realized what he was doing to her. She fought like a tiger, and he killed her."

"That could be," a reporter said to Mary.

Sure it could, she thought, *in a dime store novel, the funny papers, or an editorial feeding fears of Japan.* For a moment Mary wondered what newspapers they wrote for, and what publishers owned those rags. But, she quickly realized, that hardly mattered. Johnny's story had everything going for it—race, sex, murder, even dancing. Everything to keep their pencils scratching, to keep their readers buying papers. It had everything, Mary thought, except the truth.

*   *   *

From his travels through Europe, the baron of the five-and-dime Frank Winfield Woolworth brought back a taste for Gothic architecture, especially as it caught the pride of empire in the British Parliament Building in London. When he decided to construct a Cathedral of Commerce as his company's new headquarters near New York's City Hall, Woolworth hired Cass Gilbert to design the tallest building in the world as a modern but still Gothic skyscraper. In 1913, Gilbert completed his 58-story, 792-foot temple in steel, stone, and terra cotta, with a U-shaped lower section and an ornamental tower.

In 1930, the Chrysler Building surpassed it as the world's tallest building, but in 1937 the Woolworth Building was still among the tallest in the New York and the world, with an observation deck on its fifty-eighth floor drawing thousands of tourists a year. The lobby was made of marble and stained glass, with carved caricatures of the building's engineer, architect, and F.W. Woolworth himself, counting out his nickels and dimes. Rather than taking out a standard mortgage, Woolworth had paid off the building's entire 13.5 million-dollar price tag in cash. His private office was decorated in the French style, modeled and furnished after Napoleon's Palace at Compiègne.

No such indulgence was lavished on the thousands of shop-girls who worked the cash registers, aisles, and lunch counters of Woolworth's street-level retail stores. The company's humble price points afforded some insulation to its profit margin, since people still needed five-cent combs and ten-cent basic necessities, but the continuing Depression meant falling sales and rounds of laid-off salesgirls. Rosetta de Soto had lost her place at the perfume counter months before. Now in 1937 the company announced its intention to let go another twelve hundred employees, mostly young, working-class women without job prospects—except for the desperate options waiting for them in dance halls, brothels, and the streets.

Louisa Vitanza was not home when Mary called the boardinghouse at 228 West 21st Street. Mrs. T picked up the phone.

"Do you know what time it is, Mary?" Gertrude said. "Louisa's at Woolworth's. Least I hope she is. First of the month's coming up."

Mary took the address and caught a cab to the retail store. When she arrived, she tried the door, but it wouldn't open. Locked.That made no sense, on a weekday morning at eleven. There were people moving around inside, lots of them. Mary tapped on the glass, waited, and tapped again, harder. A sales clerk finally came over, but instead of opening the door, she just shook her head. Mouthing something. *Try? Shake* it?

Strike.

They were on strike? At Woolworths?

The sales clerk smiled and nodded.

Mary rattled the door. "I'm not a customer."

The sales clerk kept smiling but shook her head and shrugged.

Mary took out her badge and held it up to the glass.

The sales clerk peered at it, looked over her shoulder, and unlocked the door.

"We're closed," she said. "On strike."

"I get it," Mary told her,"but I'm not looking for a pillow case. I'm looking for a girl who works here. Louisa."

"Vitanza? She's on the strike committee. At the back of the store."

The overhead lights seemed dim. Half the fixtures had been turned off. Papers littered the floor, and the place was crowded. Mary headed back through the aisles, past bins of clothing, racks of magazines, rows of housewares and cleaners, all of it ready to leap from the shelves. There were sales girls everywhere, more than Mary had ever seen at any time, but they didn't have their usual attitude of patient service. They didn't have the gravity of striking miners, either. They were cheerful, energetic, calling out each other's names and running down the aisles with a bounce in their steps.

A girl from the sweater department carried a tray of chicken salad sandwiches, still wrapped in white paper from the deli down the block.

"Want one?" she asked Mary. "They're free—donated. And the fruit man is bringing apples. Everybody's behind us."

From the music department across the store, Mary heard a trumpet. Then the bass came in, and a drum. Someone had turned on a record player and cranked it up loud. Two of the girls in bedding started dancing with each other.

It felt like a party.

Louisa was sitting at the soda counter in the back of the store, her head close to two other girls. "Are the registers closed?"

"Check."

"All of them?"

"The ones in front and the one by the lunch counter."

"What about the doors?"

"Locked now. We'll open the side one when we get the picket signs."

"How many girls do we have in the store?"

"Three dozen, so far, but everyone wants to be part of it."

"It might get rough."

"They know that. But this is our chance, right? To stand up for everybody."

"Then let's stand up, by sitting down."

The three women looked rather pleased with themselves, when Louisa spotted Mary and waved her over.

"Mary! These are Shelly and Grace. Girls, Mary Shanley. With the New York City police! She's a detective."

"Good for you!" said Shelly. "Madam Officer Shanley."

"Thanks for coming," said Grace seriously. "We can use your support."

They seemed to think she was there for the strike. "Louisa, I can see you're busy, but could I have a minute?"

"Sure," she said, and the other two marched off.

"You should've seen it, Mary," Louisa sighed. "We had a man from the Retailers Union here, Local 125. He told us what we can and can't do. We called a strike around three o'clock, when a bunch of us put down whatever we were doing and lined up around the lunch counter. Maybe twenty girls at first. Some girls didn't want to strike. They made a circle around the registers in front and started chanting, *No strike, No strike.* But there was no contest. We had them. In a little while, the company closed the store, and sent the other girls home. Since then, the place has been ours."

Mary looked around at the girls talking excitedly, laughing and dancing together. Two were sitting on lunch counter stools, doing each other's hair. "Was that Rosetta's station? The perfume counter?"

Louisa made a face. "It used to be."

"What do you mean?"

"She hasn't really been working here for the last couple of months."

"She hasn't," said Mary. It didn't sound like a question.

"You knew that already?" Louisa said.

"I found out from another detective. Not from you. Didn't you think that piece of information might be helpful?"

"It wasn't my secret," Louisa told her. "Rosetta didn't want anyone else to know. She didn't get fired or anything like that. They laid off lots of girls in all the departments. She was just the newest girl in perfume."

"That's nothing to be ashamed of, these days."

"That's why we're striking," Louisa said. "But it's not what embarrassed Rosetta. She had to find another job, to pay the rent at Mrs. T's. But there aren't too many jobs around, especially for girls."

"So she took the only job she could find."

"Until she found a better one."

"Dancing."

"If you can call it that," said Louisa.

"Wasn't she dancing?"

"It's not like doing a turn with your boyfriend. Rosetta hated every night. All these men just pay a dime for a ticket and they can dance with you. She got five cents for every ticket she brought in. Most of them don't even want to dance, really." She moved her hands over her body, and shivered at the touch.

"She went all the way to Brooklyn?"

"She thought nobody she knew would see her out there. The Shanghai Ballroom. It's pretty much the kind of place a girl could get shanghai-ed."

"She must've had a lot of Asian customers."

"That's a plus," Louisa said, "according to Rosetta. Can you imagine? She said they tip better than white guys. Especially in between the dances."

"Did she ever say the name Ming-Lu Lin?"

"That's a name?"

"Yes, it is. Or Mickey Lin?"

"Not to me."

"Would Rosetta see a Chinese man outside the club?"

"No. I don't know. Dance hall girls have rules about those things."

"Would you?"

Louisa shook her head emphatically. "I told you—we're not doxies. I'd never date a Spic or bone China."

There was a crash at the front of the store, and both women turned their heads. But it wasn't Pinkertons smashing through a window. It was a gumball machine that had toppled and scattered colored balls over the floor. A shopgirl was standing over it, close to tears, with both hands on her face.

"I'm sorry!" she said. "I knew it was there, I always do, but I didn't see it behind me. I'm so stupid!"

Louisa knelt to scoop up the gumballs. "Don't worry, honey," she said, "we'll pay for it. And they'll probably fire all of us anyway, won't they?"

Nineteen. The Shanghai Ballroom

Mary had never been to Brooklyn. As far as she was concerned it was a different country. The Bronx felt like the city's countryside, but Brooklyn felt like another town, at least. The Giants played at the Polo Fields at 155th Street in northern Manhattan; the Yankees played at 161st Street in the Bronx. Both were New York City's teams. But the Dodgers played at Ebbett's Field, and they were Brooklyn's team. The players lived in Brooklyn and played stickball with the kids in Brooklyn streets. The Dodger and Giants were both National League teams—so the rivalry between their fans was the fiercest in New York. Michael had been a Giants fan.

When Mary crossed the Williamsburg Bridge, she entered *terra incognita* and had to trust in the honesty of her Checker cabbie, who knew the Shanghai Ballroom without the address. He followed Broadway, turned left on Myrtle Avenue, and pulled up in front of a brown brick storefront.

"This is it?" asked Mary. "The ballroom?"

"You don't have to go in, if you don't want to," the cabbie said. "I can take you right back to Manhattan."

She shook her head and paid him, with an extra five percent tip for his kindness. But she had not come this far to lose heart at the door.

It was not really a ballroom in the grand sense but a second-floor establishment reached by a staircase with steep steps and a handrail that came loose from the wall in three places. The interior décor was cheesy Oriental: fake jade fixtures, a checkerboard dance floor, and red leatherette booths around the perimeter. Overhead paper lanterns with smudged calligraphy allowed only a yellow light. Some booths were open, while others were closed from the dance floor by curtains of colored beads. In one corner of the room, a band played a listless rumba on a tenor sax, drum, and off-key piano. In the opposite corner, a fat man stood by a counter with a roll of green tickets. Next to his counter was a liquor bar, where he was pouring a cheap scotch.

Mary heard the sound of strung beads sliding noisily past each other. A blonde stepped out of a booth, adjusting her narrow skirt. It was red satin, slit to her thigh and gathered at the waist by a patent leather belt. The blonde looked Mary up-and-down and shook her head. "Sorry, sister. You'd want the dance hall on Avenue T. This place is strictly boy-meets-girl."

"Excuse me?" said Mary.

The blonde shook her limp curls. "There's no excuse for that hat." She slinked across the dance floor and struck a pose by the bar.

The fat man laughed. "Don't mind her. You not African, you can buy a ticket." He held up his roll.

"No, thank you," said Mary.

"What you drink?"

She looked at the fly-specked bar. "Nothing, right now."

He laughed. "You know where to find me."

A brunette came out of another booth and led her Chinese customer by the hand back to the dance floor. She raised one arm high in the air and drew him toward her with her other hand. The customer stepped up and threw both arms around her, pressing his torso against hers and wiggling his behind.

"Quite a grinder, isn't he?" Mary said to the fat man.

"Lots of tickets," he said.

"I'll bet."

"At night the floor gets sticky. Not from sweat." He laughed.

Mary heard a familiar clomp on the stairs, turned and saw Johnny Broderick step into the Ballroom. He wiped grease from the handrail off his hands with a hankie and nodded to the blonde still posed against the bar.

"Where's Lottie?"

She shook her head. "Not here."

"A friend of yours?" asked Mary from the corner.

157

Johnny looked over and saw her by the fat man. "If it isn't Mary Shanley! What are you doing, way out here?"

"Answering questions," Mary replied. "What about you?"

"Same damn thing," said Johnny. "Crossing the eyes and dotting the tees."

"Not quite sure about Mickey?"

"Oh, he did it all right. I'm just filling in some blanks about the why and wherefore. Why he chose de Soto, and wherefore he took her."

"*Wherefore* doesn't mean *where*. It means *why*. I thought you said he took her into the tunnel."

"Not at first," said Johnny. The M.E. seems to think she was beaten someplace else and then moved. Course, the M.E. could be wrong."

"Or you could," said Mary.

"Not too often, it turns out." He winked at her and looked around the ballroom. "Lottie coming in today?"

The blonde shrugged. The fat man shook his jelly head.

"Then I'm out of here. You need a ride?"

Mary rode with Johnny back to Manhattan. He drove an unmarked Pontiac Deluxe Series 26, all-steel construction with white wheels. When he turned the key, its six cylinders roared to life. As he pulled into traffic, Johnny reached for a contraption attached to the dashboard between his knees and Mary's. He disconnected a hand-piece and brought it near his mouth.

"This is Sergeant Broderick, on Myrtle Ave in Brooklyn, calling in."

"Hey there, Sergeant," a female voice replied.

"I'm riding with Officer Shanley."

"Irish Mary? Why?"

"Hush up—she can hear you. We'll both be back at Centre Street in twenty-two minutes. You got that?"

"Got it," the voice said. "See you, Johnny."

Broderick hung the hand-piece back on its hook and shifted into third. He gave Mary a sidelong glance. "You ever see one of these before?"

"A radio?"

"Two-way. They're going in all the cruisers, to keep the man on patrol in touch with the precinct. If anyone needs back-up, all they got to do is call."

"The girls in the ballroom could use one."

"The dime-a-dancers? Come on, Mary. You're not still saying Rosetta de Soto was a good little girl. You saw the Shanghai. You know why men buy tickets? So they can get their rocks off on the floor. Dime-a-dance is cheaper than a hooker."

"She wasn't like that."

"Now how would you know that? All right, so the girls aren't pros, exactly. They can't get preggers through their dresses. And no one gets them all alone, so they don't get beaten very often. But it happens. Your Miss Rosetta paid the cost of doing business. She paid the highest price anybody can, and that was a rotten deal. It always is. But it's up to us to make damn sure that Chinaman pays it back."

"She won't see a dime of it."

"No, she's seen all the dimes she's ever going to see. And you know how she earned them, now."

Mary tried to keep silent, but couldn't quite. She understood how Johnny made his case and why he thought as he did. But she thought differently.

"It doesn't feel good to me, Johnny."

"It never does. But you've got to be logical about it."

"It doesn't *sit* right with me, either. It doesn't feel like the woman I was getting to know. Rosetta might have taken this job, if it was all she could get. But she'd never go off with a man she didn't trust, and put herself in a place where he could do that to her. A woman on her own has to look out for herself, Johnny. She gets to know the difference between one kind of man and another."

159

Johnny wasn't buying. "I know lots of skirts who can't tell the difference between a prick and a prickly pear."

Mary knew them too. "Rosetta wasn't one of those. I know her, Johnny. I've got a feel for her. And what you say she did doesn't make sense to me."

"That's a woman's logic," said Broderick. "It won't hold up in court, so I can't make cases by it. All I can do is put together the pieces, one by one. Mickey Lin told me he never met the broad, and he was lying about that. Why should he lie to me, Mary, unless he had something to hide?"

"Maybe he did," said Mary. "Maybe he still does."

Johnny snorted. "When you find a doll's body half buried in the dirt, it's not so hard to figure out what a guy is hiding."

"To guess, you mean."

Johnny shook his head. "What if I told you they had a big fight outside the club on Wednesday night?"

"De Soto and Lin? Did they?"

"That's what Lottie told me. That's what I came to double-check. Is she sure it was Rosie and Mickey? Will she testify to that?"

"So you're not sure."

"You can never be sure, with these ditsy dames. But, you know what? From the way she told it the first time, I'll bet she is. And will."

"Maybe. But can anyone believe her?"

"Are you impugning the credibility of these ladies, Mary? Just because they'll do whatever you want for ten cents a dance?" Johnny shook his head. "It's hard to picture sweet Rosetta dancing beside them."

Twenty. Money to Burn

When Johnny Broderick arrested him, Ming-Lu Lin must have been wearing a suit. When Mary approached his cell, he still had the trousers on and the white shirt buttoned to his chin. No jacket nor tie or belt, of course. Both sleeves were rolled to his elbows, and Mary saw why—he had torn the cuff off one sleeve and knotted it around his slender bicep. He was kneeling in the center of the cell, bent over something. Mary sniffed, smelling carbon. And smoke.

The precinct jailor must have smelled it too, who rushed in from the outer room and fumbled his key in the lock.

"What did I tell you about that stuff? What are you burning? Oh, gee!"

Ming-Lu was crouched over a small pile of paper, which he had set on fire using the sunlight through his glasses. When the jailor burst in to stamp out the flames, Mary saw he was burning dollar bills.

"What is this, now?" said the jailor. "A protest against the government? Or some kind of *voodoo Chinee witchcraft?*"

Ming-Lu didn't answer, but watched bits of blackened currency scatter around the floor. His face was as sad as any face Mary had ever seen. She stepped inside the cell and asked the jailor to give them a little privacy.

The jailor looked doubtful about leaving her alone with a *Chinee murderer*, but Mary stared him down. "Your chili must be congealing."

The jailor wiped the red sauce from a corner of his mouth, locked her in with Lin, and went back to his supper.

Ming-Lu man sat on his bunk with his legs drawn up and his back against the wall. There was no other seat, so Mary sat down gingerly on the edge of Lin's mattress and propped her purse on her knees.

"Mr. Lin, my name is Shanley, Officer Shanley," she said. "Can you spare me a few minutes of your time?"

His bloodshot eyes seemed to say he had nothing else but.

161

"I'd like to talk to you about Rosetta de Soto."

His eyes filled with tears, which he blinked away. From the redness of his lids Mary guessed he must have been crying for some time before she arrived.

"You do know who I mean, don't you?"

He shook his head.

"You don't? You never met her?"

He shook more violently.

"Mr. Lin, I'm afraid that cat is out of the bag. Right now my partner is typing up a statement from the ticket seller at the Shanghai. Can you guess what he said?"

No response.

"That you bought a big roll of tickets on Wednesday night and kept her dancing with you until the ballroom closed."

"The fat man is a liar," Lin said bitterly.

"I can believe that," said Mary, pleased to hear he could speak English. "Easily. But there are half a dozen other girls ready to testify you did that more than once. In fact, two of them claimed as soon as they saw you enter the club, they knew Rosetta would be out of circulation for the evening."

Lin wrapped his arms around his knees. "They're all liars."

"Every single one?"

He shrugged, but wouldn't look up.

"Weren't you two fighting outside the dance hall, Wednesday night?"

He shook his hanging head.

"You weren't."

"No."

"Mr. Lin, I don't think you appreciate your position, here. We have witnesses who swear they saw you together, red-faced, on the street. Saw you dancing. What is a jury going to think, when witness after witness gets up on the stand to testify they saw you do what you keep insisting you never, ever did?"

"Whatever they think already."

162

"They'll have to conclude you're the liar. They won't have any choice. Are you a liar, Mr. Lin? Or are you going to tell the truth?"

He was silent.

Mary waited, until she saw his shoulders shaking. Sobbing. "Isn't there anything you can say to save yourself from the chair?"

He mumbled something into the space between his arms.

"Excuse me."

"Ask Mr. Fischer," he said. And that was all she got out of him.

*   *   *

Randall Fischer was Ming-Lu Lin's employer at the Queens County Reclamation Corporation. The company had been created for only one purpose—to bid on the job of leveling the mountains of ash and trash that had piled up for years at the municipal dump. The land was chosen as the site of the 1939 World's Fair. Somebody had to march into that wasteland and make it look inviting to companies and governments around the globe.

That job fell to thirty thousand working men, who picked up shovels on June 29th, 1936, and kept digging for twenty-seven weeks and a day.

Despite the scarcity of employment opportunities during the Depression, thirty thousand local men did not volunteer. To hire the requisite laborers, it was necessary to import them. Randall Fischer and his partners did not have the connections they needed in China, but they located a subcontractor in Queens who spoke Mandarin and enough Cantonese to manage their recruiting. That man was Ming-Lu Lin, an immigrant from Hong Kong, whose six-year status as a naturalized citizen made him eligible to receive federal funds.

Mary found Mr. Fischer in a temporary trailer on a hill of new grass over the site. When her taxi picked its way through the mounds of fresh earth and crept up to the boss's office, Randall sat in a green-and-white beach chair, sipping a thermos filled with gin. He was dressed in khaki shorts and a regimental shirt. His trailer didn't look temporary at all. Thick wires ran from a tilted pole behind it, and a gas generator belched on a yellow patch of ground at the foot of the telephone pole. The screen door of the trailer was ajar, and a thin extension cord wiggled out between his knees, where a radio blared Arturo Toscanini and the NBC Orchestra's spirited rendition of *The Ride of the Valkyrie*. As the horns rose, so did Randall Fischer, standing to sucker-punch the foul-smelling air. "Dum-dee-dee dumb-dumb...dum-dee-dee dumb-dumb...dum-dee-dee dumb-dumb...dum-dee-dee dumb!"

Mary stepped out of her cab. "Mr. Fischer?"

"Dum-dee-dee...eh?"

"Randall Fischer? Of the Queens County Reclamation—"

"That's me. What can I do for you?"

"Do you mind turning down that thing? Lower, please. Thank you."

"All right? Miss?"

"My name is Mary Shanley. I'm a police detective. Working on a homicide."

"Who died?"

"A young lady named Rosetta de Soto."

"Never heard a her."

"But you do know a contractor named Ming-Lu Lin?"

"Mickey," said Fischer, dropping back into his beach chair. "Sure, I know him. I heard about that whole business. What a shame!" He scratched his navy haircut. "What can anybody say?"

"He thought you might say something."

"Me? About what?"

"About whether or not he's guilty."

"How should I know that?"

"You know Mr. Lin, don't you? Personally?"

"Personally? Oh, yeah. The sweetest guy you ever want to meet. Hard worker. Reliable, when he makes a deal. A credit to his race, as they say. Though I'm not sure it is a race. China's a country, you know."

"Yes."

"Who did you say he killed?"

"I didn't. He's accused in the death of a young lady who danced at the Shanghai Ballroom, in Brooklyn. He did frequent the place, didn't he?"

"I don't know how frequently, but he sure liked the dancers. They all do."

"The Chinese men?"

"All the Asians. You know why? Because they're all here by their lonesomes. We don't let their womenfolk come. So long as they can show they have a job waiting, a Chinese man can get a visa. Or a Jap. But there's nothing an Oriental woman can do. They have to leave their wives and girlfriends behind. So what do we expect them to do, except find a place to dance for a dime?"

"We don't expect them to beat their dancing partners to death."

Fischer stared. "Is that what Mickey did?"

"That's how she died."

"I can't see that," he said. "Not Mickey. I could see him doing something wrong by accident, you know? If he didn't know better. Or running someone over with a car. But beating a woman to death? Nope. No way. I doubt if he's ever raised his voice to a woman, let alone his fist."

"That's what I thought," Mary said. "Or rather, that's what I felt when I met him. But he is keeping a secret."

"He's pretty good at that," said Randall Fischer.

"Know what it is?"

"Nope. But if Mickey's keeping mum, he must have a reason."

"So tell me—what could be worse for a Chinese immigrant than being accused of murdering a white girl?"

165

Fischer smiled knowingly. "You and I would say, *nothing*. But they have their own way of looking at things. If one of these young bucks dies, for example, if he falls under a tractor or something, his family won't bring his body home from the funeral parlor. His parents can't even say prayers for him. Because a Chinese elder never shows respect for anybody younger. He has to be buried in silence. I've seen it."

Mary thought of Ming-Lu kneeling in his cell. "They don't by any chance burn wads of money, do they?"

"Not legal tender," said Fischer, "not sawbucks. They burn this special prayer money, so the dead will have enough cash in his pocket when he gets to the afterlife. They put a candle at the foot of the coffin and burn incense, paper, and prayer money in the flame. Is that what you're talking about?"

"I don't know what I'm talking about," said Mary, "but when I saw Ming-Lu Lin, he was burning money in the middle of his cell. With a white strip of cotton torn from his shirt tied around his arm."

"That's what they do," said Fischer. "The full funeral rites go on for like 49 days, with prayers every week, if the family can afford it."

"And if they can't?"

"They do what they can. What else? They go into debt, if they have to."

"Is that what you think Ming-Lu was doing?"

"In his cell? Sounds like. The best he could, under the circumstances."

Mary thought of the jailor stamping out Lin's burning cash. "Is that what you're supposed to do? When you can't get ritual money, use the real thing?"

"That, I'll bet, was Mickey's own idea—which is rare, because usually the whole affair's so organized."

"What do you mean?"

"Didn't you ever see a Chinese funeral?"

Mary shook her head. All the dead cops were Roman Catholic.

"Tradition with a capital T, or whatever they call their scribble. They stand around the coffin arranged by their rank in the family. The children wear black, grandchildren wear blue, and great-grandchildren a lighter shade of blue. A son-in-law can wear white or even bright colors, since he doesn't really count as a member of the family and isn't expected to grieve. The ladies are another story. Sometimes they pull a sackcloth hood over the head of a daughter-in-law."

"So, Mr. Lin—"

"That's right," said Fischer. "I'm not Chinese myself, but that's my best guess. Mickey must have been mourning."

Twenty-one. Rocking the Cradle

The first thing Mary heard the next morning was a ringing in her ears that started and stopped but would not leave off altogether. The second sound she heard was the voice of an angry man.

"Is there any proof at all that girl was raped and murdered in my tunnel?"

Was she still dreaming? No, she was propped on one elbow in her floral flannel nightgown with a heavy black receiver at her ear.

"Who is this?"

"This," echoed the outraged voice, "is Robert Moses."

Mary rubbed the sleep from her eyes. "How did you get this number?"

"My colleagues and I are building this city," he said, "the model city of the future. I could give you the serial number off your gas meter."

"No thank you." Mary yawned.

"I thought you told me Herbert Handley was responsible for this crime."

"You told me he wasn't."

"How should I know something like that?" Moses roared.

"It looks like you were right."

"It does?" He sounded mollified and somewhat surprised. "Then believe me—there is no way a Chinaman could have carried a doped-up girl into my tunnel for the purpose of rapine and homicide. Do you think we have no security on the site?"

"I'm sure you do."

"The *World* apparently does not," said Moses. "Have you seen the paper?"

"No," said Mary, "but I can imagine. That's Johnny's version—my partner, Sergeant Broderick's. They take down every word he says like gospel. It's not the only theory we're investigating."

Moses said, "You're working your own angle?"

168

"No. Well. Something like that."

"Then let me talk to you. Let me tell you what we do to keep our people safe."

Mary leaned against her quilted headboard and propped the phone with her shoulder. "Go ahead."

"Have you any idea how dangerous it is, building a tunnel under a river like the Hudson? You take the usual risks of a construction site, add the problems of building in a tiny, dark space, and then multiply the whole thing by the pressure of thousands of tons of water overhead. Work crews have to be extensively prepared and then rotated so that nobody works more than a couple of hours a day. Our tunnel was built as a succession of pressurized chambers. The sandhogs rested two hours for every hour they worked in the tube. It was an incredible job of planning, training and organizing labor, anticipating and responding to threats. But it was all worth it, because thanks to our safety engineers we haven't lost a single soul. Our mortality rate was zero for the entire construction project...until that story came out in the *World*."

"Your perfect record ruined," said Mary. "Not to mention the clean-up expense. This must have been trying for you."

"We're not insensitive to the tragedy. The death of a young girl always is. Edgar Allen Poe thought it the most moving story one can write. It's not a question of money. We created a Casualty Fund, to cover the expenses associated with the usual accidents on a jobsite. Every penny is in it, unspent. But it does create a special problem for us. Our ability to do these projects depends on the public's trust. The tragedy of this young lady's death would be magnified immeasurably if it interfered with our plans for the city."

"Rosetta would have hated that."

"Your sarcasm is understandable, Detective Shanley. I can imagine how heartless I must sound. But every great enterprise has its casualties, and we have done our utmost to minimize ours. We don't need to be blamed for other people's crimes. If this murder took place in the Lincoln tunnel, that's our misfortune. But if, as I believe, that could not have happened, I would be grateful to anyone who proved it had occurred elsewhere."

Mary said, "If it did."

"I am not offering a bribe to compromise your integrity. I am appealing to you to do your job with more than the usual diligence."

He wasn't really a bad old bird, Mary decided, just a bureaucrat protecting a labor of love. In the silence between his careful statements, she heard the suppressed emotion of a man struggling to act rationally in the wake of senseless violence. The horror of a young girl's death was made personal for Robert Moses by her burial in his tunnel. This was not the city of the future he and his boys had in mind.

"I'll do my best," she said.

He hung up.

Mary sat against the headboard with the dead phone in her hand. Moses hadn't asked her to do anything she hadn't been doing for herself. He just reminded her that the stakes were bigger than her own conscience, or justice for Rosetta de Soto. Johnny had the story wrong. She knew that. But how did it go right?

The last reported sighting of Rosetta alive came from Freddie Arlington, who gave her taxi fare at the Edison Hotel and headed off to Grand Central. She never made it home to Mrs. T's boardinghouse, so she must have met somebody else, either deliberately or by accident.

But who?

Mary was aware of a widening gulf between her generation of women and Rosetta and her friends. Michael had courted Mary in her mother's front parlor. He would never have asked, and she would never have consented, to go out alone together, just the two of them, after dark. Her father did not approve of the new fashion among the daughters of New York's native-born, middle-class families—the date.

Mary needed to know where a girl like Rosetta might go, but her own experience provided no clue. She needed a young informant who could tell her what people were thinking these days. And she had an invitation to find out.

*   *   *

Whatever his true intention had been, Mary decided to take at face value Mark Gamble's invitation to sit in on an open rehearsal of *The Cradle Will Rock*. That young man might have been offering as a courtesy, but she hadn't seen any reluctance in his frank blue eyes. She planned to take a cross-town bus but while she was waiting at the stop a light rain started to fall. A few minutes later, it was coming down hard. Mary thought *what the hell* and hailed a passing cab.

She found Rachel and Mark in the lobby of the Maxine Elliott Theatre on 39th Street. But the two young radicals didn't seem to notice each other. Or rather, they were doing whatever they could not to notice each other. Mark was reading the poster of an earlier production, and Rachel was inspecting the carpet swirls.

As Mary approached, she heard Rachel say, "If you didn't want to dine with them, you could've told me."

"I did say it," said Mark. "Remember? You thought we really should."

"They're *your* parents."

"So maybe I know what I'm talking about."

"You can't just turn your back on them," Rachel insisted.

"Rache, it's them who turned their backs on me."

"They."

"I said I would eat with them, didn't I? I said you could arrange it."

"Then you backed out at the last minute."

"Only when I heard where they made a reservation. The Mayflower Club? Of all places! You know how they treat their help?"

171

"Your mother likes the fish soup. Your dad just wants to please her."

"Yassum, boss lady. Dat fish soup comin' right up!"

"He's calling you," said Rachel.

"Who? Uncle Remus?"

She pointed to the far side of the lobby, where the stage manager was signaling to the actors, gathering them into the theatre. Mark glanced at Rachel, who wouldn't give an inch. He bounded into the aisles.

"Like a big, happy puppy!" Rachel sighed.

Mary smiled. "He is cute. Have you seen Louisa lately?"

"Can you believe it?" Rachel lit up. "Our own little Louisa! Who never, ever responded to any of my arguments for unionizing retail. What did they need to pay dues for? That sort of thing. And now --"

"Woolworth's is letting people go," said Mary. "Business is down."

"Business goes up and down," Rachel said. "That's what a union is for. To look out for the little guy—or in this case, the little gal—when it tanks. I'm planning to bring her a cake, later. Want to come along?"

"If I can."

"We'll make a union maid of you yet, Officer Shanley." The lights dimmed and came up again.

Mary said, "Shouldn't we find some seats?"

They sat toward the back of the theatre, trying to be inconspicuous. Mary often sat there, watching for pickpockets. It took discipline on this occasion to direct her gaze to the stage, where a slender man, six-foot-two with black hair, loomed over the actors, lecturing on the significance of a new theatrical genre.

"It isn't easy finding a title for a new art form," he said, pacing back and forth, while the actors watched from folding chairs. "Mr. Blitzstein calls it a *music drama*, and that seems to me a fitting name for this love-child of the arts of Music and the Play. Its Muse is Bertolt Brecht, to whom Mr. Blitzstein has dedicated his script. You know the work Mr. Brecht has done in Berlin, do you not?"

Mary heard a rumbling from the folding chairs. Some of the actors might have, though no one spoke out. Mary had never heard the German name before, but a nicely dressed gentleman at the end of her row evidently had. He sat leaning forward, one knee crossed over the other, resting his classic chin on his fist, nodding. Rachel followed Mary's gaze and smiled.

"That's Pesach'ke Burstein," she whispered, "a star of the Yiddish theater. You should see the ladies swoon when he sings at matinees."

"Does he ever act in English?"

"Why should he?" said Rachel. "Do you know how many Yiddish theaters are running right now in New York? Six. Ten years ago there were twenty. Unfortunately, he's married, to the actress Lillian Lux. But he is handsome, isn't he? And just about your age, I'd say."

Mary hushed her and pointed toward the stage, where the slender young director was still pacing before his cast. "In order to make his audiences think about his drama, Brecht does whatever he can to alienate their sympathies from his characters. Of course, his uncanny ability to write interesting people allows them to reconnect immediately to his thieves and whores. Our task is precisely the same."

"To alienate the audience?" one actor said. "Isn't the WPA enough?"

The others laughed.

The director didn't. He seemed to totter where he stood, like a treetop in the wind. "All right. Let's start with Gus and Sadie."

Two actors stood in front of their folding chairs.

"The text tells us these are simple people, recently married, and terribly in love," the director said. "The gangster Bugs is about to set them up as patsies for an explosion that will take out Union Headquarters. Our druggist, here, is being forced to

173

blame them for the bomb that will take their lives, while his son Steve reacts, horrified, for all of us. Our job is to make sure the audience thinks about the collusion between the mob and the anti-union forces, rather than merely feeling sorry for poor old Gus and Sadie. Do you understand?"

"Yes," said the actor playing Gus, while Sadie nodded beside him.

"Good!" The director waved his hand.

Gus held up his script and read, "The Manager he come to me yesterday, say I keep away from union, I getta good job; then Larry Foreman, union fella, come to me, say, Gus, don't be fool, you belong with us. Look like I very pop'lar, everybody want me, I dunno." He turned to his play-wife. "Sadie, you gonna have kid soon?"

"Gus!" she said, coloring.

"Less emotion," said the director. "Alienate."

Gus tried to flatten his delivery, but it wasn't easy, given his lines. "I wanna kid, I wanna son! What I care what they hear? Now I got first papers, pretty soon I be real American citizen. The fella say they need men like me; sure, good hands, strong— He say American need men like me. ... Sadie—I tink maybe—You getting big already! We gotta buy you new kinds dress soon, huh?"

"Gus, stop it!"

"Now the song!" shouted the director. "Gus and Sadie go right into the song!"

The pair came a little closer together, standing in front of their folding chairs. They sang: "We wonder if anyone could be as much in love as we;

> We wonder if anyone ever was before.
> They couldn't be any more than we are.
> There never was such a day or such a night time.
> There never was such a boy as we will have,
> And all in the right time."

They finished and looked up hopefully. The audience clapped.

"Excellent!" said the director. "Just a little less pathos, next time around, and it'll be excellent."

The stage manager called out, "Take five," and Mark stood for a moment on the edge of the stage, shading his eyes. He spotted Rachel in her seat and bounded over.

"So? What did you think?"

Rachel shrugged. "Kind of heavy-handed, isn't it?"

"What?"

"The innocent immigrants blamed for blowing up the union hall. When it's really the mob in cahoots with the bosses."

"You got that, huh?"

"Uh, yeah. Isn't it obvious?"

"To who?"

"Anybody paying attention to what's going on in this country."

"Nobody is, in the theatre. Except Blitzstein."

"Well, maybe there's a reason."

"Are you kidding? The guy's a genius. Ask anybody."

"They ought to know."

From her seat Mary could make out only the top of Marc Blitzstein's head, where the playwright sat hunched over in the front row. Standing before him was the slender director, smiling like a cat. From the pocket of his stylish coat he drew out a silver flask and swigged discreetly.

"Who is that man?" Mary asked.

"That," said Mark, turning around too late to catch sight of the flask, "is His Highness Orson Welles. The Federal Theatre Project created this unit for him and his producer, John Houseman, who staged *Macbeth* in Harlem, using only black actors. The word is the two of them are planning their own troupe—the Mercury Theatre—to play on the radio. I'd love to get into that."

Rachel asked, "Why should they start their own theatre troupe when they have this one already?"

"Have you any idea how much bureaucracy is involved with the Works Progress Administration, the Federal Theatre Project, and the rest of the government's alphabet soup? Besides, the WPA is planning to close us down, using a phony union excuse. The truth is, they're taking some heat. One Congressman asked if Christopher Marlowe was a Communist. Orson swears we're going on, if not here in a theatre on Seventh Avenue. We'll do it without sets or costumes, if we have to—just a piano and Blitzstein's lyrics."

The stage manager whistled, and Mark sat up. "I have a surprise for you," he told Rachel. "I'm changing my name in the program."

"To what?"

"Wait and see!" He galloped off toward the stage.

Rachel watched him go. "He's a knucklehead. But he does have his moments of brilliance, doesn't he?"

"What about his mother and the fish soup?"

Mark found his place on the stage and winked at Rachel.

She scowled at him and shrugged. "You always fight with the one you love, don't you?"

Mary didn't remember fighting with Michael. There had been long stretches of silence, however, when she wasn't talking to him and he was his usual taciturn self. But Michael was an old-school Irish cop, and Mary was cut from the same cloth. She had noticed, however, that younger women didn't seem to mind raising their voices, and supposed that Rachel was right.

And then she remembered Rosetta de Soto fighting with Ming-Lu Lin outside the Shanghai Ballroom.

Twenty-two. Woman's Logic

When Mary saw Ming-Lu Lin in his basement cell again, he no longer looked like a Chinese businessman who had forgotten his suit jacket. His white shirt was torn at the pocket and stained below his jaw, where the grizzle had clotted around a new purple welt. A gash in his left eyebrow had not been bandaged either.

"Who did this to you?" Mary asked, when the jailor left them alone.

Ming-Lu shook his head. "Nobody."

"Not this time," Mary said. "You can't deny the bruises right there on your face."

He touched his jaw and winced. "It make no difference. Doesn't matter."

"It matters to me," Mary insisted, "if Sergeant Broderick was responsible. Or any other policeman."

Ming-Lu smiled. Then he shook his head. "You a police, too, aren't you?"

"That's right," she said. "But not that kind."

"A different kind?" said Lin. "What kind is that? A kind kind?"

Mary was about to answer indignantly, defending reform, when she realized he was making a joke. Not too funny, but in a foreign vocabulary. She smiled to show him she got it. "Something like that."

"Another prisoner," said Ming-Lu Lin.

"Beat you up? I'll have to speak to the jailor. Who was it?"

He shook his head. "Not the jailor's fault. Mine."

"You picked a fight in your cell? I find that hard to believe, Mr. Lin."

"What you believe?" he asked. "Not what I say, any time."

"I believe you were mourning her loss, because you and Rosetta were involved," Mary said plainly.

He looked at the floor, as if he didn't know the word. "Involved?"

"Romantically. You cared for one another. She wasn't just a dance hall girl, and you were more than a customer."

He shook his head. "No. I came for a dance. She danced for a ticket."

"At first, maybe," said Mary. "But when the dance was over, what did you do? Bow and say *Goodnight, Ma'am?*"

He was silent.

"You bought up all of her dances. Night after night."

"I was a good customer."

"Yes, you were. But you became more than that. Those tickets aren't specific to the dancing girl, are they?"

"Specific?"

"You can use the same ticket to dance with any of the girls. If Rosetta kept dancing with you, instead of telling you her next dance was taken, she must have wanted to dance with you too."

"I'm a good dancer," he said and did a quick two-step.

"Maybe that was the first thing she liked about you. Maybe you didn't paw her so much as the other men did."

He straightened in self-respect. "I am not that kind of dancer."

"No," said Mary, "you're the kind kind. I'll bet that makes a big difference to a dance hall girl. I'll bet, after all the sweaty bodies rubbing up against her, she could care for a man who treated her with kindness."

Ming-Lu hesitated. Mary could see he wanted to speak up, to claim the respect he had shown her and the gratitude he had earned. But something held him back. "You have me confused with another man," he said. "Not a Chinese."

"It was you," insisted Mary. "You were seen fighting on the street outside the Shanghai Ballroom after it closed for the night. What kind of fight could that have been? If you were just an annoying customer who couldn't let go when the last dance ended, Rosetta would have called a cop. Or some man on the street would have intervened. But she wasn't looking for help, was she? She didn't appeal for a rescuer, because she was already with her rescuer. It was a lover's quarrel."

"No."

"You were just harassing her?"

"No."

"Then what were you fighting about? With just another dance hall girl?"

Lin said nothing.

"A silent defense is going to get you hung," Mary told him. "If you have nothing better to offer, the jurors are going to assume the worst. And the judge will show no mercy in sentencing a cold-blooded murderer who doesn't seem to care what people think of him."

"I care," said Lin, almost audibly.

"You do?"

Again he lapsed into silence.

"Were you planning to get married?"

Ming-Lu smiled bitterly. "How could a man like me marry a girl like Rosetta? Here, in this place?"

"So what were you planning to do? Run off together?"

"We talk about it," he said finally. "I talk mostly. She listened. But I see in her eyes how much she like to hear about it."

"Did she ever say *Yes*?"

He nodded. "Two week ago, she agreed. To go to San Francisco, where nobody knows us, and we can be man and wife. I ask her on Wednesday, did she tell them? Did she tell the ballroom she was quitting? Not yet, she said. Not anybody."

"Is that what you fought about?"

"Yes." But he looked at his shoes when he said it.

"Was there more to it?"

"She didn't tell anybody yet. So she has to tell them all. Not just her boss. All her friends too. At the place where she live, and everywhere else."

"Was that a problem for you?"

179

"Not the girls where she live. Not Mrs. T."

"Then who?"

Mary waited a long time for an answer, as Ming-Lu stared at the wall over his cot. She almost prompted him with another question, but she held her tongue and at last he spat out the single word. "Freddie."

"Arlington?"

Lin shrugged. "She always call him just Freddie. She has to see him one more time, to say good-bye. I tell her, No, no more times with Freddie. But Rosetta is proud. She bring down her foot," he stamped his. "She say, Freddie, he beg her to see him. He is always so generous. And we not married yet."

"Did that make you angry?"

"Of course. But even more sad. I could not tell her what to do, or how it make me feel. So I leave her there, on the street. She calls after me, calls me names. The other girls hear those names. But I never fight with her. She fight with me."

"You left her there?"

"Yes."

"And you never saw her again?"

Lin said nothing for another long time. Then he smiled. "So, Officer Shanley—how do you think the juror feel after they hear this story? That a Chinese man fall in love with a dance hall girl, who have a fight on the public street, because she want to see a rich white boy?"

It was Mary's turn to fall silent. *Then we find her dead.*

"They hang me for sure," he said. "Faster than if I say nothing. Am I right? Or do you still think me a silly old Chinaman, too much a fool to speak up?"

*   *   *

The party at Woolworth's had settled down considerably when Rachel Lipinsky made her way through the store to Louisa Vitanza, at the lunch counter. The strikers were still there, determined, waiting in the aisles with grim faces for their turns to picket outside on 13th Street. They had made a deal with the municipal police stationed at the doors: only one picketer per door on the street at any time. The company had brought in their own private cops to back up the city police and to try to keep food out. The girls had responded with a hunger strike, until a group of supporters had climbed to a window fifteen feet off the ground and tossed in food and other supplies.

None of the girls would change their clothes into any of the store's merchandise, because, as Louisa said, they weren't thieves or shoplifters. They were honest workers, who put in a hard day's labor and expected to be treated as the company assets they were. When customers came into the store on an ordinary business day, they were met with courtesy and reliable service—as they expected at Woolworth's. But that reputation had been earned for the chain by scores of young women who moved through its aisles, folding clothes, making lunches, staffing its cash registers. They couldn't be tossed out like last month's penny candy. If nobody else in the company was willing to stand up for them, they would sit down on the job for themselves.

The energy with which Louisa made this case had taken its toll on her. Her eyes blinked from sockets that seemed to have receded deeper into her skull. Her hair was clean and combed through, but the ends had all but uncurled. Her mouth looked dry and wrinkled from too little lipstick and too much talk. An unhealthy pallor had settled on her cheeks that could not be covered over in blush. When Rachel swept into the dimly lit store, she carried a large handbag. Once inside, past the eyes of a watchful policeman determined to keep out food supplies, she produced an oblong wrapped in a paper napkin. Both she and her gift looked fresher than anything inside the store.

Louisa was sitting with two other girls at the lunch counter in the back. She got off her stool and hugged Rachel. One of the other girls took the oblong from her and set it on the counter, sweeping away the napkin as if she were unveiling a

181

work of fine art. And so she was—rich swirls of deep brown icing over moist yellow pound cake, with a teaser of soft brown filling. Louisa sank a knife over and over into the goo, as one of her comrades-in-arms brought a stack of plates and forks while the other ran off to summon the troops.

When half a dozen shop-girls were happily scraping the last trails of icing off their plates, Louisa carried her own to a sink behind the counter and washed it. Rachel went with her to dry, as one by one the other plates arrived with forks to be cleaned. Standing together by a sink, washing and drying, restored some sense of their boarding house life to the two young women. Louisa asked about Mark.

"He's in his glory, as usual," said Rachel, and tried to use the story of the open rehearsal to amuse and distract Louisa. "Welles was there, drunk as a skunk, as usual. Mary watched him wobble all over the stage until her cop's nose got the better of her and she said, 'Who is that man?'"

Louisa laughed. "What was Mary Shanley doing in the audience?"

"Mark invited her to come! Mark would invite the marine corps marching band, if he thought they would clap for him."

"Is she making any progress? On her case?"

"About Rosetta? It's not so easy to tell. She keeps asking more questions."

"I hate that."

"Answering questions?"

"No—thinking about Rosetta. I can't stand remembering the sight of her, lying on a slab. And the idea of her alone in a pauper's grave—"

She wiped away a tear with her sleeve.

Rachel said, "I don't know what they'll do with her now."

Louisa said, "I heard about those graves. You know they bury them four to one? Four corpses buried in each hole! Lying forever next to some strange body."

"How much would it cost, if we did it ourselves?"

"I don't know, exactly," said Louisa, "but it's a lot. We're not making much money in Woolworth's these days. We can't expect them to pay us for the hours we aren't working. They're not going to hire all these girls back and give us all a big raise! So I don't expect to have any extra money for a while, after this is over. I'm not even sure how I'm going to pay Mrs. T this month."

"She'll understand," said Rachel, drying the last fork.

Louisa shut off the faucet with a squeak. "Oh, everybody understands," she said. "But they still want their money."

"That's just why you're striking," Rachel said. "That's why we need unions. So that girls like you don't have to worry where your next rent check is coming from. And girls like Rosetta don't have to worry where their bones will be buried. You're doing the right thing, Lou—not only for yourselves and the salesgirls here but for all the rest of us, too."

"You're a lot surer than I am."

Rachel used her towel to wipe off Louisa's cheeks. "There's only one question in my mind. What kind of cake do you want next time?"

"Lemon meringue," said a girl from housewares, dropping off her plate. "I mean, if anyone's asking."

Louisa turned the tap back on. "If life gives you lemons—"

Rachel grinned. "You buy lemon meringue."

*   *   *

But a different kind of pie was chalked upon the blackboard in a conference room at the top of the Woolworth's Building at the southern tip of Manhattan. The men who raised their eyes to the chart were in no mood for meringue. This was a complicated risk assessment—daily losses in revenue, public relations and investor confidence to be weighed against an hourly rate increase that would have to be paid in five and dimes all over New York City and across the USA. There was the question of authority within each store, and the perception of personal grit and corporate resolve in every boardroom on Wall Street. The whole city was watching, and the rest of the nation behind them. Accountants pushed pencils with scowling faces, while the senior men smoked and looked out the window, consoling themselves with the view.

"You see, gentlemen, the wisdom of our founder," said one smoker, the most high Managing Director. They all admired his perspicacity, because through the sunlit glass, across a few blocks of slow-moving traffic and bustling pedestrians, shone the gleaming roof of New York's City Hall.

Twenty-three. Strike Out

The street outside the Woolworth Building was hardly the same place Mary had left Louisa on her last visit. The ragged line of salesgirls bearing strike signs, marching down the pavement and sitting on the curb, had vanished into the store. Now a fleet of black-and-white police cars occupied 14th Street, blocking the fire hydrant and crosswalk, their engines running. Sitting inside those cars, or leaning on their hoods and trunks, an entire squadron of bluecoats waited for the order to move. On the opposite side of the street, behind police barricades, a crowd of three hundred civilians had gathered in support of the striking salesgirls.

On the far side of the barricade Mary saw Erich Tanenbaum, propped on a pair of crutches, leaning against the trunk of a sour gum tree. His nephew Leon Catalan stood beside him with both hands on the crossbar of the barricade. A bluecoat passing in front of them rapped his nightstick on the wood. The boy snatched his fingers away just in time to spare his knuckles a bruising.

As Mary drew closer to the door of the store, where the bluecoats were thickest, she found a uniformed brass with a bullhorn addressing the women inside. Mary recognized Captain Kent, from the Mercer Precinct. Whatever patience had been in his voice when he began his exhortation had long ago run out of it, which was now hoarse and threatening.

"I'm telling you girls for the last time," he was sputtering, as Mary approached. "You have only two choices. You can walk out quietly, one at a time, with your hands where we can see them. Or we're going to come in and get you."

There was silence. Then a thin, wavering voice from inside the store replied, "We are sorry, Captain, but we've talked it over and decided. You can't really agree to meet any of our demands, can you? So, as much as we appreciate your offer to help, we're going to wait to negotiate with the Woolworth Company representatives."

185

Kent shook his head. He took off his hat, wiped the sweat band, and put it back on his head. The uniforms waiting for his order did not look disappointed, smacking their billy-clubs into their palms.

"I'm not here to negotiate," the Captain said. "We've had a complaint filed by the owners of this property. You and your girlfriends are trespassers."

"We're all employees here, in our place of employment," the voice inside replied. "We aren't trespassers or loiterers. We're strikers."

Mary recognized Louisa's voice and knew the girl did not understand the point of view of the force. Police were taught to recognize only three kinds of people in the city. The first were themselves, other police and by courtesy the members of their immediate families. They made in fact a huge extended family, which included all of the rivalries, petty disputes, and long-simmering grudges of any family—but collectively the good guys. The second kind were the citizens. They were often liars, usually stupid, almost always lacking appreciation for the sacrifices of the first group—but still to be treated with basic respect, since the police needed people to serve and protect. The third kind were mugs, criminals, and other lowlifes, who should always be expected to cheat, steal, and murder. Once a citizen crossed the line and became a lowlife, there was no reason to show him—or her—any consideration. You would always regret a break.

What Louisa failed to understand, as she stood with her salesgirl comrades in the dark store, was that sometime in the last few hours someone in Woolworth's executive office had reached somebody in the Mayor's office and changed his view of the strikers. Louisa Vitanza and her shop-girls had traded away their status as citizens in crisis for new ones as lowlife Commie trespassers. Having crossed that line, they were no longer considered the same sort of women as the wives of the police family, or even the morally wayward daughters of the city's general citizenry. They no longer required the respect these officers would have shown any young lady on the street. The shop-girls peering through the plate glass, shivering at their stations in Woolworth's, could no longer expect their skirts or basic humanity to offer protection against the armed troops massing on the street. They had guts, those girls, but very little idea of their danger.

Mary moved toward the street door, but was stopped by a uniform. "Where do you think you're going, Mary?"

"Sergeant Tully! I know that girl, inside. Let me talk to her."

Tully shook his graying head. "It's too late for that."

Mary started to object, but Tully pointed to Captain Kent, who had again raised his bullhorn. "Well, ladies? Are you coming out?"

A long silence. Then, "We want to talk to somebody from the sixteenth—"

He did not allow her to finish. Captain Kent pointed.

"Go."

The troops responded with the pent-up energy of a released slingshot. Broad blue backs stormed the front entrance with their nightsticks raised. Mary heard shrieks, female screams, and the sickening thumps of wood falling on soft flesh and bone. For several minutes, there were only police rushing into the store. Then the first girls were dragged out. They looked terrible—haggard and worn from their time in the store, but energized by the terror of the police assault. Some came out kicking and screaming, still fighting to hold onto the store, their rights, and their dignity.

But it was hopeless. They were carried out of the store like struggling sacks of potatoes, hauled across the pavement, and dumped into the backs of paddy wagons waiting double-parked at the curb. Some women hung limply, with bruised bodies and faces. Some came out cursing or choking.

Mary made a dash for the door and this time got through it. Inside, the scene was more of a madhouse than the street outside. The lights were off, but she could hear the whimpers of women all around her. Some of the police were talking as they tried to pry loose the salesgirls' holds on display cases and cabinets. Others were treating the girls as they might have treated a gang of mobsters, scoring their points with clubs.

"Stop that!" cried Mary, as she stood between one officer and a teenage girl who hung onto the base of a lunch counter stool, despite her torn dress and bloodied face.

The officer was twenty-five. He wavered in Mary's face. "Who are you?"

Mary flashed her badge. "I'm a cop," she said, "Though I'm not particularly proud of it at the moment."

The officer looked at the stubborn salesgirl, then at Mary. "It's orders."

"To beat this girl to a bloody pulp?"

He blushed, looked away, and hurried down the aisle.

Mary could not find Louisa in the chaos. She thought she heard Louisa's voice hollering hoarsely, "Let go of me, you big bully!" But Mary saw only the silhouettes of burly men overpowering tired young women.

She ran outside, but the standoff on the street had broken into something uglier. The sight of young girls being dragged out of the store, across the sidewalk and into the vans, provoked the crowd to anger. They surged against the barricades until driven back by the clubs of the uniformed officers. New York's finest had lost their patience, and so had the citizens they were sworn to protect.

Erich Tanenbaum left the shade of his sour gum tree and was pressed against a barricade, which seemed to hold him up as much as hold him back. He raised one crutch in the air as she shouted to the police, "Take your hands off those girls! They have a right to be here! Let 'em go!"

A few voices behind him picked up the cry, *Let 'em go!* But there were other voices too, one of which seemed to rise above the din of the crowd to make itself heard over their shouting.

"Shut up, you stupid kraut," it said. "What do you know about rights? Go back to Deutchland, where you belong!"

Erich spun around, stung. "Ziss is where I belong! Where I earned the right to belong! What have you done to earn the right to talk such shit?"

"I was born here," his accuser said. He was a large man in a camelhair coat, with eyes bulging from a face that seemed redder on one side than the other. He planted himself right in front of Erich, who wobbled on one crutch, resting his other crutch on the crossbar of the barricade. "I can say whatever I like," the big man insisted. "Something you Nazis will never understand."

"Nazis? Are you calling me a brownshirt? You haf no idea!" But the angrier Erich grew, the more he sputtered, and the deeper he lapsed into his boyhood accent.

The red-faced native drew closer to Erich. "Heil Hans!" he sneered and thrust his open palm into Erich's face.

Caught by surprise, Erich reared back and smacked him with the crutch. It landed on the man's elbow with a crack of wood against bone.

At that moment, a bluecoat on the far side of the barricade looked over. He saw the crutch rise and fall and reacted to the violence by joining into it. Up went his baton and down it came once, twice, three times…falling like *Stielhandgranates* on the World War veteran.

Erich tried to defend himself with his upraised crutch, while supporting himself unsteadily on the other. But his ineffective resistance only made the officer angrier, who raised his baton to deliver a final rain of blows—

When he felt a small hand in the crook of his elbow. He turned and saw the boy, Leon Catalan, standing to his left with something in his hand. It was a brick, dug up from the earth that surrounded the sour gum tree. Before the bluecoat could turn away, Leon raised the brick and smashed it into his flushed and sweaty face.

That touched off the bedlam that followed. The police lost all restraint and began beating the crowd in the streets, without bothering to ask if they were for or against the strike. The crowd fell on the officers whenever they could, and when they couldn't, they fell on each other. Mary heard whistles and thuds, the grunts of officers swinging their batons, the crunch of bone, and shrieks of women trampled underfoot. Mary saw outrage in one cop's eyes and stepped out of his way. Then she stepped back into the store and watched the chaos through the picture windows.

It didn't take long—less than an hour from the Captain's "Go." When it was over, Mary wandered the store, looking over the destruction that had been wrought. Clothing bins had been wrecked, skirts and tops, trousers, shorts, bras, girdles, and underwear strewn all over the floor. Shattered glassware glistened in the aisles. Cleaning liquids and beauty lotions seeped through the floorboards. The salesgirls had kept the store stocked throughout their occupation. They respected the merchandise—they lived with it and worked with it, and made their handling another reason for customers to buy it. The same could not be said for the police, who trashed everything in their enthusiasm to carry the young women off.

Someone must have anticipated all that, when they decided to call in the law to throw out the strikers. An accountant in the executive suite must have calculated the cost of the police raid and decided it was cheaper than negotiating with their sales force. It had cost Mary a chance to talk to Louisa Vitanza, to confirm the suspicion in her head. It had cost the shop-girls' families a great deal more. But Fiorello LaGuardia clinched the Republican nomination for his second term as Mayor.

One pair of eyes assessed the damage by a different slide rule. His patience had not been rewarded. He had found his victim and waited for his chance. He had kept a low profile and taken no risks, except to rile the Nazi, but that was just for fun. He had resisted all temptations, but who could anticipate a labor dispute disrupting his plans? Not only preventing him from getting to the girl, but bringing in half the NYPD as a *cordon bleu* between them? If patience was a virtue, his own should have been rewarded. But how often did that happen? Which was why he was not a virtuous man.

The laws of nature did not seem to work that way. The hard-working ant can be swallowed at a gulp by a lizard on a rock, or burned by a boy with a magnifying glass. The squirrel works all winter laying away nuts, only to be snatched by a hawk just as the leaves start to turn. There was no percentage in breaking your back like an ant or squirrel when you could just as easily swoop down and steal it all away.

The red-faced man squatted down in the square of bricks beneath a sour gum tree and fed bits of his cruller to a sparrow standing on a root. The little bird hopped closer for each bit of sweet roll, until it fell under the shadow of his hand. Its tiny beak dropped for one more bite, when he struck—seizing its body around the wings, so they couldn't open and fly. Its head bobbed back and forth, striking his fleshy hand with its beak, as he raised the bird to face its doom. Twittering was useless. His grip only tightened, as its frightened eyes blinked at his bulging irises.

That was how it should be, the red-faced man thought, and that was how it would be, when he got his second chance. The laws of nature would make good in the end. A man like him would always be given a fat second chance.

Twenty-four. Mercy Street

The Mercer Street Precinct House was a madhouse when Mary arrived. People sat on benches, bleeding through bandages that had been hastily wrapped around their cracked limbs and heads. Uniformed officers dragged suspects through lines of wounded, who hung on columns and corners, fighting back with their shoulders when their hands were cuffed behind them. The noise was deafening, of voices shouting, women shrieking, and doors slamming with unexpected force. Somewhere a window scraped and then shattered.

Mercy Street, the cops called it. But nobody else did.

Mary picked her way through the cops and collars, the bruised and angry officers and their detainees, searching for Leon Catalan. Erich Tanenbaum had not made it to the precinct house. His paddy wagon drove him straight to Bellevue Hospital, where Gertrude Tanenbaum found him on the ward. He sat silently tugging at his bandages when his mother came in, but by the time she left, he asked her to bring him his radio. Gertrude called Mary, anxious for word about the boy, and Mary had promised to do what she could to help.

Now she searched through the Mercer Street Precinct House without much hope. She was prepared to make the case for Leon, who had stood up to an officer beating his uncle. What would we not do for our family? But Mary knew the Mercer Street squad would not give up Leon, even if blood were spurting out through his nostrils. He had hit one of their officers square in the face with a brick. They would insist on their right to get even with him first.

She was surprised, therefore, when she reached the second floor and saw Leon through the glass wall of Captain Kent's office. He was sitting in a chair meant for a man twice his size, gripping the wooden armrests. Across the desk in the Captain's chair was not the weary commander who had overseen the riot, but a dapper detective in a checkered vest, who sat grinning with his fingertips together.

Johnny Broderick.

Mary couldn't believe it. She broke into the Captain's office without stopping to knock. Inside, she smelled fish and got her first good look at Leon Catalan's face. The boy's left eye was swollen and his lower lip purple, just as the Chief liked to see when an adult offender was hauled in. On Leon, Mary thought it looked obscene.

"For Christ's sake, Johnny," she said, "he's ten years old."

"I never laid a hand on the kid," Broderick protested. "Though he did hit a cop in the face. With a brick."

"It looks like they gave it back to him."

"They'll do that," said Johnny. "But here he is now, sitting in the Captain's office, eating a tuna fish sandwich."

Mary stared at both of them. "What are you doing here?"

"Trying to help this nice young man," Johnny said, "keep himself out of prison. Have you met my friend Leon?"

Mary found a hankie in her purse and pressed it against the corner of his dripping eye. Leon winced but held it there with his free hand.

"You have," Broderick said. "I thought you might, since you know his Grandma. And you probably know who he saw on 22nd Street, Thursday night."

"Who?" Mary sounded skeptical.

"Tell her," said Broderick.

Leon sat silently, until Johnny nodded at him. Then he said, "The Chinaman."

Mary rested on the edge of the desk. "Ming-Lu Lin?"

"How about that?" Johnny grinned. "And you never thought to mention it."

"It's the first I'm hearing it," said Mary.

"Leon works at a candy store, didn't you know? Or he did work there, until Hizzoner axed the slot machines."

"Pinball," said Leon.

"Excuse me. The pinball machines. Anyway, who do you think stops in for a pack of Luckies, just before they close at eleven?"

"Ming-Lu?"

"Our own Mr. Lin. Shaking, the boy says. His hand so unsteady he had to strike three matches to light his cigarette."

Mary looked at Leon, who nodded seriously. *Was it possible*, Mary wondered, *the boy was lying to get himself out of a spot?* His big brown eyes held hers, and she knew that couldn't be true. No one had put him up to this.

"Now, Leon, tell the nice lady—how far did you say the candy store is from the boardinghouse where you live?"

"Couple of blocks," said Leon. He looked at Mary again, to see where she fit into the story, but she was staring right through him.

"How did you find this out?" she asked Johnny. Her voice cracked, but Mary kept her face calm and composed.

"Kent deserves the credit for that," Broderick said. "They brought the kid in for assaulting an officer, inciting a riot— everything short of drunk and disorderly. They had a few words with him in the basement. But when they brought him through the bullpen, he spotted a photo pinned to the wall. The one we used for canvassing."

Johnny tossed a glossy eight-by-ten onto the desk. It had a picture of Ming-Lu Lin and a headline across the top that read, *Do you know this man?*

"He pointed it out and nodded, *Yes*. The uniform didn't believe him, at first, but Captain Kent thought they might as well check it out. That's why he's a captain, and the rest of these bozos will spend their careers swinging nightsticks."

Johnny settled back in the Captain's chair, as if it were his own. The way the case was breaking, Mary couldn't blame him. Leon's eyewitness testimony might have spared himself another beating, but it tied a neat bow around Johnny's story and reserved a seat for Ming-Lu Lin in the electric chair. Broderick's eyes glinted as his heavy lids closed in satisfaction. Only Mary was convinced he had it wrong.

*   *   *

"What's with all the taxi receipts, Mary?"

The Captain had the reimbursement slips for her rides to Choate and back to New Haven, to the Shanghai Ballroom in Brooklyn and the World's Fair garbage dump. She hadn't even submitted the cross-town taxi fares yet. McVeigh was sitting in his office chair on Centre Street, while Broderick sat in the other with one foot up on the seat, trying to tie his shoelaces evenly.

Mary had never learned to drive. When Michael was alive, she never had to drive, and after his death she gave away the car, since she couldn't stand to ride in it without him. But that wasn't the answer to the Captain's question.

"I'm just tying up one or two loose ends," she said.

"On De Soto?"

"Poking around a closed case," Johnny mumbled, undoing and retying a shoelace. "She's trying to unsolve it."

"Except it isn't," Mary insisted. "Did you bother to read the autopsy report? After you spoke to the press, Johnny? The M.E. found no opium in Rosetta's blood."

Broderick shrugged. "So he used another Chinese chicken-feet drug. The M.E. can't test them all. I have a witness, Captain, who can place Lin at Seventh Avenue and 22nd Street on the night of De Soto's death. Mary knows the boy, don't you? Considering the fact that Lin lives in Chinatown and works in Queens, any idea why he should've been hanging around her neighborhood?"

"Leon Catalan is ten years old, and they were beating him. He would've said anything they wanted to hear, just to make them stop. Are you even sure your witness can tell one Chinese man from another?"

"You mean, because they all look alike? We don't talk about Chinks that way anymore. Do we, Captain?"

McVeigh leaned forward, closer to Mary. "Have you got a better idea?"

"He wasn't her customer, Captain. They were involved."

"Who?"

"Rosetta and Ming-Lu."

"The vic and her killer, she means! She wants to let him go because he loved her, Pat. If that's not woman's logic, I don't know what is."

"De Soto and Lin?"

Johnny grinned. "Wouldn't they make a lovely couple?'

"Mary, most homicides are committed by people the victims know," said the Captain. "For females that's usually their husbands or boyfriends."

Mary shook her head. "Not this female. Or this boyfriend."

"We have different ideas about this dame," Johnny explained. "Mary thinks she was a sweet young thing. I think de Soto would've lifted her skirt, whenever the right sort of guy came along."

"Did she have to be one or the other?"

The two men exchanged a glance. "They usually are," said the Captain.

"You see?" Broderick smirked.

But Mary wasn't laughing. "She was a decent person."

"All right." McVeigh's face declared he had heard enough. "Can you show me any evidence of Mr. Lin's innocence?"

"Not yet," Mary conceded. "Give me a little more time."

The Captain shook his head.

"I know it doesn't seem satisfying, Mary. It often doesn't. We rarely get the full story in cases like these. We get a fact here and there, attached to some evidence, and have to fill in the gaps with conjecture. We know Mickey Lin had a thing for Rosetta de Soto. We know he waited for her, after work. We know they had some—"

"Altercation."

"Thank you, Johnny—some altercation on the street outside the ballroom. And the very next night, she was dead."

"But he grieved for her, sir. In his cell."

"Or bemoaned the fact that we caught him," said Johnny.

"He claims he never met her, isn't that right? Yet the kid—your kid, Mary—puts him in the neighborhood on Thursday night."

"There's so much we still don't know, Captain. She had a date on the night she died, before she was found in the tunnel. We don't even know the scene of the crime, where Lin supposedly beat her to death. We don't know when she was killed, or why. In the absence of all that, how can we say with any certainty *who*?"

Johnny said, "He lied, didn't he?"

The Captain nodded. "We don't have all of it nailed down, but we do have enough for the District Attorney to get a conviction. That's our job, Mary. The case is closed. Why don't you start considering your schedule for the next few weeks? The Pickpocket Squad is short-handed again. I told them to expect you back."

Twenty-five. The '35 Airflow

Whenever Mary needed to spend some time with Michael Shanley, she knew just where to go. She didn't go to his graveside, where his bones lay in the earth. Mary had seen his corpse in the open casket and decided that his spirit had left it behind. She didn't go to Saint Patrick's on Fifth Avenue either, the scene of his public funeral. That ritual had been for the sake of his colleagues, who marked the death of a police captain with all their bagpipes and ceremony.

Mary went to Old Saint Patrick's on the corner of Prince and Mott Streets, where she and Michael had been married. That's where she felt his presence, sitting on the aisle she had walked as a bride while Michael waited at the altar, surrounded by marble and gold. The vaulted ceiling rose 85 feet overhead, and behind her the organist practiced on an instrument built in 1852. In the churchyard were the graves of New York's first Bishop and of Pierre Toussant, born a slave in Haiti in 1766, whose cause for sainthood the Vatican was debating.

Mary didn't pray in the church, or speak to Michael either. She didn't expect an answer to either one. She had gone to church every Sunday with her mother, and then with Michael as a young wife. When Edward was young, they attended the church of his parochial school. But when Michael died, Mary discovered she didn't feel the need and realized it was his desire that prompted them to go to church on Sundays.

Yet, from time to time Mary still liked to sit in the silent church or listen to the practice of the organist. It felt like the only place that couldn't be changed. But as Mary watched the parishioners sidle into the pews, she saw not only Irish and Germans and French, but Italians and Dominicans and Puerto Ricans kneeling in the pews. No place was immune to change. And Mary was changing too.

She was trying to earn a place for herself in the ranks of male detectives. She had tried to rely on the difference between them, the point of view she could bring to the job. But it had failed—or she had failed to prove she could do the job as well as one of the bare-knuckle boys. Now her chance at homicide was over. She was going back to the Pickpocket Squad, and all her work on the case counted for nothing. Mary felt she had let down Gertrude, Rachel, Louise, and all the people who were depending on her.

Maybe they were right. Maybe Johnny Broderick had a point, after all. Maybe Ming-Lu had murdered Rosetta in a typical domestic homicide. Mary wondered if she doubted it only because she didn't want it to be true. She remembered the sobs she heard from Ming-Lu's cell and the smell of burning money in his makeshift funeral rite. Then she heard Michael's voice in the echoes of the organ:

I do, I do, I do ...

Mary could taste the tickle of fear in her throat when Michael was late coming home. She would ask him to be careful while she kissed his grizzled cheek, perhaps for the last time. Sometimes she worried that her fear itself, if it made him too cautious, might increase the risks he faced. It was to do something about the danger out there that she had asked for a job, when she went to see McVeigh. Now it felt as if the shadows lurking in dark alleys had won, had taken him away again. Mary could pinch a dip here and there, but what did that really amount to? A recovered wallet or purse—while the murderer who left Rosetta de Soto under a shovelful of tunnel had washed his hands of earth and blood and tucked them safely in his pockets.

Mary felt a stultifying spasm of powerlessness tighten its grip on her muscles. The only way to shake it off and wake herself up was to take some kind of action. But what if she got it wrong? What if all she did was raise enough doubt to set the killer free? Wanting to make a difference was one thing, but she had to make it right. Mary felt a shadow fall over her.

"I thought I'd find you here," said Edward, standing over his mother in the third pew off the nave. His body blocked the light from the upper windows. Mary opened her eyes and saw his pinstriped suit jacket unbuttoned, his fedora in one hand, and his baby face over the cockeyed knot of his tie. He wore the same expression—compressing tight lips and squinting eyes—he wore when he came to her after Michael's death. "I hear you're been having a rough time, Mother."

"Are they talking about me at Tammany, now?"

He sat down beside her. "The bulls pass in and out. You know that. And some of those boys are none too sorry to hear you're going back to the Dip Squad."

"Including you?"

Edward shook his head. "You've got me wrong, Mother. You've always had me wrong. You think I want you to fail at this, don't you?"

"No," said Mary, "I don't think you'd wish that for me. But you wouldn't mind seeing me installed in my parlor."

"No, I wouldn't mind seeing you there. I don't like seeing you putting yourself in danger. But I'd rather see you happy, one place or another. And after all you've done, I can't picture you in a Queen Anne wing, knitting your lifetime away."

"I don't have that chair anymore," said Mary.

"I carried it out," recalled Edward, "when we donated Father's things."

"I miss him," she said.

"I know. So do I. What would he say to you, now?"

"I have made a mess of it," sighed Mary. "I let Johnny Broderick under my skin. He thinks he knows, and no one else! I was sure he had the wrong man."

"Maybe he does."

"Maybe. Or maybe I just want him to."

"Is that what you think?"

"No. It's not what I feel. But he has convinced the Captain, and the papers, and just about everyone else."

"Not me."

She looked at Edward closely. "You don't believe in his evidence?"

"I believe in you. You don't believe his evidence, do you?"

"No."

"Then go with your gut, Mother," he said. "Isn't that what you always told me? If you don't trust yourself, who will?"

A priest entered the confessional along the south aisle. Mary set her hand on Edward's shoulder and brushed a bit of lint from the wool. Then she stood and walked out, without looking back. She had nothing to confess, after all.

*   *   *

When Mary reported for her tour of duty at the Pickpocket Squad the next day, she found a cardboard file sitting in her mailbox. Inside were two sheets of paper stapled together. There were checked boxes on one and a typed summary on the other, reporting the results of a forensic analysis of a piece of wax paper.

From Joey's American grocery.

Mary learned that detective cases were rather like boxers: a lug as big as a wall can go down at a punch, while a little mug who looks like a pushover can put up a hell of a fight. The pussycat missing-persons case McVeigh had given Mary had turned itself into a tiger of a homicide investigation, while an anonymous burglary suddenly turned personal, specific, and handily solved.

There was a readable fingerprint on the wax paper. It took some time to compare it to the prints in the precinct's card file, but they did find a match. The wax paper print belonged to a sixty-year-old ex-con thought to have given up safe-cracking, who worked with his son in a locksmith's shop on Houston Street. And that wasn't all.

Detective Johnny Cordes had been staking out the shop in his spare time, itching to prove that Kmetsky and Son were still in the burglary business. Cordes had busted Father K eight years before and testified against his release when the senior safe-cracker came up for parole. Johnny Cordes was a bona fide hero, the only man ever to win the New York City Police

Department's Medal of Honor twice. He was very good at his job, which he usually did alone. But he was not above working with a partner.

Mary made a call to Cordes, who agreed to meet her by the locksmith shop on Houston Street. She found him across the street, watching the door from a Plymouth. She first recognized his straw-colored hair, but when he turned his head, those blue eyes under thick eyebrows made him unmistakable. Picked out of the academy by "Honest Dan" Costigan, Cordes's slight build allowed him to impersonate a sailor or longshoreman, a playboy, a streetcar conductor, and a whole shantytown of stumblebums. His toughness and persistence had made the gossip columns of Walter Winchell and Ed Sullivan. If Boffo Broderick was the bull of the Detective Bureau, Johnny Cordes was the matador—light on his feet, focused on his foe, disappearing in a sweep of his cape.

"Mrs. Shanley?" he asked in a soft voice, like the man who delivered her seltzer. "Are you ready to make this town safer?"

"I think so."

"That-a-girl! Then, please, lead the way."

They found the younger Kmetsky in the storefront, copying a house key. Cordes came up behind the much larger man and in the blink of an eye had him doubled over, hands behind his back, handcuffs around his wrists. Johnny left Mary to keep an eye on their first suspect and made his way into the back, where the senior Kmetsky hunched over an ancient Yale, filing its sticky tumblers. He didn't look up or remove the jeweler's lens from his eye socket.

"Hello, Johnny," he said pleasantly.

"Mr. Kmetsky," replied Cordes. "You're going down this time."

"Hmm. For what?"

"The Farinacci grocery job."

The old man finished filing and wiped off his tool. He unscrewed his eyepiece, wrapped it in black velvet, and tucked it into his shirt pocket.

"The wax paper?"

"The wax paper," said Cordes.

"The *prosciutto* tasted fine. Thin, the way I like it."

"When did you start eating on the job?"

"I was hungry."

"No," said Johnny. "*He* sliced it. And gave you a taste, didn't he? Why did you leave it behind?"

The old man sighed through his nose. "He couldn't get it open."

"The safe?"

"So I left the wax paper where he set it down, and knelt to do my work."

"And then forgot all about it?"

"I remembered after we left the store. Too late, I'm afraid."

"Too bad."

Johnny took a second pair of cuffs from the back of his belt. Kmetsky held out his wrists and Cordes snapped on the loops. The old man studied their mechanism and smiled. Johnny took him by the elbow and led him to the outer room, where Mary waited with Kmetsky *fils.*

"Sliced ham on wax paper." The old man shook his head. "Nincompoop."

"Don't be too hard on him," Cordes said. "You'd have left something behind, sooner or later."

"He couldn't open the safe, after all my training. He doesn't have the fingertips for this line of work."

"Maybe he'll find another trade," Mary said, "in the can."

Kmetsky looked curiously at Cordes.

"This is Officer Shanley," Johnny explained. "A colleague of mine whose detective work made the case against you."

"Charming," said Kmetsky, and then *sotto voce* to Johnny, "You brought in your auntie to help?"

But the only word Mary heard was Johnny's *colleague.*

Cordes gave the bust to Mary and let her share the news with Guiseppe Farinacci, the grocer.

Mary taxied back to the store on Mulberry Street and found American Joey bagging plums at the fruit scale, near the front. His customer was an old man in a brown felt hat, who took a plum out of the bag as soon as it was weighed and sank his yellow teeth into its juicy red flesh.

"You solved it?" said Joey. "My robbery?"

"With physical evidence as proof," Mary said. "They didn't have all of your money, of course. They spent quite a bit. But you should be able to recover a hundred, at least, once the case goes to court."

Farinacci slapped his customer's arm. "Can you believe it?"

The old man shook his head. Maybe that meant he couldn't believe it. Maybe it meant he could. Mary couldn't tell.

When the old man walked off, Joey offered her a peach. She refused, and he bit into it himself. He wiped the juice on the back of his sleeve and leaned against the bumper of a black Chrysler parked at the curb.

"Nothing on Rosetta, still?"

Mary said, "They booked a suspect. A Chinese man, from Queens."

Joey shrugged. "A Chinaman?"

"You don't believe it?"

"What do I know? Could be. She wouldn't hold a thing like that against a man," said Joey, with another bite of peach.

"But what?"

Joey chewed. She waited. "Her family wouldn't like it."

"I didn't know she had one."

"Not here. In Italy. Sardinia. You know?"

"An island, right? Did you know her back in Sardinia?"

"No. We met right here, on the street. She was looking at dresses in the window. I was stacking plums."

Mary could picture it—the pretty young girl window-shopping, Farinacci sucking his plum, leaning on a bumper like the one supporting him now. Mary looked at the black metal car, its elegant grille of three chevrons rising to a graceful hood

ornament. Decorative hood, small windows, curving corners...
all of which had been parked in the same spot before.

"Whose car is this?"

"The dressmaker's, next door."

"Is it always here?"

"*Si*. He parks it in the morning, and it sits all day."

"Was it sitting here the day you first met? When Rosetta
window-shopped?"

"Was it here? It's always here."

"You know what they call this car?"

"He told me. My neighbor. The Airflow, thiry-five. His
Christler, he calls it. Those are good cars, no?"

Mary didn't know if they were good cars or not. She didn't
know one company's models from the next. But she could see
the signature across the trunk, where the name was spelled out
in bright silver script.

De Soto.

Twenty-six. Butcher Paper

It took Joey Farinacci a minute to understand what Mary was trying to tell him. "You told her your name, didn't you? That first day you met?"

"*Si*."

"What did you tell her?"

"Guiseppe. Joey. You understand?"

"Which was it? Guiseppe or Joey's American grocery?"

"Joey."

"That's not what your mother named you."

"In Italy? No. But here? Joey."

"Exactly," said Mary. "Then you asked her name. And what did she tell you?"

"Rosetta. De Soto."

"But was that really her name?"

"Rosetta?"

"De Soto. You see? She found it right here." Mary tapped the Airflow. "She named herself after the car."

He turned up his palms. "Why would she do that?"

"I don't know why," said Mary. "It's a big American car. Maybe she wanted an American name. Maybe she wanted to hide from somebody. Have you any idea what her name was, before you met? In Sardinia?"

Joey shook his head. Yet he didn't say *yes* or *no*, and his eyes shined.

"But you know who would, don't you?"

Joey did, and half an hour later Mary found herself in a cold butcher shop on 14th Street. The walls were white tile and the floors black and white check. A white freezer case ran the length of the shop to a wooden butcher block toward the back. Beyond it, a steel door sealed a walk-in freezer, through which the butcher emerged with half a calf's hindquarters.

Aboulafia was evidently a well-fed man, who had some trouble breathing and pushed out each exhale through pursed lips. He was round at the middle, bald on top, with a ruddy complexion made redder still by frequent exposure to cold. His apron was stained with blood, as were the cleaver and knives lying across his wooden cutting block. He stuck the calf's thigh onto the last of a row of hooks behind the counter, where three plucked chickens also hung, wiped his hands on the front of his apron, and offered a pink paw to Mary.

It felt as if the bones of her hand had been packed in a snowball.

"Detective Shanley, is it?" said the butcher. "Anthony Aboulafia. Half the local precinct stops by here for lamb. The other half comes for a rib-eye, or a tender diaphragm. What can I trim for you today? I have a fresh pork loin in the freezer. Would you like a nice, juicy piece of pork?"

"No thank you," said Mary, still recoiling from the sight of the raw butchered calf. "I'm not here to pick up dinner."

He looked slightly offended. "The health inspector came by already."

"I'm working a homicide," Mary said, with a stab of guilt. She might've been sent back to diptown, but Rosetta was still in the morgue.

Aboulafia's eyes widened. "What do you need from me?"

"I need to ask a few personal questions."

He picked up the cleaver from his chopping block. "If you need to ask, go ahead. Mind if I work while you do?"

Mary shook her head, and he lifted the first plucked chicken off its steel hook. Laying it across the smooth wooden block, he raised his arm and hacked off its head in one stroke. Another two removed the feet, and a fourth opened the belly. The butcher scooped out the guts and shoved them onto a corner of the chopping block.

"So tell me. What do you need to know?"

She took out her photo of Rosetta de Soto, the second one she had taken from Gertrude Tanenbaum. "You know who this girl is, don't you?"

He studied the picture a moment. "Yes," he said finally, "or I should say, almost. I sent for her from Sardinia. She almost came."

"Almost?"

"She crossed the Atlantic."

"And then?"

He turned back to the chicken. Whack! Whack! Each of the thighs came off. With a smaller, sharper knife he separated the legs from the thighs. "Then she saw me on the dock, and refused to get off the ship. Is that what you came here to ask me?"

"Not entirely."

"Then what else do you need to know?"

Mary looked him over. He was younger than she expected, an energetic fifty, with rosy cheeks and moist brown eyes. From the lines around them, he must have laughed easily or often, and his pink lips looked soft and expressive. He was probably an excellent catch, Mary thought, though she understood how a twenty-year-old who had crossed the ocean to join him might not notice from the deck of a ship.

Whack! He cut the breasts halves from the back of the bird, snapped the wings off with his hands, and put them in a pile with the neck. He saw what she was watching and smiled. "You want me to wrap up a piece?"

"No thank you."

He placed the chicken parts into a clean white tray and swept the guts and organs into another. Then he puffed out a sigh. "No more questions?"

Mary felt for the man, but she had a job to do. There was no choice but to ask. "When was the last time you saw her?"

"That was the last time—on the ship. She looked over the railing and waved but wouldn't come down the gangplank. I watched from the dock as she stood on the deck and argued with the officers. I stayed to watch as they packed her on a tugboat and shipped her out again."

"To Ellis Island? For a deportation hearing?"

"Is that where they took her? They never told me. All I saw was her back, when the tug blew its whistle and chugged away from the dock."

"Haven't you heard anything recently?"

"Why? Has she done something remarkable?"

"Not exactly."

"Notorious? Even criminal?"

"I'm sorry to disappoint you. But the poor girl is dead."

"That is a disappointment," the butcher agreed. He turned and grabbed a second chicken from its hook. She saw the muscles bunch in his powerful arm as the cleaver flew into the air and fell again. "Especially for her."

He was playing it cool, Mary understood. But she couldn't let it go so easily. "There's more to it. Her body was found in the new midtown tunnel, in a pile of earth. She had two crosses with her. Gold crucifixes."

"I sent her one of those," he said. "When she was still in Italy."

"And a schoolboy gave her the other. We have the story on that. A lot of the stories, in fact, that followed yours. But we haven't identified the person who killed her. I was hoping you could fill in one piece of the puzzle."

"What piece is that?"

"Her name," said Mary, watching his eyes. "Rosetta, they called her."

"So did I," agreed the butcher.

"De Soto," said Mary.

The butcher stopped chopping. "No. That's not right."

He looked over his shoulder. She waited while he turned to the register and opened its cash drawer. He took out a red-brown envelope wrapped in a string and tied in a loopy bow. He carried it flat with the bow on top, like a dusty wedding present.

"These," he said, untying the ribbon, "are the papers I filled out to bring her over from Europe. Here is her ticket, on the Strathmore."

209

He offered Mary the used ticket, uncovering a second document—an unsigned marriage license. He flipped that over, face down, as soon as he noticed. Mary accepted the ticket and read out the name of a second class passenger.

"Sarotte, is it?"

Whack! Whack! Whack!

The cleaver came down three times, and the head and feet of a third bird flew off the chopping block. Mary looked up and noticed that the butcher's eyes had changed. They seemed to sink deeper into their sockets and blacken in the shadow of his brows. His mouth pinched in annoyance, perhaps, or distaste at a memory. And he refused to meet Mary's gaze.

"That's the name of her family in Italy," Aboulafia said. "The same name on the ticket." The name she had glimpsed on the license.

"I'm sorry," Mary told him.

Whack! The cleaver fell again, and little bits of thigh flew up from the carcass. "You know, she left me at the dock, humiliating me. But I still imagined that sometime we might meet at a bus stop, or she might drop in for a beefsteak. We would strike up a conversation, and before she even realized who I was, she might decide she liked me after all."

"I'm sure she liked you—"

He cut her off with a steely glance. "That day at the dock would be forgotten, and we could tell our children how we almost met, and then met, and almost missed meeting altogether. It would have made a lovely story. But it won't happen now."

"No, it won't."

The butcher's neck grew redder, not in shame or grief. He was angry, Mary saw, and growing angrier. "To hell with her," he said.

Whack! Mary watched the rhythm of the cleaver and wondered if the butcher had it in him to chop other meat. The strength he had in his shoulders. The requisite anger was there. He had motive. And he made his living in blood.

"There's one more thing I need to ask," Mary said, as he cleared the entrails. "Where were you last Thursday night?"

The butcher understood the question. "I was here," he said, "with customers. Where else would I go? There was no one waiting at home."

"All night?"

Aboulafia exhaled. "I was here until ten o'clock. Then I closed up and went home. I have an apartment on Prince Street, on the top floor of the building. I set a beach chair on the fire escape, opened a bottle of wine, and put a record on the phonograph. Caruso's last recording of Rossini's sacred music. You know it?"

Mary didn't. She watched him draw a breath, and for a moment she thought he might give her the first couple of bars. But he puffed out the air between his soft lips and his shoulders sagged.

"You can ask my neighbors about it. They heard."

Mary told him she would. A bell jangled over the door. A customer entered, and the butcher welcomed her by name. Mary made her way to the street, where the traffic was brisker and less personal than on Mulberry Street.

Mary's mind was rattling like a jigsaw puzzle in its box. She had all the pieces needed, but how did they fit together? A blur of brown and blue could be a bulrush at the shoreline or a bit of cloudy sky. But which one was it?

Sarotte.

Rosetta Sarotte.

Where had she heard that name before?

Louisa Vitanza had been unable to recall Guillermo's last name. *LaMotte*, she said, *something like that*. But if he and Rosetta had the same last name, could they have been married? If they were, where did that leave Ming-Lu Lin? Angry enough to take matters into his own hands?

Mary wondered if Johnny Broderick had it right all along. Did Leon Catalan really see Ming-Lu Lin, lurking around the neighborhood on the night Rosetta was killed? Had Ming-Lu

211

discovered that Rosetta was already a married woman? Was Mary actually making Johnny's case for him?

Mary's speculations were racing ahead of her facts. She took a deep breath and tried to slow herself down. They might have sounded alike, but Sarotte was not LaMotte. Mary wasn't certain she had heard Guillermo's name correctly. There were too many holes in her picture puzzle yet. But she knew where to fill them in.

Twenty-seven. The Good Girl

Mary never regretted her inability to drive as much as she did during her taxi ride from Fourteenth Street to West 23rd. It wouldn't be her biggest fare, but it followed the Captain's complaint about her receipts, and Broderick's silent smirk. Johnny would have driven an unmarked car too fast through the streetlights, parking wherever he felt like leaving his vehicle. Taxi receipts left a trail of your movements visible to superiors, and the fares added up so quickly.

It occurred to Mary that Rosetta de Soto would have been equally aware of the extravagance of a private taxi ride. When Freddie Arlington gave her cab fare in the Edison Hotel and headed off to catch his train at Grand Central, would she really have used the cash to travel home? Rosetta was dancing with strange men for five cents a ticket. That cab fare would have meant hours of gripping sweaty palms. No, Mary felt sure Rosetta would have caught a bus or a train for a nickel and pocketed the cash. It might have been difficult to determine which she would have taken, until Mary realized that it made no difference. Both stopped at the same place.

The corner of Sixth Avenue and 23rd Street was bustling when Mary's taxi pulled up between the bus stop and subway entrance. The marquee overhead was illuminated, and a line of audience members shuffled past the ticket office into the theatre entrance. Inside, the seats were filling with a crowd of women and children. The show advertised on the marquee was *Jack and the Beanstalk*, a family matinee. Mary made her way down the aisle, sidestepping skinny elbows and skinned knees that jutted out suddenly from seats on either side.

Backstage, the scene was even more hectic. Behind the curtain was a narrow stage, three or four feet deep, and then a cloth scrim, painted with a country scene—rolling hills, a blue sky, fleecy white clouds. Behind the scrim, a wooden platform had been erected, reached by a stepladder, so the puppeteers could work their marionettes on their knees, reaching over the top of the scrim. At the back of the wooden platform were pegs on which hung Jack, a giant chicken, and a pair of enormous feet, rising on legs that connected to nothing above the knee. Three puppeteers were already on the platform, crawling back and forth, untangling wires, fixing Jack's tiny clothing, testing the rings of a telescoping beanstalk so that it grew evenly when the center strings were pulled.

Mary climbed the steps to the platform and waited to catch Lucy's eye. "Miss Morelli," she said. "Can I speak to you for a moment?"

"Officer Shanley! I'm sorry, but this isn't a good time. We're about to go on! We can talk after the show."

Mary shook her head. "We can go someplace private and talk now," she said, "or I can take you down to the precinct house and we can talk there."

Lucy sat up. "Are you arresting me?"

"Let's see," said Mary.

She stepped down and Lucy Morelli followed her. There was a spot at the edge of the stage where the curtains did not open, hiding the backstage area from the audience. Mary led Lucy there to talk. The thickly folded fabric of the curtains hid them from the audience, puppeteers, and other people working backstage.

"I don't have a lot of time," Lucy said.

She was dressed in a black sweater, black slacks, and flat black shoes. Mary did not know a lot of women who wore slacks, but crawling around on that wooden platform had to be rough on the knees. Lucy's eyes were outlined in black, which made her deep brown irises look almost black. There was a purple tint on her lips too, which could have been from her lipstick or all the time she spent in the dark.

"Miss Morelli," Mary repeated, officially. "Or should I say Mrs. Sarotte?"

"No, I told you. We're not married yet."

"But that will be your married name. Sarotte?"

Lucy hesitated. "It's Guillermo's name, if that's what you mean. Billy's."

"And it was Rosetta's, once."

"Was it?"

"Don't tell me you didn't know that. Were they married?"

"Billy and...?" Lucy laughed. "No. Never."

"You're Catholic, aren't you?"

"A good Italian girl. As I'll bet you are yourself, Officer Shanley. Only the blowsy Irish model."

Mary stuck to her line of questioning. "We both know, if Billy and Rosetta were married, in the eyes of the church they still are and always will be. That would be the end of your plans for a life together, wouldn't it?"

"I suppose it would."

"So what would you do, if you suddenly discovered that you couldn't marry Billy, because Guillermo Sarotte already had a wife?"

"What would I do? I can't imagine. What do you think I would do?"

"I think you might have killed her."

Lucy stared. "You think I'm capable of that?"

"I've seen you swing that painted sword, Miss Morelli, and haul around those heavy wooden puppets."

"Marionettes."

"You have the upper-body strength you would have needed to beat Rosetta de Soto to death. I've heard about the Mediterranean temperament, but even without a temper, I could understand a woman in your situation losing control of herself."

"But I have an alibi," Lucy said. "I was putting on a show. A hundred strangers watched me do it."

"They saw puppets dance—excuse me, marionettes. They didn't see you pulling the strings."

"They don't dance by themselves."

"That could have been done by your partners, here."

"Have you ever heard Tony's falsetto? He could've worked the strings, maybe, but the voices? I voice all the ladies. Besides, they'd have to know, wouldn't they? Enough to cover for me?"

"Just that you needed an alibi."

"Why would anybody risk doing that for a murderer?"

"They're your family members, aren't they?"

"Cousins. Maybe one of them—Antonio—would lie to the police for my sake. But all of them? They'd be afraid of being deported."

"Perhaps I should threaten them now."

"That isn't necessary."

"What about your audience? If I brought in a couple of officers and asked these people for their papers, how many do you think would head for the door?"

Mary and Lucy both knew that the most common slur for Italians—*wop*—came from the immigration stamp With-Out Papers. Lucy's eyes hardened. "You're a bigger bitch than you seem at first, you know that, Officer Shanley?"

"Shall I make the call?"

"I told you it wasn't necessary."

"Then why don't you tell me what I need to know?"

"Look...do you really think I would kill some woman just to marry her husband? If you are a good Catholic, you must know murder is a venal sin. Why should I spend forever in hell for a few guilty years as a housewife?"

Mary shrugged. "People don't always think their actions through."

"I do. What sort of marriage do you think that would be? Blessed with children? Or damned from the moment we exchanged our vows?"

Mary felt the younger woman's logic creeping over her skull. Lucy made sense. But Mary couldn't afford to be distracted by theological speculation when she had a good, clean line of facts to follow.

"Rosetta de Soto was given cab fare on Thursday night at the Edison Hotel on 47th Street. That's just a mile north of here, and a couple of blocks to the west. She would never have taken a taxi cab instead of a bus or subway. Do you know where either of those would have dropped her off?"

"Outside the theatre."

"Exactly."

"Who do you think was waiting for her to get off the train? Me? Don't be silly. It was the Chinaman. "

"You mean Ming-Lu Lin?"

"That's him."

"Why would he do that?"

"You have him in a cell—ask him. How should I know?"

Mary shook her head. "One way or the other, Miss Morelli. Did you see him here or not?"

Lucy took a breath and let it out slowly. "Billy usually comes on Thursday nights. Early. But it was getting close to curtain and he still hadn't showed, so I went out to look for his truck. The Chinaman—"

"Ming-Lu Lin."

"Was waiting under the theatre marquee. Watching people get off the bus and climb up the stairs from the subway."

"Just waiting? Quietly?"

"During the first act, we heard a disturbance. Shouting from the street outside the theatre. After my character exited, I went out to shush them."

"Rosetta was there? With Lin?"

Lucy glanced at the stage, where marionettes were clanging swords. "They had a fight at the dance hall, didn't they?"

"That's right."

"Ming-Ling, or whatever his name is, couldn't let it go."

"Is that what he said?"

"He said he was sorry for fighting with her in Brooklyn. That he understood if she had to say good-bye to her old friends. That he trusted her not to do what she used to do with them. And you know what she said?"

217

"What?"

"She did. She slept with one, for one last time. Because he begged her and had always been so generous. It was the only way she could think to say good-bye."

Rosetta and Freddie Arlington at the Edison Hotel.

If Lin had been waiting for her on 23rd Street, she might have said that to piss him off, to get back at him, to test him—who knew? She was angry, probably tipsy, caught unawares in the dark. Maybe having some doubts about tying the knot with Lin or annoyed at finding him waiting for her.

"After she told him all that...how did Ming-Lu react?"

"How do you think? He got angry. What did she think she was doing to them? Which only made her mad. She said she was still her own person, and whatever she did was her business, wasn't it?"

"She told him that in the street?"

"That's right. The bus had come and gone. No train emptying in the station. The show had started inside, so there weren't a lot of people passing by."

"And then what?"

"He hit her."

"With his fists? You heard him beating Rosetta?"

"Right."

"And didn't do anything to help her?"

"We didn't know what it was, at the time. But when the story came out in the paper, we figured that's what it must have been. Him beating her for sleeping with somebody else."

"But you didn't think it worth reporting, the last time you spoke to me. Who's *we*?"

"Excuse me?"

"You just said, '*We* didn't know.' Twice. You and who else heard her?"

"Nobody."

"Nobody says *we* when they were alone."

"I do. I mean, I did."

"No, you didn't. You're lying. You didn't hear any of it, did you?"

"I did. That's just what they said to each other."

"Maybe it was. But you didn't hear him beat her. I'll bet that's what you and Guillermo worked out, after the body was found. Rosetta was fighting with a Chinaman on the street, so he must have killed her."

"Is that a question?"

"The question is *why would you need a story*? Was Sarotte here by then?"

"No! Billy never showed. I heard them."

"So you listened to Mr. Lin beat a white girl and said nothing to anyone else?"

"I opened the door and chased him off. But that doesn't mean he didn't beat her to death on the way home."

"Somebody did," said Mary. "She never reached Mrs. T's."

Lucy said, "You don't think Billy found her?"

"He never showed up here, did he? He could have been waiting for her. Sitting in his truck outside the boardinghouse, or any place in between."

"To see her safely home? He could have—like a gentleman from the old country. That's what they do in Italy."

"With strangers on the street? Or old girlfriends? That's very understanding of you. When you and he were supposed to get married."

"What do you mean, *supposed to*?"

"You're still planning to marry him, after what you heard? You knew she was Rosetta Sarotte, but still wanted Guillermo. Why? What else did you know?"

Lucy shook her head. "It was never like that."

Mary felt a tingling behind her ears. "Because Billy was never her husband, was he?"

Lucy screwed up her face. "No. Never."

"So why did they share a last name, if he wasn't her husband?"

"Maybe she liked it," said Lucy.

But Mary was not to be shaken from her lines of reasoning. "Too young for her father or uncle. A cousin...or her brother," said Mary at last. "Guillermo was her brother from Italy."

Lucy refused to confirm it, but the answer was written on her face.

Mary went on as if she had. "Only they weren't in Italy any more. Her landlady told me how important a daughter's virtue is to her Italian family, how much of the family's honor rests on her virginity. What happens when a sister isn't such an angel? When her brother gets off the boat and learns she's out on the town with men who never intend to marry her?"

Lucy glanced toward the stage. "The curtain's about to go up."

Mary caught her by the elbow, keeping her there. "That's when he beat her up the first time, wasn't it? When he arrived and found out how his sister had been living. He heard about her nights as a charity girl and tried to end them. By beating the devil out of her."

"You don't have to make him sound like an animal. That's what they do in Italy, to keep their women in line."

"But it didn't work here, did it? Rosetta changed her name to protect her family's reputation, but she wouldn't stop living the way she wanted to."

"Like a slut."

"That's how Guillermo would have described it. Rosetta might have said, like an American girl."

"Is there a difference?"

"Isn't there? They were engaged to be married."

"Rosetta was? To...Lin?"

"You didn't know that? Billy did. He must have heard it around the neighborhood. His sister and a Chinaman running off to get married. I'll bet it drove him nuts."

Mary watched Lucy, who wouldn't say a word until her cousin's curly head poked through the curtain. "*Scusi*, Lucia— we need you. To work the giant's strings."

"I'll be right there, Antonio."

220

"The house is full."

"I know. Just give me one minute."

He looked doubtful but headed back to the platform.

"I have to go," Lucy said.

Mary shook her head. "Ming-Lu would never have beaten her. He would have walked away in disgust and confusion, the way he did outside the dance hall in Brooklyn. Guillermo would have beaten her. He did it once before. If she had run off with a Chinaman, the family reputation would have been ruined, here in New York and in Italy. So he hit her—like a big brother, looking out for his sister and the family honor. That sounds like him, doesn't it?"

"I don't know," Lucy said, listening to the audience beyond the curtain. "It sounds like a lot of guys I know."

"Guillermo was the one with a charity girl for a sister— which gave him a reason to beat her. Because Rosetta refused to back down this time. She told him to go to hell. Has your fiancé got a temper, Miss Morelli? When a woman refuses to listen? Having thrown his first punch, and getting nothing for it but lip, Guillermo kept beating her out of rage, or fear for his family name, or whatever other excuse he gave himself. He probably talked while he hit her. She must have talked back. And before he calmed down enough to realize what he was doing, he had beaten his sister to death."

The lights in the theatre dimmed. Lucy said, "That's not what he told me. He got stuck at work. His truck kept jamming on the cement. I don't know any more than that."

"And you don't want to know," said Mary. "Didn't he ever hit you?"

"Billy would never do that."

"Because you're a modern girl? Or because you're not married yet? He beat his sister to death. That's how he treats the women in his family."

Lucy shook her head. "It's not so easy to leave your whole world behind. You walk down that gangplank and they expect you to become a new person by the time your feet hit the dock.

221

But it takes longer than that. I hope you find whoever killed Rosetta. I hope the Chinaman did it. That's all I can tell you, Officer. That's all I know. Now, if you're not going to arrest me, you'll have to excuse me. I have a show to put on." Lucy said it calmly, but a blink of doubt closed her eyes.

"There's one thing more you can tell me," Mary said. "He's a sandhog, isn't he? Still working on the tunnel to Jersey?"

Antonio's head popped through the curtain again. "Lucia, please—"

"No," Lucy said quickly. "They pulled him off that job four months ago. He drove a truck for a while to a park in Queens. Now he's working a new treatment plant on Ward's Island."

Twenty-eight. Toilet Water

The Ward's Island Water Pollution Control Plant, the first facility to treat sewage water in New York City, was nearing completion in the spring of 1937. Like everything else built at the time, it was a project of Robert Moses and his indefatigable team of city planners and visionaries. Having trained their own corps of sandhogs, Moses' managers moved their crews from site to site, allowing the coordination of their workforce and a high return on their investment in training.

Rising from the soil of Ward's Island was a tower of steel and concrete supporting one section of the Triboro Bridge, an architectural wonder completed the year before by Robert Moses' Authority, linking Manhattan to the Bronx and Queens. It was the largest public works project in the history of New York, built by five thousand laborers over seven years for fifty million dollars. To follow it, Moses agreed to develop Ward's and Randall Islands in the bridge's shadow. Landfill linked the two islands, and a railroad bridge was built over Hell Gate, connecting Ward's Island to Manhattan. A sports arena was constructed on Randall Island, and a park on Ward's Island with the world's most capacious sewage treatment plant.

Wastewater in the plant is treated in four stages. During Preliminary Treatment debris in the sewage water is screened out and ground up. Sticks, rags, toys, sand, gravel, and chunks of food are removed to protect the pumps inside the plant. The second stage is called Primary Treatment, when wastewater is held in a quiet tank, so that particles settle down and grease floats to the top. Grease and particles are skimmed off and treated as sludge, while the clarified water is pumped into another tank, where biological agents are used to remove dissolved organic matter. In this stage, Secondary Treatment, micro-organisms are added that feed on the matter in the wastewater. In the final stage, Disinfection, chlorine is added and the wastewater exposed to ultraviolet light to kill off any disease-causing organisms that remain in the water.

The Ward's Island Water Pollution Control Plant was fitted with huge ceramic tanks for each stage of the process, so that thousands of gallons of wastewater could be pumped from one to the next and purified differently in each tank. In the spring of 1937 the tanks had all been built, while the last crews labored on landscaping the park. Guillermo Sarotte worked on a crew turning up the dry earth with a hand-cranked rototiller, planting trees, seeding grasses, paving the walkways with tar. He was building a concrete bench with slats of green wood, when Mary Shanley arrived at the island on a police launch and marched a group of bluecoats from the boat landing to the trailer where the grounds-crew boss kept his office.

Sarotte could hardly keep his eyes on his bench while the police officers talked to his boss. He didn't even try, when they exited the trailer and started down the black tar path to the ground where Sarotte's crew-mates were installing steel poles for a chain-link fence. When they spoke to Sarotte's crew chief, and his eyes met Guillermo's, that was the final straw. Sarotte left his bench and started to walk and then run in the opposite direction, where the new treatment plant loomed on the edge of the island.

As he picked up speed, Guillermo imagined the gang of policemen starting after him. He didn't look back and tried not to listen, except to the sound of his own rubber soles pounding the tar. He burst through the plant's steel door into a huge, tile chamber and heard an ear-splitting *gush* echo off the concrete walls as gallons of filthy sewage poured from one tank to another.

Mary Shanley had worked hard to convince Pat McVeigh to send four uniformed patrolmen along with her to pick up Guillermo Sarotte on Ward's Island. The uniforms had sensed the Captain's uncertainty, or Mary's own doubts, but had gone along for the boat ride. Once they saw Guillermo Sarotte start to run, their reflexes kicked in, and they started to chase him as if he had robbed the widows and orphans fund. An old hand never runs from a bear or a cop, but Guillermo Sarotte had very little experience with either one. The faster he ran, the more he inspired the boys in blue to chase after him, so that by the time he reached the western entrance to the pollution control plant, the cops were falling further behind but growing angrier.

Sarotte was tall and skinny as a water bird, with long legs that carried him farther with every loping stride.

Mary wore low heels, but her legs were shorter than the uniformed officers, and the narrow hem of her skirt slowed her even more. When she passed through the doors of the treatment plant, Guillermo Sarotte had already made his way halfway around a large grit tank, where a lake of fetid water bubbled through Secondary Treatment. Sarotte was sidling along the far edge, one foot after the other. Three bluecoats stood on a wider ledge, waving him onto steadier ground and cursing him under their breath. The fourth uniform was going after him, sidling along the narrow wall that ringed the goo in the tank. With each step, he seemed to wobble, recovering his balance only by setting one foot ahead of the other, like a tightrope walker with a ten-foot drop on one side and a pit of hungry microbes on the other.

"Mr. Sarotte!" shouted Mary, afraid that either the fugitive or the cop following him might take a false step into the slime. "Stop running! There's no way to escape. Stay where you are and we'll get you down safely. Please!"

But Guillermo couldn't hear her. Or else he didn't believe her. Or he might have been more afraid of the cops than reassured by Mary.

The bluecoat behind him was on his knees, crawling after Sarotte, who seemed to float along the edge of the tank as if he were made of air. The uniform must have weighed fifty pounds more than the fugitive, which would have tilted the scale in the officer's favor if the two men traded punches on solid ground. It only slowed him down along the tank's slippery perimeter and made his every move awkward and treacherous.

"You stupid sonuvabitch," he mumbled, tottering on one knee. "I'll break your scrawny neck."

That only motivated Sarotte to run faster, until the ceramic edge beneath his feet met the far wall. That left him nowhere to go, while the uniformed cop kept crawling closer.

"Mr. Sarotte!" Mary called again. "We're almost there. Please don't try to resist! You want to get out of here alive, don't you?"

Sarotte's eyes widened as the uniform inched toward him. He raised his foot to kick the cop off the tank's edge.

"You sick bastard," the officer hissed, breathing hard. "Don't even think about it! Shake of that fucking foot again and I'll kill you."

The cop was close enough to lunge for Sarotte's knee. But he missed, lost his balance, and nearly rolled sideways into the tank. When he finally caught his balance, lying flat on his stomach, he reached again for Sarotte's skinny ankle. And this time nearly snagged it.

"One more step, you crazy bastard…"

That was enough for Guillermo. He stretched behind him, brought his hands over his head, pressed his calloused palms together, and dived into the sludge.

The uniform who followed him around the rim of the tank stood and leaned back against the wall. He watched as Sarotte's head emerged from the black goo and pulled away from the tank's edge with a few graceful strokes. The fugitive swam off as if he were doing laps in Astoria pool, unconcerned about the sewage or the organisms digesting organic matter. The cop against the far wall looked at his three colleagues, but no one dared go after him into the glutinous scum. Guillermo kicked, and a foul-smelling bubble burst the surface behind him.

"Mr. Sarotte! Wait!" cried Mary, but her voice echoed off the tiles, unanswered. With a few long strokes he had crossed the tank and approached the far side. It was just a few seconds before he pulled himself up on the opposite edge, sidled along the last few feet, and escaped through a service door on the far side of the tank. Two of the uniforms still near the entrance headed out to cut him off. But they were on the wrong side of the plant, with no hope of running around the mammoth building before the fugitive slipped through the service door and disappeared into the trees.

Sarotte's hand reached up, grabbing the edge of the tank. His muscles grew taut and his shoulder followed, then his head and opposite arm. One elbow found the edge of the tank, and then the second elbow. Sarotte hung there a moment, catching his breath, his torso still hanging in the sludge, as the black grease dripped off him and he tried to fill his lungs for the last push onto the ledge.

At that moment a bell rang, loud as heaven's alarm clock. It clanged off the ceramic tanks and the chamber's damp walls. Mary wanted to cover her ears, but like the four patrolmen and the dangling Guillermo, she stood stock still, waiting to see what the bells announced.

Brrrring. Brrrring. Brrrring. Brrrring.

The bells stopped suddenly and Mary heard a roar. At first she thought it the sound of her own blood rising. But no, it wasn't in her ears—the noise was in the chamber, echoing off the tiles. Then she saw the sluices open, and a flood poured through the wall on the opposite side of the tank. It knocked Sarotte off the edge and caught him up in an eddy of sewage that swept him under the surface.

In another moment the dark water surged again, foaming a sickly yellow as it was pumped out of the Secondary tank into the last tank for the final stage of treatment.

Disinfection.

For an instant Mary thought Sarotte's fingers reached out of the swirl of sewage, grasping for hold. But there was nothing to catch onto and no way to help him. Sarotte's hand spun around in a curl of black water, roaring into the tank for Disinfection. Then a second bank of sluices on the far side opened, dumping in gallons of chlorine.

The surface glistened and boiled.

An acrid stink, like sulfur, arose from the roiling soup.

But Guillermo Sarotte never appeared again.

*　　　*　　　*

The news reached Centre Street before Mary did. By the time she got back, the press were already gathered around the steps, waiting for Lin's release. When he stepped out of the building, blinking at the daylight, the photographers snapped their pictures of him, and reporters asked a few questions. Their real enthusiasm was not for Mary, who watched through the window in the Captain's office, but for Johnny Broderick, who always had a snappy line for the columnists.

"Well...we got him, boys. The case is solved!" Broderick declared.

"What about the Chinaman, Johnny?" one dared to ask.

"We used him to flush out the real killer," Johnny confided, clapping his hands and leaning into them, as if he were spilling an official secret. "Then we flushed that bad boy right down the drain."

The pencils of the press scribbled away.

The Captain laughed, standing beside Mary. "They're onto him, you know. But he always gives them a headline, a lead—a caption, at least. They pump him up, and he keeps them happy. Everybody wins."

"Except for the readers, who want the truth."

"Do they now?" asked McVeigh.

Mary listened to the baby birds chirping in the tree. There were three of them, English bullfinches. Most people confused them with sparrows.

"Congratulations to you, Mary," the Captain said. "I know the truth. You wrapped up your first case. And did it alone."

"Not entirely," Mary said.

"You had a little help at the end," he granted. "Still—"

Mary shook her head. "I'm not so sure it is wrapped up."

"The man jumped into a cesspool, Mary," said McVeigh. "You think he would've done that if he wasn't guilty as sin?"

"I'm sure Sarotte beat her," Mary said. "What I can't figure out is why."

228

"You explained that already, didn't you? She was going to marry the Chinaman. That would've shamed the family in Sardinia. You're not changing your story now, are you?"

Mary shook her head. "But how did he know? How did Guillermo find out his sister was planning to run off with Ming-Lu Lin?"

"She must have told him."

"Rosetta? I doubt it. He beat her up once before, without a Chinaman."

"He must've heard it from her friend, then. Vitanza."

"Louisa wouldn't even tell me that Rosetta had lost her job. It wasn't her secret to tell. I don't think she knew this one. From some of the comments she let drop, I doubt she would have understood Rosetta falling for Lin."

"Sarotte found out somehow."

"Yes, he did," she said. "But I can't wrap it up until I figure out how."

The Captain shrugged, done with it. "You keep on thinking, Mary."

A leaf struck the window, still attached to the sycamore. At the far end of the branch, the mama bird landed with a bagel in her beak. The nestlings sat up, twittering, while on the street below, the reporters kept laughing at Johnny's jokes.

229

Twenty-nine. Cherry Pie

Louisa Vitanza was the last girl released from the Mercer Street station. She was named as a "ringleader" by the Woolworth manager and taken to a separate room, where she was questioned by two plainclothes officers. The older officer asked a lot of questions about her housemate Rachel Lipinsky, while the younger officer beat around the bush and finally asked her out. When she had said *No* to the latter and *I don't know* often enough to the former, they left her alone in the room, until a clerk came in for a file from the desk and told her she could go home.

Outside the precinct house, Louisa realized that her purse was still in her locker at the store, and she didn't have a dime for the subway. She started uptown, pausing at bus stops along the way to ask if the drivers wouldn't let her ride without the fare. But there were lots of people without dimes in New York. By the time she turned onto 21st Street, Louisa was beat tired, and the streets were dark and empty—which made the mug idling on the corner even scarier, when he tossed his toothpick against the curb and started strolling after her.

Sweet Jesus, she thought, *I don't have the strength for this.*

He had broad shoulders under his camelhair coat and a hat pushed back on his head to show his face. Louisa didn't want to stare at the man, but even from the glance she gave him as she passed she could see that his cheek was smeared with a scarlet stain, as if someone had hit him in the face with a cherry pie and he hadn't bothered to clean it. Except the stain wrinkled with his skin when he smiled, and it wasn't a comforting sight. Louisa didn't want to know what thought provoked that smile, and especially didn't want to know if it was meant for her. She focused on the steps to the porch of the boardinghouse at the far end of the block and quickened her pace towards them.

As she moved more quickly, so did the man behind her. He wore soft-soles shoes that made no sound, but Louisa could feel his shadow hovering closer. She lengthened her stride and doubled her steps, but the rounded toes of his oversized shoes kept drawing nearer to her heels. There was something wrong at the boardinghouse. The bulb over the door was out, and the porch was a shoebox of shadow. Still, it looked safer than the street below it, with a strange man lumbering after her.

No one else on the block. Where were the nosy neighbors, when you needed one?

Louisa tried to keep her wits about her, her pace brisk but confident, her back straight and her head held high. Projecting an air of authority, she told herself, controlling her own space. Then she heard the man's breath near her ear, and ran. When she clattered up the steps to the porch, he was half a short step behind her.

Louisa didn't have her key. It was still in her purse in the Woolworth locker. She banged on the front door with her fist, calling, "Mrs. T! Please, let me in!"

But no one answered inside the house, and the man reached over her shoulder to set his palm against the door, so it couldn't be opened at all.

"Nobody home," he said, smiling again.

The cherry skin buckled like red leather, and his green eyes bulged. His breath smelled of licorice. "Your Commie friend was called to an emergency meeting, down at the union hall. Somebody beat up a rag picker outside a sweatshop. The old lady's at Bellevue, visiting her Nazi. Regular little Europe she's got living here, isn't it?"

"Eric's not a Nazi. He's her son," said Louisa.

The man shrugged. "Even Hitler's got a mum, I guess."

"Eric's an American. A war hero."

"I'll tip my hat, the next time he hobbles by."

Louisa twisted the knob behind her, but the mug only grinned when it rattled. She tried to steady her voice when she said, "What do you want from me?"

His red splotch grew redder. "Just your pretty neck."

She raised a hand to the base of her throat and felt her pulse race. "Why?"

231

"Does it matter?"

It seemed to, yes—the mug was enjoying her terror. She tried desperately to think of something else to say, to keep him entertained and delay whatever he was planning to do next. She stared at the stain on the left side of his face, which was not from a cherry pie. Maybe a dribble of acid. But she couldn't ask him about that, could she? For the life of her, and the very first time, she could think of nothing to say.

He reached forward and set his thumb over the spot her fingertips had touched.

"This shouldn't take but a minute."

"It should take less than that to put down your hand very slowly," said a voice from the darkness behind him, in a warm, familiar brogue.

Louisa turned to see Mary Shanley step out of the shadows at the end of the porch, with a 32-calibre revolver in her fist. Its muzzle stuck comfortably against the mug's head, where the hairline met his neck.

Louisa felt the pressure drop from his thumb, as his fingers opened and went first down and then up into the air as the gun pressed into his skull. As soon as she had room, she slipped away from him. Her dress was damp and she felt cold, and to stop her teeth from chattering, she asked, "Mary, what are you doing here?"

"I was restless," Mary said, "and needed to talk. I took a cab to Mercer Street, where they said you'd left hours ago. When I found the house empty and the porch light unscrewed, the little hairs on my neck stood up. So I made myself comfortable here."

Louisa touched the bulb over the door, and it lit—which started her chills all over again. "He was waiting for me?"

Mary nodded.

Louisa blinked, and not from the light. The mug tried to use the moment to free his cramped head, but Mary moved in closer, using the barrel of her gun to force him back against the doorframe.

"You came to twist her neck? Now why should you want to do something like that to such a pretty girl?"

The thirty-two dug into his flesh until it rested against his skull. "No reason. I spotted her walking down the block and thought she might be fun."

"You're a liar," said Mary, "and not a good one. I saw you in the crowd outside Woolworth's didn't I?"

He shrugged.

"What were you doing there?"

"You tell me."

"Waiting for her, is my guess. But you couldn't get to her once the strike was on, and the police dragged her away. So you waited here. What I want to know is why? Who told you to wring Miss Vitanza's neck?"

This time she let him turn his head, since Louisa was now safely out of reach. The gun was still pointed between his gut and heart, but Mary allowed him space enough to back off from the door. He looked her over and said, "Nobody."

"I called you a liar already."

If that was supposed to get him riled, it didn't work at all. The mug set his palm against his jaw and pushed, cracking his stiff neck. "You can call me whatever you like," he said, "so long as you're holding the gun."

There was a threat in that, and Mary's grip tightened.

Louisa moved to the low wooden wall separating the porch from the street. She leaned against its edge, catching her breath in gulps. She had not felt breathless earlier, running for the porch, but she couldn't take in enough oxygen now to stop her heart from pounding through her ribs. She must have held her breath the whole time they stood at the door. She had hardly felt afraid then, but the fear was rushing in now like hot liquid, together with a feeling like indignation. How *dare* he? Take such *liberties*! It felt strange to respond to her near murder as she might to an unwelcome kiss, but both Mary and the mug were staring at her as if they expected her to slap his face.

"She knows something, is that it? Or somebody thinks she does. Something they don't want her to tell?"

The mug sneered at Mary. "Why don't you ask her?"

Louisa shook her head. "I don't know a thing," she swore, crossing hers chest. "Not one blessed thing."

He grinned through his scarlet stain. "You tell her, sister. Just like I said. She don't know a thing, and neither do I. We're a couple of innocent bystanders. I was hanging out on this corner when I saw her walking home. She looked like it had been a long day and she could use a little company."

"Is that what you call company?" Louisa demanded, the blood rushing into her face. All of a sudden she could breath again. "Creep."

"Maybe I got too affectionate," he said. "Maybe I moved too fast."

"Maybe you did," said Mary.

"All right, I misread the signals. So shoot me."

"Do it," said Louisa, nodding at the gun.

"I can't, right now," Mary said. "I'm a police officer. He's in custody."

"Well, I can," said Louisa and kicked him in the shin.

The mug let out a whelp of pain and grabbed his wounded leg. "I want a lawyer," he said.

Louisa's eyes were still fixed on hard targets. "Just give me one more minute, Mary, before you take him in. One good shot, you know where—"

Mary caught Louisa by the crook of the arm, and kept her out of kicking distance.

"That's not how we do it."

"You want to know who sent him, don't you? To kill me, for Chrissake! I mean, I want to know."

"I know already," said Mary.

The red-faced man smiled. "Sure you do."

But Louisa caught something in the tone of Mary's voice that made her stop and wonder. She followed the detective's gaze to the mug's raised leg, which was still crossed over its partner to protect the bruised shin. And then down the leg to the foot, where his soft-soled shoe jiggled nervously, shaking off specks of powder.

Trapped between the treads on the bottom of his shoe was more of the stuff—fine white particles of something like talcum. Or chalk.

Thirty. Rockaway

On the narrow peninsula in southwestern Queens, a bathhouse had been built in 1932 on the site of the Rockaway Naval Air Station, a strip of land alongside Fort Tilden. Four years later Robert Moses redesigned the beach as a getaway spot for New Yorkers with cars. He removed Moorish designs from the original bathhouse, extended both ends, and raised the height of its central tower. To cover the difference in architectural styles, his crews repainted the whole thing white. They replaced the beachfront pavilion with a modern facade, added a boardwalk, concessions, and sports facilities, and landscaped the grounds with his favorite tree, the Japanese black pine.

In a gesture toward social justice, the park was named for Jacob Riis, the muckraking photo-journalist whose 1890 book, *How the Other Half Lives*, exposed desperate living conditions in New York's tenements. The design of Riis Park, however, like so many Moses projects, had car-owners in mind. The park provided a destination for drivers who crossed over Rockaway Inlet on the Marine Parkway Bridge, connecting the Queens peninsula with Flatbush Avenue in Brooklyn and the Belt Parkway, which was also built by Moses and his minions. To accommodate the traffic, the lot at Riis Park had spaces paved for five thousand cars.

When Mary's taxi found its way to the park, three days after Ming-Lu's release, the driver gripped his steering wheel with none of the usual confidence expected from a cabbie. When he dropped her off, the park looked deserted. It was not yet open to the public, but the cabbie wouldn't wait. He drove off faster than he drove in, leaving Mary alone with the gulls and the glistening brown sand.

Only not quite alone. There were bulldozers rolling back and forth across the beach, smoothing the sand where the dunes had been flattened. It was after five o'clock, but there were still a crew painting the last buildings white and contractors inspecting the brickwork and tiles, the railings and half-buried jetties running out through the sand to the waterline. Mary found Bertram Boone kneeling on the plaza in front of the bathhouse, checking the squares of the boardwalk. Behind him, Irene sat on a bench with her elbows on the railing, watching the whitecaps. She was wearing an oversized navy sweater with its sleeves covering her hands. As Mary approached, Irene mumbled, "Christ, Bert. Look what's coming."

"Pipe down," he said. "I'll handle this."

Irene gazed out to sea.

"How does it feel?" Mary asked him. "Solid?"

Boone stood, rising to his full six feet. "Officer Shanley, isn't it?"

"Will it hold my weight?"

"The concrete? You and a hundred more like you. We built this for the people. A whole lot of them."

"It has a nice view, doesn't it?" Mary asked Irene.

"I guess. I've seen better."

Mary looked up and down the boardwalk. "It looks like the place you stopped on Tuesday night."

"There are lots of pretty spots along this beach," Boone said, moving closer to Irene.

"I think it's the very same one," Mary insisted, pulling out a photo from her purse. It was a copy of the second shot Moses had in his limo. "Look," she traced the outline. "There's the Empire State Building. The same angle."

Boone frowned at the photo. "You tailed us?"

"Not me! A Pinkerton, who must have snapped this from the bathhouse behind us." Mary lined up the photo with the scene. "See?"

"Maybe it is, and maybe it isn't," Irene said. "I was drunk."

Boone said, "So what?"

Mary glanced down the beach. "Your office said I might find you here."

"Did they? I'll have to talk to them about that."

"Come often?"

Irene said, "All the fucking time."

"It's my job," Boone snapped. "Do you mind?"

Irene looked at the ocean, and he turned back to Mary.

"See all this concrete? We poured it for Moses."

"For Herbert Handley, you mean."

"For the city, all right? I'm a civic-minded guy, doing his bit for New York."

"Even when the district attorney tries to put you away?"

"They dropped that indictment," Irene told her.

"Did they? Why?"

"Blind justice," declared Boone. "They had no evidence against me."

"They have Mr. Handley's account books, don't they?"

"For Chrissake," said Irene. "It's not his fault if some little twerp on the city dole decides to take his bid."

Boone shot her a nasty look. "I said I'd handle this."

Irene shrugged, *Go ahead.*

"Explain something to me, Detective Shanley. How is it my problem if a cautious civil servant decides to go with Booligan instead of some fleabag outfit?"

"It's not," agreed Mary. "Handley made the call and he takes the fall. Unless they can prove conspiracy to defraud the people of New York."

"Now, how could anybody do that?"

"I don't know," said Mary. "Things turn up. Handley might talk, if they offered a deal on his sentence."

"Herbie?" Boone shook his head. "He'd never take it."

Mary turned to Irene. "Wouldn't you?"

"It would still be his word against ours," Irene said. "Who'd believe him?"

Boone could have socked her.

"That's true," Mary said. "Now that Rosetta is dead."

Boone eyed both women. "Are you driving at something, officer? Because that girl little wouldn't testify. She already refused."

"Any idea why?"

"What?"

"Moses told me the same thing. I was just wondering why she wouldn't."

"I don't know. She must have been sweet on Herbie."

"Is that what she told you, Irene? She cared too much for Handley to speak up in court? Even when she was summoned, under oath?"

"We weren't that close," said Irene.

"It's been a real pleasure to see you again," Boone told Mary, "but we've got work to do. The beach is opening to the public in a couple of weeks, and somebody's got to check out the concrete." He took Irene's arm and turned her away.

"I'm coming," she told him. "Jeezus."

"Because I have another idea," said Mary. "Why Rosetta refused to testify."

Boone looked toward the parking lot. A last work-crew were making their way up the boardwalk. One man hoisted a pick, another had a shovel, while two others made a Mutt and Jeff team of foremen.

"What's your idea?" asked Boone.

Mary stamped on the concrete. "You poured this?"

"That's right."

"When? Four or five months ago?"

"Six or seven, maybe."

"Lucy Morelli told me Guillermo Sarotte drove a truck for you, four months ago. This is where he drove to in Queens, wasn't it?"

"Who?"

"Sarotte. Lucy calls him Billy. Rosetta de Soto's brother."

The cement man glanced at Irene but said, "Never heard a him."

"You paid his payroll taxes."

"No kidding? Concrete is a big business these days in New York. I don't know everybody who drives a truck in and out of our jobsite."

Mary said, "Maybe you should get a partner."

"He had one," said Irene. "It didn't work out."

"That's right," Mary recalled. "You did, didn't you? The other half of Booligan."

Boone clamped his teeth together.

Irene heard the click but said, "Mitchell Mulligan."

"That was the name I saw them scraping off your door," Mary said. "Too bad he disappeared with all that money."

"Yeah," Boone said. "Too bad for everybody."

Mary clucked in sympathy. "Wasn't that four months ago?"

"Something like that."

"I read the report when you opened the safe. That must've been a shock. Ninety thousand dollars missing. Not to mention Mulligan."

Boone shook his head.

"Any idea where he could be now?"

"Probably lying in the sun on an island someplace," Boone said, "sipping a drink from a cocoanut, mixed by a hula girl."

"A beach guy?"

"Not really." Boone grinned. "But he did like those brown-skinned girls."

"*Does like*, you mean, don't you?" said Mary.

"Sure. He probably still does."

Mary nodded thoughtfully. "I had an idea about that."

"You're just full of ideas," said Irene, rising from her bench to stand beside Boone. "Can we go? I'm hungry."

"I'll bet you said the same thing last Tuesday night," said Mary, "when the four of you stopped by here on your way to dinner."

"That was a long time ago," said Irene.

"That was before the indictments came down, but it wasn't too long ago. And it wasn't your first party together, either. Rosetta must have heard something compromising, as you all got drunk in the past. She could've made life uncomfortable by talking about your nightlife, with Booligan making concrete and Handley buying so many yards of it for Moses's public works."

The last work-crew was drawing close to them. The shorter foreman kept stopping to check the welding of a handrail or to note holidays in the paint job. The taller one seemed focused on the twisted left strap of his overalls and the jelly doughnut dribbling down his chin.

"Please lower your voice," Boone said. "You're forgetting that they had us tailed, by a Pinkerton. Why should we bother about the girl?"

"Because you didn't know that, did you? Just as you didn't know what Rosetta would say, if she were questioned by the police. So you drove to the beach, to watch the waves roll in. And while you were here, you threatened her. I think you told her what happened to Mulligan and warned her the same thing would happen to her, if she ever decided to testify."

"Nothing happened to Mulligan, except running off with my money. Check your police report."

"That's what the report says, but they took it down from the victim—his partner, Bertram Boone. My guess is that Mulligan learned what you were doing with Handley, and he wanted out. You couldn't risk his going to the law, so you offered to buy him out. You gave him ninety grand as a down payment. That lulled his suspicions and bought you a story to tell the police when Mulligan disappeared. I don't see you letting him walk or sail away to Tahiti."

The work crew members were now close enough to hear Mary's story. They stopped in their tracks for Boone's reply. "That's a screwy idea you dreamed up, lady. What have you got to back it up?"

"Only Mulligan."

"You can't find Mitch," he said, "any more than I can."

"We both know where he is," replied Mary.

For the first time, his booming voice wavered. "You're bluffing."

"Am I?" said Mary. "let me introduce my colleagues." She gestured toward the work-crew members standing around them. "The gentleman with the jelly on his collar is Detective

John Broderick. The officer standing behind you"—the smaller foreman—"is Detective Johnny Cordes. They've brought along two members of the East Side Drive road crew to assist us in gathering evidence."

The pick man lifted the tool from his shoulder. "Where do we start?"

Mary took out her copy of the photo again and tapped a point in the foreground. "There," she said. In the background, Handley and Irene were gazing out to sea, while in front of them, Boone was showing Rosetta his Italian shoe. Except that wasn't what he seemed to be doing now. He was pointing with his toe at a certain square of concrete on the boardwalk, to the right of Irene's bench.

The pick hit the walk in just the same spot, cracking the concrete. "What do you think we'll find, Mr. Boone? Another false accusation?"

Boone turned pale. But it was Irene who spoke up.

"I can't believe it!" she said. "You killed him? Your own partner? How could you do such a thing?"

Boone said, "Don't you ever shut your trap?"

"You must still have the money!" she cried, incensed even more. "So all the time you were telling me you were short because of that rotten embezzler, you really had fifty gees socked away?" She marched up to Boone, her heels clicking on the concrete, until she stood two feet from his face. "Asshole!" she declared, then turned to head down the boardwalk.

But she didn't get far. Before the end of her first stride, she was stopped by a grip on her shoulder. Mary said, "Why don't you sit down?"

Irene sat sullenly. "Great," she muttered. "Another idea."

Boone watched the pick-man swing at his boardwalk.

"Once the indictment came down," said Mary, "you knew we'd pick up Handley. I collared him myself. You weren't sure you could rely on Rosetta's silence, even after you'd shown her Mulligan's tomb."

Crack! The concrete shattered underfoot.

"That was stupid of you," Mary said. "If she talked, she had even more to say. You needed to silence Rosetta de Soto, but you couldn't do it yourself. You had to get somebody else to beat her to death for you.

"That was where Sarotte came in.

"You already had him driving a truck. The sandhogs move from job to job, and Handley had a hand in their assignments. Rosetta must have asked him to find a softer job for her brother than digging a hole to New Jersey. All you had to do, when his truck drove into the yard, was strike up a conversation. Talk about his sister. How many men were showing her the town, hinting at what they expected in return.

"Sarotte was primed to believe it. Then another stroke of luck—she agreed to marry a Chinaman.

"That made it too easy, didn't it, Boone? All you had to do was remind him what people would say about him and his family. I'll bet you rubbed it in pretty good, last Thursday night. Once you had him riled enough, you gave him the night off. He drove straight to Mrs. T's boardinghouse and waited in his truck. He'd done it before. Eric Tanenbaum told me the noise of an idling cement mixer kept his mother awake at night, until Handley chased it away. They thought it was working a jobsite there, but anyone who looks at that sidewalk could tell it hasn't been paved in years.

"Rosetta showed up late, after her date with Freddie Arlington. Still shaken by her fight with Ming-Lu Lin outside the marionette theatre. Guillermo confronted her, before she climbed the steps. He must have repeated everything you said. Imagine what she told him in reply. Maybe she stood up to him. Maybe she stood by Ming-Lu Lin. Sarotte would have answered with his fists.

"Maybe she fought back. Or maybe she ran and he caught her. Either way, he did what you sent him to do. He beat his sister to death, to protect his family's name in Italy. He saved your dirty secret accidentally, as a bonus."

243

"You bitch!" Boone lunged at her but was stopped by the *click* of bracelets closing around his wrists. Cordes raised the handcuffs higher up Boone's spine, forcing his elbows apart. Then the diminutive detective wagged a finger at him.

"I can't believe it," Irene said, wiping her nose on her sweater. Her eyes were puffy with tears.

"Oh yes you can," said Mary, "because one other thing kept bothering me. How did Guillermo Sarotte find out his sister was planning to marry Ming-Lu Lin? Lucy Morelli didn't know it. Somebody else had to tell him."

"You just said," Irene stammered, "that Bertie told him."

"But how did Boone find out? Rosetta wouldn't have told him. She didn't even tell her landlady, or her closest girlfriend. You thought she had, didn't you? You thought she must have told Louisa Vitanza. That's why you sent the red-faced man to keep her quiet. But Rosetta couldn't even tell her best friend, because of the way Louisa talked about Chinamen. She never heard about Rosetta's plans."

Irene turned to Boone. "What red-faced man?"

He glared at her.

"He didn't tell you about that? I'm surprised. Because you're such a good listener. Isn't that what Rosetta thought? When she told you, last Tuesday, at your final party together. Maybe in the powder room. She said she wouldn't be seeing Handley again. She might even have kissed you good-bye. She was going to get married. Why not ask about the lucky guy? If you kept at it, she would've answered. She was happy about it and proud too, in a scared, daring way.

"You told Boone, and together you figured out how to play the angle. Sarotte wouldn't know about Rosetta's elopement. She asked you to keep her secret. Which meant the surprise would work for you. You knew what he did to her that first time they talked. If you played it just right, you could get him to explode.

"Or maybe I should say *just wrong*.

"It makes you an accessory before the fact. You might even have whispered a little extra something into his ear yourself. We'll never know exactly what pushed him over the edge. But either way, sister, you're pinched."

Thirty-one. Casualties

On a clear morning in December, Mary Shanley stood with Louisa Vitanza, Rachel Lipinsky, and Gertrude Tanenbaum on the slope of a hill in Woodlawn Cemetery. The sky was a hard powder blue, stretching out to the south over the Bronx and beyond. At their feet lay the freshly piled earth of Rosetta de Soto's grave, where a cold, new tombstone stood cleanly perpendicular, its letters etched sharply into the unblemished marble, paid for by Robert Moses out of the Lincoln Tunnel Casualty Fund.

The tombstone read:

Rosetta de Soto
born Sarotte
1910 - 1937
An American Girl

"I tried to think what she would want," said Louisa, "and realized that's what she always wanted, most of all. She wanted to be American—too fast maybe for her brother and the family in Italy. But that's what she wanted when she was alive, when she couldn't be. So I thought at least she should have it now."

"It's perfect," said Rachel.

"You think so?"

Getrude trembled in the chilly air. "Beautiful."

Rachel hugged her housemate. "I think this is a lovely spot. I can't imagine any place that would please Rosetta more."

Gertrude had come with a bouquet of mixed flowers she purchased from a cart at the entrance to the cemetery. When she laid them on the grave, she found a clutch of Chinese roses already starting to wilt between the earth and the base of the stone. Mary read that to mean Ming-Lu Lin had found his way to the grave, which gave her a very private sense of personal accomplishment.

Mary looked out over the bare winter treetops of the borough and imagined the city beyond them. Cars were passing through the Lincoln Tunnel on their way in from Jersey, up the East Side Drive to the Triboro Bridge, and out to the former garbage dump in Flushing, Queens, where Moses had already broken ground for the 1939 World's Fair. Downing Stadium on Randall's Island was ready for the track and field events of the coming Olympics, as was the pool in Astoria, Queens, where the swimming and diving competitions would be held. On Ward's Island, sewage water was being treated and returned for use by the people of New York in the tides of the harbor.

In far Rockaway, Jacob Riis Park was drawing visitors. Its opening had been delayed by a last-minute repaving of the boardwalk outside the bathhouse, where Mitchell Mulligan's body had been unearthed. The papers were full of the *Scandal in Cement*, as the headlines called it, playing up the partnership between Booligan Concrete and the late beer baron, Dutch Schultz. La Guardia promised to investigate the mob's role in the paving industry.

Erich Tanenbaum was home in his mother's parlor, listening to broadcasts about the scandal and news about the strikes in steel, coal, and retail. Leon Catalan's busted lip healed completely. He kept a permanent scar over his left eyebrow as a souvenir of his battle with the New York police. Leon liked it. He rubbed it for luck and showed it off proudly to his mother and father, who returned from Spain on crutches but upright on two legs, waving to a small crowd of Loyalist supporters.

In the middle of all this activity a peaceful hillside in the Bronx seemed the perfect place to watch the modern city emerge. In 1937 the Bronx was sa place people moved for their health. In the West Bronx, the Grand Concourse was already grand; in the center of the borough, Bronx Park, the Bronx Botanical Gardens, and the Bronx Zoo maintained a swath of unbroken foliage. In the Gardens' greenhouse bloomed a fifteen-foot flower, the *Amorphophallus titanium*, which was dubbed by the Borough President James Lyons "the official flower of the Bronx," even though it stank and was naturally found only in the jungles of Sumatra.

On the eastern edge of the park some friends of Rachel Lipinsky organized the first cooperative housing development, with a dozen buildings of fine brown brick, six stories tall, grouped around three courtyards. The Coops had collective activities for adults and clubs for children of every age, all of it owned by the residents. Farther east were farmers growing vegetables among empty lots and open space for refugees from Brooklyn and the Lower East Side, looking for a different life. Robert Moses had not yet built the Cross Bronx Expressway, severing the borough from the George Washington Bridge to the East Bronx, ruining the neighborhoods through which the highway passed and those to the south as well. At the lower end of the Concourse, near the Bronx Municipal Courthouse and the Bronx County Jail, the Babe was knocking them out of Yankee Stadium. That summer, the Yankees beat the Giants in the World Series for the second year in a row, but Rosetta de Soto was not around to see it.

"Such a *luffly* girl," said Gertrude Tanenbaum.

Louisa wept. Rachel wiped a tear from her nose. Mary let the cold air fill her lungs and emptied them. She had spent so much time thinking about Rosetta, trying to get into her head, it had felt for a while as if she knew her. But of course she didn't. Alone among the women at the graveside, Mary had never met the girl. And it was going to be that way every time she worked a homicide.

She sighed. "I'll bet she was." And she let the others grieve for a while.

On their way back from the grave, Gertrude said to Louisa, "Did you tell Mary about Detroit?"

Louisa shrugged. Mary said, "What happened in Detroit?"

"The Woolworth girls sat down in Detroit too. Only they had more support from the C.I.O. than we did. And you know what happened?"

248

Her eyes beamed.

"We won. They dragged us out of the Brooklyn store and they dragged us out of the Bronx. But in Detroit the company got tired of dragging us out. They recognized our union and even gave us a raise. Five cents an hour. Every hour."

"That's terrific," said Mary.

"We're all very proud of her," Rachel said. "I'll bet you can tell."

Louisa blushed, but didn't object.

They were approaching a Pontiac parked at the curb near the chapel.

"Can I give you ladies a ride?"

Rachel and Louisa stared at the car. "In that?"

Mary opened the driver's door and ducked inside. She flipped down the sun visor, revealing a card that said *Official Business Detective Bureau.* Then she slid across the seat and opened the passenger door.

"Get in."

They did—Rachel first in the front seat, then Louisa and Gertrude in the back. When they were all comfortably settled, Mary turned the key, and the engine purred into action. She worked the clutch and slid the shift into gear. Smoothly they pulled away from the chapel.

"Look at you," said Rachel. "You're driving."

www.ingramcontent.com/pod-product-compliance
Lightning Source LLC
Chambersburg PA
CBHW061615170626
46811CB00001B/436